THE
VAST
CONFIGURATION

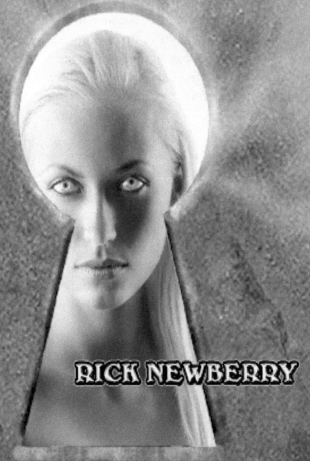

RICK NEWBERRY

NewLink Publishing
2021

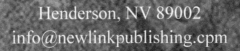

Henderson, NV 89002
info@newlinkpublishing.cpm

The Vast Configuration
Rick Newberry

This book is a work of fiction composed from the author's imagination. It is protected under the copyright laws of the United States of America. No part of this publication may be reproduced or transmitted in any form or by any means, electronic or mechanical, including photocopying, recording, or by an information storage or retrieval system, without written permission from the publisher. Contact the publisher at info@ newlinkpublishing.com.

Line/Content Editor: Janelle Evans
Interior Design: Jo A. Wilkins
Cover: Janelle Evans

p. cm.—Rick Newberry (Science Fiction)
Copyright © 2021 / Rick Newberry
　　　All Rights Reserved
ISBN: 978-1-948266-28-4/Paperback
ISBN: 978-1-948266-42-0/E-Pub

1. Fiction/Science Fiction/Action & Adventure
2. Fiction/Science Fiction/Alien Contact
3. Fiction/Science Fiction/Military

www.newlinkpublishing.com

Henderson, NV 89002
Printed in the United States of America

1 2 3 4 5 6 7 8 9 10

A writer's group is a supportive team of writers
who gather together to pursue the craft of writing.

Thank You,
Carrie Ann Lahain, Derone Rankin, and Chris Arabia

THE
VAST
CONFIGURATION

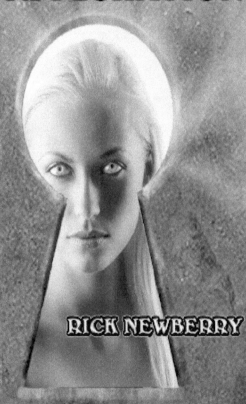

RICK NEWBERRY

Professor Carlos Huerta craved another Quaalude, his third for the day—usually not a concern, but the fact he had already taken two so early in the morning gave him pause. The first pill came after the call from a former student, Payton Sinclair.

"I'm so sorry to impose, professor, but I'm desperate for your help."

Carlos chuckled. "Are you in the middle of a physics emergency, my friend?"

"I'm dead serious. Are you able to travel?"

Carlos's grip tightened on the telephone. "Of course, for you, my friend. Where?"

"The Nevada Test Site. I can't say anything more than that. Please follow the instructions of my aide. He's on his way to your house as we speak."

The second pill came after the limo ride from Sedona to Flagstaff Pulliam Airport.

"Nervous?" The aide cocked his head. "They tell me you haven't flown before," he said with a grin. "Shoot, it'll be fine."

"Oh, the flight is no concern," Carlos said, "but the destination puzzles me." Something about the Nevada Test Site sounded an alarm. Although he had never been there, the name stirred memories—vague recollections lying dormant in the back of his mind.

Cruising at thirty-five thousand feet above endless miles of

1

desert, Carlos used the time to reflect on his relationship with Payton Sinclair. The man had shown true promise at MIT—a brilliant student of physics. Later, he had joined the Air Force and became involved with some top-secret government program—very hush-hush—in a facility just north of Las Vegas, Nevada.

Carlos bolted upright, the pieces falling into place. Top-secret site... Air Force... Las Vegas... Area 51.

The aide roused. "Are you okay, professor?"

Yes, another under-the-counter "happy pill" would be required. "Will there be aliens?" Carlos said. "Little gray men?"

The aide turned away, sat back, and said nothing.

"Please, I must know. I have not felt this way for a very long time. As if my life once again has meaning—some higher purpose."

The aide faced Carlos, a sparkle in his eyes. "Then, I guess, it's meant to be. You know, professor, someone once said God doesn't gamble with the cosmos."

"Actually, Einstein said, 'God does not play dice with the universe.' Meaning, there is a reason, a purpose, for everything."

The young man smiled. "Hope to shout."

Ding-ding. "Prepare to land."

"Is that the driver?" Carlos said.

"You mean pilot. You really haven't flown before, have you? Just relax. Breathe in nice and slow. Close your eyes. We'll be on the ground in no time."

Carlos leaned back and faced the window. Automatic blackout shades energized, covering the portholes and shrouding the fuselage in shadows. "What is this?"

"Sorry, professor," the aide said, "it's protocol—for security purposes. Same reason you couldn't bring your cell phone. Don't worry, you'll get used to that kind of thing."

The jet slowed, then tilted, thousands of pounds of metal, plastic, and steel falling to the ground in a controlled, sweeping curve. The combination of darkness and movement reminded Carlos of the first maddening plunge of a roller coaster. Chaos on the edge of disaster.

He shut his eyes, rehearsing the principles of flight in his mind. *Weight is a force of gravity. Lift is the force acting at a right angle to the direction of motion. Thrust is force. Drag is the opposite of force.* The sensation of control, the power he'd enjoyed earlier while glancing down on a quiet, distant earth had vanished. He shoved his hand into his coat pocket in a frantic search for the pill bottle.

Esperar—wait! Would there even be enough time to pass out if he swallowed another pill? Probably not. The aide said they would be on the ground in no time. He forced himself to hold still.

Sweat coated his brow. He concentrated on the equation making flight possible. Bernoulli's equation. Lift and drag and weight and thrust and power...*Ay Dios, Bernoulli isn't even on this plane.*

Breathe. Bounce. Rattle. Bounce. Breathe.

"See," the aide said, "no big deal. C'mon, let's go, professor. Follow me."

The jet had rolled to a stop. They strode up the center aisle toward the uniformed flight attendant opening the exit door. A brilliant white light accompanied by a burst of hot wind raged against Carlos's face. He cowered back, raising an arm against the searing heat.

"We're in Hell."

"Calm down," the aide said. "We're in the desert is all. Shoot, it's about a hundred and ten degrees out there. You might want to take off that peacoat—makes me sweat just looking at you. We're safe and sound on the ground. We'll be at The Shelter soon."

"*¿Donde?* Where?"

"The Shelter. I promise it's not Hell. Although, between you and me, some of the men call it a whole lot worse than that."

"What could be worse than Hell?" Carlos stared into the man's eyes.

The aide grinned. "Listen, just follow me, okay? Do you think you can do that?"

"*Si*, I can." He slipped off the peacoat, wincing at the ache in his shoulder. Another mystery pain he had awoken with. "Take my advice, never get old."

"Easy does it." The young man turned, beginning his descent down the gangplank.

Carlos's mind ventured to thoughts of home, his safe haven on the edge of the Coconino National Forest in Sedona, Arizona. The town known for art-filled shops, hiking trails, and quaint bed and breakfasts, also boasted the vortex.

He trusted in the power of the vortex, a whirling force of nature conducive to healing, meditation, and introspection. He imagined the vast energy as something being guarded by Sedona's massive stone formations rising from the desert floor. Carlos had always believed their protection extended to him. He whispered the guardian's names. Cathedral. Bell. Chimney. Steamboat. Devil's Bridge. Moving his lips, he repeated the names to himself, envisioning each giant creation at sunset aglow in vibrant shades of red and orange. Cathedral. Bell. Chimney. Steamboat. Devil's Bridge.

Once again, the vortex provided. He opened his eyes and hurried down the steps after the aide with a renewed vigor. "Tell me, young man, what is your name?"

"Once again, Sergeant Henry Sandoval, sir."

"Sandoval. *Habla Espanol?*"

"No sir. Well, just a little."

"*Por qué no?* Why not?"

"Shoot. I'm a Texan, just like my daddy. My mother's maiden name is Fitzgerald. English is the only thing we ever spoke in our house. You?"

"I came to this country from Guatemala." They continued their trek down the ramp, Carlos no longer faltering. "They taught us English in grade school. So, when I arrived in the United States, I spoke both Spanish and English."

"Here we go, professor. Watch your step." Sergeant Sandoval helped Carlos transition from the steps to the sticky, black asphalt of the tarmac. He opened the rear door of a waiting sedan, ushered Carlos into the back seat, rushed around to the other side, and hopped in. "Wow, them door handles are hotter'n fire. The air feels good in here though, don't it?"

"*Si*, quite pleasant." Carlos patted his forehead with a handkerchief and glanced out the tinted windows. He folded the heavy peacoat on his lap.

The sedan hurried away, rushing toward a butte about a half mile in the distance. Other than a couple of men unloading supplies from the bottom of the plane, the landing strip seemed deserted. A dozen wooden and brick structures at the far end of the runway baked under an unforgiving sun. The car bounced off the smooth blacktop and onto the bumpy surface of the desert. Carlos peered through the back window to see a column of dust billowing up behind the vehicle.

He swiveled around, ducking to peek through the front windshield. "What are those shapes up ahead?"

4

"Shapes?" Sergeant Sandoval lowered his head even with the professor's. "Oh, those are Joshua Trees. The Mojave's lousy with 'em."

"No, what are *those* structures? They look like old telephone booths."

"Oh, right, those are emergency exits. There's over a hundred of them out here."

"Exits? Exits from what?"

"Right up ahead, professor. Do you see it?"

Carlos leaned over the front seat. A dark cave loomed ahead. *"Ay, Dios mio."*

"What's the matter, professor?"

"Forgive me, but it reminds me of the open mouth of Xolotl."

"What the heck's that?"

The sergeants lack of knowledge made Carlos snort and lean back. "Supposedly, Xolotl is a canine god responsible for accompanying the dead from this world to the next."

"I thought you were a man of science."

"*Si*, I am," he said, grinning. "But I'm also Guatemalan—filled with superstitions, myths, and obsessed by dark magic."

The sedan slowed and entered the giant cave, the opening devouring them. Carlos detected a rapid change in temperature, the strong odor of fresh paint, and a sensation of travelling over smooth concrete. "This is quite impressive."

"Shoot, you ain't seen nothing yet."

The sedan came to a halt. Sandoval hopped out of the vehicle and glanced back. "C'mon, professor, you'll see what I mean in a moment."

The gleam in the young man's eyes dared Carlos to follow. From the vial in his pocket, Carlos pulled a small pink pill and placed it under his tongue. He stepped out of the sedan and followed the sergeant to an elevator door. Glancing above the threshold, he searched for arrows, numbers, anything that might indicate whether they would be going up or down. The sergeant pressed a single red button on the wall and turned back to Carlos, a smile growing on his face. At the sound of a "ding," the elevator doors slid open. Entering the stainless-steel box made the sergeant's grin widen.

Carlos cleared his throat. "How far are we going?"

"All the way." Sandoval chuckled. "Sorry, but everybody asks, how far? It's just an old joke."

No problem—the Quaalude had already begun working its magic. He smiled at the sergeant as the elevator's motor hummed. Pressure in his ears told him they were dropping deep into the earth. He swallowed hard, grinned, and tried to enjoy the ride.

The metal box stopped its descent with a soft thud, and the doors parted. Carlos shivered from the extreme temperature change. He threw the peacoat back on, jamming both hands under his armpits. A vast cavern stretched out before him. Distant swaths around the perimeter were swallowed in shadows. Total illumination of the underground expanse appeared impossible. He glanced up at a nearly unlimited ceiling. Frigid air stung his throat.

"C'mon, professor," Sandoval said, "we still got a ways to go."

Uniformed personnel rushed about in all directions. Some were dressed in the same crisp black outfit as Sergeant Sandoval, others wore camouflage fatigues and carried rifles. Their demeanor reminded Carlos of the soldiers in Guatemala City, cold and unsympathetic.

"Tell me, sergeant," Carlos said, "is this facility a military base... uh...by that, I mean is the US military in charge?"

"No, sir. Well, it used to be. You see, the military hasn't been in control of this site for years." He drew close and whispered, "I guess they didn't want any snoopy congressmen calling the shots. So, they fired them and hired us."

"Oh? And who is *us*?"

"Gatekeeper, a private company contracted to the Defense Department." Sandoval motioned to his uniform. "Black shirts, black pants...kind of intimidating, don't you think? Most of us are ex-military. In any case, Gatekeeper represents the rule of law down here. A word of warning, professor, those weapons hold live ammo."

Carlos nodded. He observed men and women in green coveralls carrying toolboxes, and a number of civilians wearing casual clothes. A group of technicians in white lab coats strolled by. He also noticed others he could only describe as watchers—men clad in dark suits roaming the perimeter of the cavern, lurking in the shadows, observing.

"Uh, we really should pick up the pace, professor."

"What do they call this place—this giant hole in the ground?"

Sergeant Sandoval stopped and turned back. "I told you, this is

The Shelter."

"No. You said some call it other things—things much worse than Hell. Remember? What do they call it?"

Sandoval leaned in and whispered, "Most of us call it The Pit. Some actually call it the Underworld. Then there's some that say it's Hades, they're just joking though."

Carlos glanced around the vast cavern, taking in the soldiers, technicians, civilians, and "watchers" in dark suits. He detected a palpable gloom infusing every inch of the strange site—some type of physical presence promising ill will. Where were the aliens he had anticipated, the joyful encounter with curious, wide-eyed extraterrestrials?

An unexpected item in the middle of the cavern caught his attention. He trembled. The tall, rectangular object defied explanation, although it did help him conjure his own name for this dark and forbidding place. *"La tumba."*

The grave.

CHAPTER 2

"Ay, Dios mio. **What** is that thing?" Carlos's eyes wandered across the width of the rectangular object. He tilted his head back, examining the monolith's colossal height. "An ancient relic? An antiquity perhaps?"

"Hold up." Sergeant Sandoval put his hand on the professor's shoulder. "You gotta follow me first. Right over there and up the stairs."

Carlos spun, brushing the man's hand away. "Please, do not touch me. Tell me, what is this object? *Por favor.*"

"Sorry, professor. You're gonna have to talk to the general about that."

"General?" Carlos glared at Sandoval.

"Yup, General Sinclair. He's the CO." The aide glanced at his watch. "Shoot, and we're late. Now, please, follow me."

Carlos did not move. *"No señor,* not until you tell me what that thing is."

Sighing, the aide moved his eyes from left to right like a secret agent making sure the coast was clear. Finally, he whispered, "Technically, it's called the Transport Delivery System—TDS for short."

"Delivery system? What does it deliver?"

The aide said nothing.

"But those of you who work here every day, you call it something different, yes?"

"That's right." The sergeant grinned. "C'mon now, professor, we really got to go."

"Please," Carlos said. "I would appreciate an honest answer."

The sergeant pursed his lips but then lowered his voice. "This is just between you and me, professor. We call it the Tombstone."

"*Gracias*, Sergeant Sandoval, thank you for your honesty." Carlos turned from the object, motioning forward with a wave of his hand. "After you."

Sandoval led the professor past the elevator vestibule, toward a metal staircase. The perforated steps rose to an industrial mezzanine facing the underground cavern. An open hallway at the top of the stairs fronted several office doors. Every window was dark, save one.

Carlos gave the Tombstone another lingering glance before climbing the stairs. At the landing, he re-examined the cavern from this fresh angle. Black and yellow warning tape on the floor around the monolith suggested a safety perimeter.

Sergeant Sandoval cleared his throat. "General Sinclair's waiting. It's the third office, down the hall."

"Is it always this quiet?" Carlos shimmied between Sandoval and the tubular railing, avoiding contact with both. "It reminds me of a cathedral."

"For now." Sandoval winked.

Carlos ambled down the corridor, his heart thumping. He grabbed for the railing, his hand wrapping around the metal in a white-knuckled death grip. It seemed ridiculous that standing just ten feet above the ground in this mysterious cave caused him more concern than being at thirty-five thousand feet earlier in the day.

Yellow lamplight from an opened door spilled across the hallway. The silhouette of a man obscured by shadows caught his eye. Carlos forced himself forward, using slow, cautious steps.

"Thank you for coming, my friend. It's good to see you." General Payton Sinclair extended his hand.

Carlos beamed but avoided the handshake. "Payton, where are the aliens?"

"Whoa. Slow down." Sinclair winced. "What have you been told?"

"Nothing. But we are in the middle of the desert, in a secret underground cavern housing an ethereal monolith, guarded by armed soldiers. I believe it's a fair question."

"Please, professor, follow me." Sinclair strode into the office and glanced back. "It's okay, Carlos. Come in. First, we have to make the lawyers happy."

The room laid bare save for an imposing conference table, surrounded by plush leather chairs. A dull and yellowed "No Smoking" sign hung on the wall. The odor of stale tobacco clung to the room like the smell of bad food in a microwave. An enormous picture window offered an unobstructed view of the cavern.

The general closed the door and waved toward a chair. Carlos sat without a word, placing his hands on his lap. Sinclair strolled around the table and sat opposite him.

"Now then, what we're about to discuss is, of course, highly classified." Sinclair tapped a manila folder on the table and slid it in front of Carlos. "In fact, you're going to have to sign this non-disclosure agreement before we go any further."

He had signed many such agreements while at MIT. The government insisted his theoretical research be kept confidential. He never balked. To him, the agreements were a mere formality. After all, who would he tell? Lilly did not care about his work, and he cared even less about having a social life. Carlos opened the folder. Sinclair produced a pen. Carlos took it and scribbled his name without hesitation. The general attached his own name as witness.

"Good." Sinclair folded his hands on the table and leaned forward. "Let me give you the short version of what we're looking at. You may have already heard this base is called The Shelter—"

"But some of the men call it something worse—The Pit, Hades. In fact, I have my own name for—"

"Yes. Well in any case, The Shelter used to be at the heart of the Nevada Test Site for atomic research. In July of 1963, they tested the very first MOAB here."

"Excuse me, Payton, the acronym?"

"Massive Ordinance Air Blast. All the force of a nuclear explosion, minus the nuclear material. The explosion created this cavern. During excavation, they uncovered—"

"The Tombstone." Carlos rose and strolled to the window. "Did the Tombstone exist before the detonation in 1963, or did it appear because of it?"

11

"We don't know. Go ahead and get used to that answer, you'll hear it often. There's a myriad of things we don't know about the object's existence or application. In fact, there's only one thing we *do* know about it. ENOs emerge from it—"

"ENOs?" Carlos faced the general.

"E–N–O. Entities of a Non-categorized Origin—those *aliens* you asked about."

"I knew it."

"We don't call them people or humans because, quite frankly, we don't know what they are." Sinclair joined Carlos at the window. "They enter the facility from the Transport Delivery System—the Tombstone—arriving at random times, and in random numbers."

"And why are they here?"

"Unknown at this time." Sinclair shook his head. "But they've been arriving steadily since 1963. Lately, in greater numbers."

"*Ay, Dios mio.* Do you think—"

A sudden illumination lit up the room, forcing Carlos to shield his eyes. The two men squinted at the Tombstone. The monolith vibrated, bathed in a concentrated light radiating from within. Uniformed security forces gathered around the pulsating object.

A black male and light skinned female, both naked, emerged from the base of the monolith. The woman, tall and slender, and the man, muscular and chiseled, shared the same color hair—pure white.

"Their eyes…" Carlos mumbled.

"A bit larger than ours."

The beings strolled across the yellow and black warning tape at an unhurried pace, as if strolling through a park. Soldiers raced up alongside them, taking hold of their elbows, and escorted them away from the Tombstone. The enormous cavern returned to its cathedral-like mix of shadows and secrets, silence and calm. The two beings were ushered toward an opening near the back of the cave, vanishing in the shadows.

Cathedral. Bell. Chimney. Steamboat. Devil's Bridge. Continuing his internal chant, Carlos felt for the pill bottle in his coat pocket.

"Please," Sinclair said, "sit down."

Carlos trudged back to the table and plopped into a chair. He wiped his brow with a handkerchief then spun to face Sinclair. "Why do they come?"

"Again, we simply don't know."

"Where are they from?"

"Unknown."

"What do they want? What do they say?"

"Nothing—and that's our biggest problem. The ENOs have never spoken—not a single word. They arrive in a sort of trance—a catatonic state. We recently started a CLP...er...a Communications Link Program, but I'm afraid it may be too little, too late."

"What do you mean too late?"

Removing his glasses, Sinclair rubbed the bridge of his nose. "Sorry, but it's been a long day, as most of them are **anymore**." He put his glasses back on and lit a cigarette. "Suffice to say, it's a race against time now—time we simply do not have."

"Why, Payton?"

"We're desperate to know where the ENOs come from. Why they're here? Who they are? *What* they are? That's why the CLP is so important."

"And have you made progress?"

The general shook his head. "But all options are on the table at this point. We've even explored the benefits of utilizing gifted people to communicate with them. Telepaths, mind readers, mediums, for God's sake. Bottom line is we're desperate. The CLP coordinator, my second in command, Colonel Bloodstone tells me a promising new alternative is being investigated, but it's too early to draw any conclusions."

"Please, tell me what happens when they arrive. Tell me everything."

"They're escorted to one of two tunnels." Sinclair pulled a laser pointer from his pocket and aimed it at a detailed map hanging on the wall. It bore the title, Project Joshua. "The Southern Tunnel System leads to the older part of the caves with over ten miles of passages, channels, and burrows. Under orders from President Kennedy, the existence of the ENOs was to be kept secret. He wanted to announce their presence later in the year, at the proper time."

"1963? He would never announce their presence."

"The Northern Tunnel System is a new construction, begun in 1984 under Reagan." The general moved the laser to the top of the map. "We alternate the placement of incoming arrivals to keep the population in both tunnel systems balanced."

"*Pobrecitos.*"

"Lucky for us, their catatonic state means they're easily led—like herding sheep." Sinclair sat down.

"General, you're talking about people."

"No, I'm not. And if you start thinking of them that way... Listen to me. Carlos, these beings are nothing like us."

"How so, Payton?"

"Well, for starters, their blood is a different color, sort of light blue. In sunlight, their skin is iridescent, it almost glows. Their DNA coding is nothing our doctors have ever seen before. They say it reads like a series of circular patterns—something about unpaired chromosomes in a non-spindled housing."

"What does that even mean?"

"Exactly." Sinclair shook his head. "Also, they have no identifying marks—no tattoos, no scars. Their skin is smooth, flawless. They don't even have fingerprints. In other words, they arrive as blanks."

"Blank people," Carlos said, mumbling to himself. "So, what do you do with them?"

"The only thing we can do. We care for them and make sure they don't hurt themselves. They're completely helpless. And they just keep coming. To date, we've carved out so many underground chambers...well, we're nearly out of room."

"Out of room? Exactly, how many of these beings are down here?"

"Too many, Carlos. Too many to house, too many to feed. I hate to admit it, but our

treatment of them is almost cruel. Seven, sometimes eight ENOs are forced to live in small chambers originally constructed for just two. That's where you come in."

"Me? But my home has only two guest bedrooms. Of course, there is the *casita*, but what can I possibly—"

"Carlos," Sinclair said, frowning at his former professor, "listen to me carefully. I know things have been...rough for you lately. And I'm sorry, I really am. The way you were treated by the government is shameful. Especially after Lilly...after Lilly's accident. You know I wouldn't have called you if my back weren't against the wall."

"It sounds like you need a cultural anthropologist, not a physicist. Still, I'm happy you thought of me. How can I help?"

Sinclair bowed his head as if avoiding eye contact and stubbed out his smoke. "The powers-that-be, the new administration, is no longer willing to commit funds for the continuation of this undertaking. They've labeled Project Joshua a drain on the economy." He glanced up and drew in a long breath. "Believe me, we already have our fair share of cultural anthropologists on site. What we really need to determine is how these beings materialize. How the TSD works so we might...err... The thought is to try and send them back to where they came from."

"You must be joking, Payton. It is an impossibility."

"Maybe. But somehow, matter appears—quite suddenly—from nothing. According to the laws of physics, *that's* an impossibility. I lobbied Washington to get you involved. If anybody can get a handle on this phenomenon, it's you."

"Surely, Friedman is better suited, or Hasting perhaps—"

"Friedman rejected us outright. He said he'd never work for the government after what happened in Uzbekistan. Hasting, on the other hand, jumped at the chance, but his health deteriorated to the point of becoming a barrier to the work. I'm sorry to say, he's in our sick bay down in the main complex."

"*Dios mio*, poor man."

"Professor, you're our best hope for..." Sinclair's words trailed off.

"Best hope for what, my friend?" Carlos eased back into the leather chair, dabbing at the sheen of perspiration on his brow.

Sinclair raised his voice. "As I said, the incoming administration wants an end to this project. They've given us a limited amount of time to figure it out, or—"

"Or *what*, Payton?"

Turning away, the general took a deep breath. "The plans have already been approved. They're calling it Operation Zero."

"Operation Zero?" Carlos leaned forward. "That can't be good."

Sinclair avoided eye contact and swallowed hard. "Euthanasia."

Tick-tock—Tick-tock.

Colonel Ulysses S. Bloodstone could not wait. He stared at the Omega Speedmaster Dark-Side-of-The-Moon watch on his wrist. Could it be slow? No. The hands had always kept precise time. He put it to his ear, then glared at it again.

He had been thrilled to receive the timepiece from his wife, Peggy, a gift on his fiftieth birthday. A year later, when the heart disease triumphed, the watch symbolized their short time together. A year after that he felt the tremors in his own chest, like the "funny" feelings Peggy ignored. The Omega became a reminder of his own mortality. That health scare led to an early retirement with an honorable discharge. Gone were the dreams of making a difference in the world—of immortality. Then came the opportunity of a lifetime.

Gatekeeper's call offered him the chance to be productive again. Were the dark rumors being whispered true? Yes. Project Joshua, the clandestine effort to house, feed, and study uncommunicative beings in a secret location proved all too real. He rose through the ranks and soon found himself second in command of the world's biggest secret. Long dormant dreams of power and purpose resurfaced. Being the leader of the Communications Link Program, he resolved to establish lines of communications with the ENOs by any means necessary. An engraved plaque hung in his office for all to see.

"By Any Means Necessary..."

Then he found Prudence Wellman.

Bloodstone offered a quick smile to the team of white-coated scientists seated around the conference table. The scent of fresh coffee, stale tobacco, and cheap cologne filled the room. Sauntering to the head of the table, Bloodstone gathered his thoughts and cleared his throat.

"We've been through some interesting times. Trying different approaches to the problem, uncommon techniques, and failing time and again. It's been frustrating—challenging—but, today, I want you to forget everything we've tried in the past. Today, we start afresh."

"You must be joking," a raspy voice whispered across the table.

"No, Malcom," Bloodstone said, "I'm dead serious. Today, we attack our communication problem from an innovative new angle. Today, we begin the Wellman Study."

Murmurs came from those seated at the table. Bloodstone raised his hands, calling for silence. "And with every new project comes the protocols. The higher-ups insist."

Malcom Fitzpatrick chuckled. "That they do, boss."

Bloodstone cleared his throat again, snatched an index card from his pocket, and pressed a button to activate the multidirectional microphone at the center of the table. "This is Colonel Ulysses S. Bloodstone, director of the Communications Link Program for Project Joshua. Today, we begin Project Wellman—a new phase in establishing communications with the ENOs." He read from the index card. "In attendance is Malcom Fitzpatrick, forensic linguist, and author of the classic book on modern language, *The Final Word on Words*. Also present is Dr. Jonas Hale, the world's leading expert on language, a polyglot in his own right, and maven of all things linguistic. Dr. Hale has been selected to be the team's leader. Next to him is Professor Hans Schmidt from the Republic of Germany. Professor Schmidt is a world-renowned etymologist. And the newest addition to our team, with a PHD in comparative language and computational linguistics, Dr. Janet Shelly. Welcome aboard, doctor."

"Thank you, sir." Dr. Shelly nodded and pushed her black-framed glasses higher up the bridge of her nose. Her brown hair lay tied back in a messy bun.

Placing the index card on the table, Bloodstone let out a deep breath. He took another visual tour of those gathered in the room. These were the best and the brightest—a communications dream team. He took a sip of tepid coffee, picked a piece of lint from his uniform, and checked the Omega one more time. "Will somebody kill the lights?"

Bloodstone stepped to the side of the projector and clicked a button on a controller in his left hand. A still photograph of a red-haired child wearing a blue dress and precocious smile flashed onto the screen. By their silence, the young girl had obviously captured their full attention.

"May I introduce a very young Prudence Wellman," the colonel said, in his typical unsympathetic tone. "Her mother claimed she possessed a very special gift since birth."

"Oh no, not another psychic," Malcom Fitzpatrick said.

Ignoring the comment, Bloodstone continued. "Here, she appears to be a lively and inquisitive four-year-old. But even at this age, Prudence had the ability to light up a room. By the age of six, she became aware of her singular gift for evoking heartfelt emotions in others and declared her intention of becoming the world's greatest actress."

A smattering of chuckles and a couple of "Aws," met the statement. He waited for silence before clicking the remote again. A slightly older version of the same sweet child appeared on the screen.

"In elementary school, Miss Wellman abandoned the idea of acting and turned her attention to medicine. In her words, she intended to ease the misery of a world in pain."

Bloodstone pressed the controller again. The image changed to a tall, thin girl—almost gangly—wearing a cap and gown.

"In high school, she pursued the sciences and mathematics with a voracious appetite. She graduated early. At just sixteen, she entered Hardwick College on full scholarship."

Another touch of the remote.

"Here, in Western Pennsylvania, her studies fell to the wayside. Once again, Prudence changed the direction of her life. She decided to follow another, more ethereal pursuit—one for which there are no degrees, no academic courses. Her vocational choice? Prescience."

"I knew it." Malcom Fitzpatrick closed his eyes and placed his fingers on his forehead. "I should be a mind reader."

Quiet laughter moved through the room.

Again, Bloodstone ignored the comment. "She believed she could tune in to the wavelengths of an unseen future. She explained away her attempts at both acting and healing by saying something had guided her—an unseen force, allowing her to test the waters, so to speak."

The colonel shut down the projector and checked his watch. In a low voice, he continued the narrative. "The search to discover her true calling eventually drove her mad. We came across her at the Powell Psychiatric Institute. You see, her unique talent, the one that put her on our radar, is not acting, nor healing—not even divination. Her gift is truly one of a kind."

"And what is this so-called gift, colonel?" Dr. Janet Shelly said.

"We've coined a term. We're calling it *anti-empathy*."

"Excuse me, boss." Malcom Fitzpatrick stirred, adjusting the glasses framing his squat face. His voice did not rise above a rough whisper—more suited to a horror show villain than a world-class scientist. "Please define the term."

Colonel Bloodstone stepped away from the screen and strolled to a large, rectangular curtain hanging on the wall. He pressed a button causing the curtain to slide open along a mechanical track, revealing a window to an adjacent room.

"I'll get the lights." Dr. Jonas Hale stood.

"No, not just yet." Bloodstone lifted his eyes from his watch, then cleared his throat. "If you'll gather round. Please, come closer. This window is a one-way mirror. The patient lying on the gurney in the next room is asleep. The effects of a sedative administered exactly four hours ago. She'll wake any moment now. With the lights out in here, she won't be able to see us."

In silence, the team gathered near the mirror. A young red-haired woman, clothed in bright pink scrubs and white slippers, lay on a gurney in the center of the next room.

"Doctors," Colonel Bloodstone said, "may I introduce Prudence Wellman."

The young woman stirred and opened her eyes. She blinked several times, a childlike yawn accompanying her movements—the end of her drug-induced naptime.

The colonel said, "Her days here have been strictly regulated.

Being an anti-empath requires us to use extreme caution in—"

"Once again, boss," Malcom Fitzpatrick whispered, "can you define the term anti-empath for those of us who are a little slow on the uptake?"

"I'll do my best. While the act of empathy is the ability to walk in the shoes of another, Prudence Wellman has the capacity of slipping her own shoes onto someone else—of transferring *her* emotions, *her* decisions, *her* feelings onto others. It's actually quite remarkable."

"*Nein.* That is not possible." The flat rebuttal came from the big German bear of a man, Professor Hans Schmidt. "What proof do you have of this so-called anti-empathy?"

Colonel Bloodstone placed a finger to his lips and pointed to the next room. "The proof can be found at the Powell Psychiatric Institute, where we found her. You see, when we made arrangements to bring her here—"

"Excuse me, but is this common practice?" Dr. Janet Shelly said. "To kidnap U.S. citizens and use them as unwitting subjects in—"

"Dr. Shelly, no laws have been broken. To infer otherwise is just reckless—"

"Colonel Bloodstone," Malcom Fitzpatrick said, his eyes fixed on Prudence, "we've examined empaths before. They start out by exhibiting certain qualities that seem to fit quite well with our needs, but they soon fizzle out. Do you remember that Jennings girl? If I recall, she didn't even—"

"*Ya*," Professor Schmidt said, "these *gifted* individuals always do the fizzle."

"Colonel," Dr. Shelly said, "you haven't answered my question."

"Please," Bloodstone said, "everyone settle down." He sat at the conference table and invited the others to do the same. "Prudence Wellman possesses abilities that have never been seen before. She's not an empath. She's the exact opposite—an *anti*-empath, able to shroud people in her emotions. She doesn't feed on the feelings of others, like an empath. She releases her own sentiments, attitudes, and reactions, then directs them onto—no, not onto, but rather into—the emotional psyche of another."

After a moment, Dr. Shelly said, "Does she know we're here?"

"Yes," Bloodstone said. "I believe she has some vague idea that she's being watched."

Dr. Shelly chuckled. "Then why doesn't she...inflict her emotions on us now? Why doesn't she simply *will* us into letting her go?"

"Short answer. I think Prudence Wellman has no idea her special power exists, let alone how to control it."

Dr. Shelly shrugged as if not impressed by the explanation. "If she's unable to control it, then how do you know this so-called anti-empathy power is even present?"

"Fair question. While at the Powell Institute, Ms. Wellman exhibited suicidal tendencies. All the proper precautions were put in place to keep her from harming herself—restraints, a secured cell, constant monitoring—that sort of thing." Bloodstone sucked in a deep breath. "However, seven staff members at Powell committed suicide during her short confinement there. Seven. The odds of that happening during a one-week period are astronomical."

"Are you implying she induced her state of mind on the medical staff?"

"No, Dr. Shelly." Colonel Bloodstone stood, put his hands on the table, and leaned forward. "I'm not implying anything. What I'm saying is that Prudence Wellman, through a power she is not even aware of, persuaded seven staff members to end their own lives."

"Incredible," Dr. Hale said. "You're right, this is exactly the breakthrough we've been looking for." He loosened his tie, stepped closer to the mirror, and put his bulbous nose within an inch of the glass. "Using this young girl's talents, we could place messages in the minds of the ENOs—like planting emails in their brains. Hardwired dispatches they cannot possibly ignore. To think of all the time we've wasted studying empaths, telepaths, and the various other *paths* we've assembled here. Simply incredible."

"I admire your enthusiasm, doctor." Dr. Shelly shook her head. "However, don't you think we should reassess our position?"

"What do you mean by that?"

All eyes fell on Dr. Janet Shelly. "Well, if it's true this woman compelled seven people to commit suicide, the dangers of examining her seem quite challenging. We must approach this exceptional person with a fair bit of—"

"Exceptional person, indeed." Bloodstone clapped his hands together. "That's why I've chosen Dr. Hale to head up the Wellman

Study." He shot Dr. Shelly a sideways glance. "Might I suggest we start with a brain scan and complete physical examination? Of course, I defer to your expertise—"

"Colonel Bloodstone," Dr. Shelly interrupted, her breathing irregular. "Since I'm the newest member of the team, one with a fresh viewpoint, I insist on being heard."

"Yes?" Bloodstone turned to her with raised eyebrows.

"How long has Ms. Wellman been a guest at The Shelter?"

"Guest?" Malcom chuckled.

"Two nights, maybe three."

"And in those three nights, has she not been told about—"

"She's been told nothing, Dr. Shelly. She's been anesthetized and fed intravenously. She doesn't know where she is. With the amount of medication in her system, I doubt she even knows what year this is."

Dr. Shelly furrowed her brow. "Colonel Bloodstone, might I suggest we proceed with extreme caution? After all, we have some vague idea of what we're dealing with, the poor staff members at Powell were blindsided. We should work in teams. We should be heavily monitored for any deviation in mood or behavior. We seem to be embarking upon the study of a human timebomb—"

"Exactly what we've been looking for." The colonel edged toward Dr. Shelly. "Remember our mission. To establish communications with extraterrestrials. After weeks of failed research, Prudence Wellman may be our best and only hope."

"*Ja, ja,*" Dr. Schmidt said. "We know what our mission is to achieve, but I also agree with Dr. Shelly. She raises valid concerns. We have no idea of what this woman is capable of. Therefore, protocol dictates we must proceed with extreme caution."

Colonel Bloodstone reached for the recording device on the table and switched it off. "Gentlemen..." He turned to Janet Shelly. "... and lady, the administration insists we provide them with at least a modicum of progress in our research. I've already brought General Sinclair up to speed on the capabilities of Prudence Wellman—"

"Forgive me, colonel." Dr. Shelly cocked her head. "But we're not at war, and this is not the Manhattan Project. We *must* proceed with caution, especially given her abilities."

"Dr. Shelly." Colonel Bloodstone sucked in a deep breath. Why had he agreed to add this woman to his team? "Dr. Shelly, I know you're new here. Not accustomed to working under these kinds of conditions—"

"Excuse me, colonel—"

"With these kinds of hard targets, if you will. Let me remind you, since being formed, the CLP has made exactly zero progress. We have a real chance now for a breakthrough. Believe me doctor, this team needs a win or...well..." He jerked a thumb toward the ceiling. "That's the way things work in the real world up there. The general is being pressured for results, he pushes me, and I push you. I merely suggested to the general that we were on the brink of something quite extraordinary. I told him we should have a preliminary report on his desk, forthwith."

Dr. Shelly shook her head. "With all due respect—"

"Dr. Hale, to repeat, I want you to head up this study. I'm sorry if this briefing has left some of you with more questions than answers, but that's the nature of the beast. Testing will begin at once."

The scientists gathered around the mirror while Bloodstone slipped out of the room.

Let them continue to squawk. Let them believe communication is the goal. The bigger picture would reveal itself soon enough. Everyone remembered the father of the atomic bomb, J. Robert Oppenheimer. The bomb that changed the world. Bloodstone imagined a new weapon. One using the untapped potential of the human mind. A weapon so powerful it would compel the enemy to destroy itself. *What had Dr. Shelly called Prudence?* A human timebomb? The father of that weapon would be remembered till the end of time.

Tick-tock—Tick-tock.

CHAPTER 4

"Es una locura," **Carlos** said, pushing away from the table, his chair tipping to the ground. "I will not be a part of this insanity, this mass murder."

"Believe me, my hands are tied." General Sinclair stood. "Our only chance is that you, or one of your colleagues, figures out how the ENOs are materializing. Right now, where the aliens are from, or what they want is on the back burner. It's the Tombstone we're interested in. We need to know how the damn thing works."

"We? Who are we? You are in charge, no?"

Sinclair chuckled. "That's what they tell me."

"What is it you think I can do? Do you think I can perform miracles? Or do magic? Is that what you think I am? *¿Un mago?*"

"Carlos, calm down. That's not it at all."

"*Si,* I can tell by your tone. You think I can solve this problem. But no, general, you are in charge of this...this prison. You are *el jefe*, the king of the cave, the ruler of—"

"Stop, please."

Righting his chair, Carlos sat down and patted at the beads of sweat on his forehead. He rubbed the pain in his shoulder. "I'm sorry, my friend. Sometimes my mouth runs faster than my mind." Though the whole situation made him wonder what kind of person his former pupil had turned into. "Payton, promise me, *por favor,* you will not permit this to happen. That you will not allow all these people to...to be executed."

Sinclair let out a long, slow breath. "We all follow orders. Even me."

"*Pobrecitos—un holocausto.*" He raised his voice. "This is madness."

"Trust me, you can't possibly think I'm comfortable with the order. You know me better than that."

"I need my vitamin." Carlos pulled the vial from his pocket and twisted at the childproof lid. He tapped a pill into his palm and closed the bottle.

"Listen to me very carefully." General Sinclair sat and patted his uniform just over his heart. "My resignation is in my pocket. It's been there for days now. In all good conscience, I can't obey this order—it's an atrocity. Look, all Washington needs is a *sign* that we're on the right track. That's why I brought you in, why Hasting is here, too. Don't you see, you and I are in a unique position to help the ENOs—that's what I've decided, anyway. I promise, I'll do everything I can to find a solution. And if I fail, well, at least I will have tried."

How could he cater to his wants when so much hung in the balance? Carlos made a fist around the tiny pink pill. He stood up and turned toward the door, fighting the urge to give in to the Quaalude.

"My friend," Sinclair said, "if you walk away from this, you'll always know you could have done something to help these poor people but chose not to. Can you live with that?"

The words stopped Carlos. "You did not call them ENOs."

"Excuse me?" Sinclair cocked his head.

"You called them people." Carlos returned to his chair. "What do you want me to do?"

"A theory, an educated guess...anything. It could make all the difference."

The room lit up, signaling another arrival. Carlos jammed the pill back into his pocket. Both he and the general pushed away from the table and rushed to the window.

A nude male emerged from the depths of the sleek Tombstone. A soldier ushered him away into the shadows at the edge of the cave.

Carlos turned to his former pupil. "*Bien.* Where do we begin, my friend?"

"For starters, let's pay Professor Hasting a visit."

"Excellent. I can't wait to hear his thoughts."

Outside the office, they climbed down to the floor of the cavern. Sinclair led Carlos to a passageway which cut through a solid rock wall. Subway tiles covered the hallway. This corridor led them away from The Shelter, the ENOs, and the Tombstone.

Conditioned air whooshed from evenly spaced vents, filling the corridor with fresh oxygen. Fluorescent lights buzzed overhead. The farther they distanced themselves from The Shelter, the less Carlos thought of being buried deep below the surface of the earth.

Soon, they traversed across a synthetic gray carpet. Doors lined either side of the hallway. It could have passed for a modern office complex anywhere in the world. Sinclair leaned toward Carlos and whispered, "Nobody in this facility knows about Operation Zero except for a handful of senior staff. I'd like to keep it that way. No need to alarm anybody."

"*Si*, I understand."

Just beyond a bank of elevators, they came upon another tiled hallway, this one painted a Robin's egg blue. General Sinclair led Carlos down this narrow corridor, then stopped. "This is your suite," he said, touching the faux wood of a door on his right. "Your luggage is on the bed." A plaque beside the doorway read—Dr. Carlos Huerta.

"You were certain I would stay."

Their trek continued past another bank of elevators, a barber shop, cafeteria, and a few storefronts with signs promising various goods—from clothes to greeting cards. Groups of people strolled by, some holding shopping bags, others seemingly out for a quiet walk.

"You have everything down here, Payton." Carlos marveled at the stark difference between this section of The Shelter and the cavern holding the Tombstone.

"And more—workout facilities, restaurants, even a movie theater. Those stationed here want for nothing."

"Except the sun."

"Yes, except the sun."

Finally, they reached a hallway thick with the smell of sanitizers and disinfectants. A large, red sign hung overhead. Infirmary. Sinclair strode toward a tall, thin man wearing a white lab coat and shook his hand.

"Dr. Turnbride, how are you?"

Carlos blinked and wiped his brow again.

"Are you all right?" Sinclair leaned toward him.

"Ah, *si*. I have become too sedentary in Sedona."

"Dr. Turnbride," Sinclair said, turning back to the doctor, "I want you to meet Professor Carlos Huerta. Carlos, this is Dr. Harrison Turnbride, one of our few civilian doctors—and a damned good one. The best."

Carlos ignored the man's outstretched hand.

"Dr. Huerta, it's such a pleasure to meet you." Dr. Turnbride withdrew his hand. "I must tell you, I truly enjoyed *Law and Disorder: Physics on Trial*."

"Ah, so *you're* the one who bought my book. That explains the royalty check from my publisher last year—two dollars and a 1099 form."

Dr. Turnbride cocked his head, offering a sideways glance.

"Please excuse the dark humor, but you see, I've always had my regrets about writing that infamous book of mine. I kept a journal when I...when I moved on from MIT. Not exactly a bestseller, eh? Forgive my carrying on so, but when it comes to that book, *ay, madre mia*...uh, Dr. Turnbride, is it?"

"You're too modest. It's on my bookshelf now. I've always been kind of a physics nut. I often read a few pages whenever I want to escape."

"Or get some sleep, eh?"

"Nonsense, I truly am a fan. Tell me, would you mind autographing my copy?" He turned to the general. "That is, if it's not against some arcane, deep-state regulation." He leaned into Carlos and lowered his voice. "Honestly, if you don't have a pass to go to the toilet around here, they threaten to shoot your pecker off."

Feigning a smile, Carlos struggled to find the pill in his pocket. He woke this morning in his own bed, safe and warm. Now, he shook from the cold in this underground city and faced castration if he did not possess some kind of note to urinate. The pill he pulled from his pocket tumbled to the ground. He watched it bounce across the tiled floor. Dr. Turnbride scooped it up. Carlos thrust out his palm. "Please, may I have my vitamin?"

Dr. Turnbride examined the pill. "Professor Huerta, you and I both know this isn't—"

"*Por favor,*" Carlos said, his words echoing off the walls of the narrow passageway. He stuck out his hand and whispered, "Please."

"How's our patient?" Sinclair said. "We were hoping to have a word with him."

"His condition has worsened." Dr. Turnbride handed the pill to Carlos. "The cancer is very aggressive. Honestly, there isn't much we can do for him here. He needs to be in a facility better equipped to deal with this type of illness."

"I spoke to him myself, just a few months ago," Carlos said. "He seemed strong—in good spirits."

"I'm afraid that's the nature of the beast." Dr. Turnbride faced the general. "I want your permission to airlift him to a facility in Las Vegas."

"Of course, I'll arrange the transport. Can we still see him?"

"Only for a moment," the doctor said. "He's on a drip for the pain."

"After you." Sinclair held the door open.

Doctor Turnbride cleared his throat. "If you don't mind, professor, I'll pop into my office and grab your book for that autograph."

"Ah, *si, si.*" Carlos hesitated at the door but decided against taking the pill. He placed it back in his pocket and peered at his friend, his mentor, lying on the bed.

"Carlos," Hasting said in a raspy voice.

"Samuel." Carlos blinked back tears. "It is good to see you. Listen to me. I know this is just a temporary setback." The words came from his lips, not his heart. "I'm looking forward to working with you on this little problem they have here." He forced a smile. "I'm sure it's nothing we can't figure out. No match for the likes of us."

It pained him to watch Samuel Hasting close his eyes rather than respond. Carlos brushed strands of gray hair from the man's forehead and whispered, hoping his friend heard. "You're a strong man. You will beat this. *Si, señor,* you will beat this."

Carlos and the general withdrew from the room.

"I'll arrange that transport." Sinclair marched to a nearby telephone at the nurse's station.

Dr. Turnbride approached Carlos, a paperback book in his hand.

"I don't understand, doctor."

"I'm sorry, Professor Heurta, I know you two were close. Here, take this, put it in your pocket." Turnbride thrust the book forward.

"But I thought you wanted me to autograph—"

"Quick," Turnbride whispered, "put it away."

"I don't understand."

Dr. Turnbride jammed the book into Carlos's coat pocket.

"What don't you understand, Carlos?" General Sinclair said.

"Uh, because of his age and poor health," Dr. Turnbride said, speaking louder than he had before, "the prognosis isn't good. Myelodysplastic syndrome is difficult to treat under the best of conditions, but here, in this hole in the ground—"

"I just scheduled transportation to Vegas," the general said.

"He will recover, yes?" Carlos needed to hear the doctor's reassurance.

Dr. Turnbride glanced down. "I've recommended a facility where he'll be much more comfortable—the Mojave Hospice Center."

"A hospice? No, doctor, he is going to get better. Tell me he is—"

"Professor." Turnbride stared at Carlos. "Dr. Hasting is dying."

"Carlos?" Sinclair said. *"Are you okay?"*

"Si." He peered into the cool, blue eyes of a relaxed Payton Sinclair. "I spoke with Samuel just last month. He visited me in Sedona. He seemed fine, he spoke of complete remission. And now..."

"I'm so sorry. C'mon, follow me." Sinclair turned away from the hospital ward, bore to the right, and led Carlos into another hallway.

Negotiating yet another set of narrow passageways, Carlos found it difficult to concentrate on anything except the frail figure of Samuel Hasting. His stomach churned. He needed to think about something else—anything else. "Payton, tell me about the Tombstone. What do you truly know about it? Tell me everything."

"Well, naturally we call it the Tombstone because of its shape. Of course, technically it's called the TSD—the Transport Delivery System. No gimmicks, no magic illusions, no smoke and mirrors. Using a technology that's obviously light years beyond ours, ENOs have emerged from it for decades. We don't know where it came from or how it got on Earth. There's been speculation it's been here for centuries."

"But certainly, you can give me *some* idea about how this Tombstone—this delivery system—operates."

"Right now, you know as much as I do. We're like a bunch of Neanderthals who've stumbled across a rocket ship. We've poked and prodded it for years. We've had it cut, drilled, x-rayed, thermal imaged—hell, we've even blasted it with fire, water, and lasers."

"And...?"

"And nothing—it's solid and impenetrable." Sinclair turned and waited for Carlos to catch up. "Are you okay? I'll slow down. Better?"

"*Si*," Carlos said, his heart pumping at top speed.

"By the way, I do have some good news. I've heard from another physicist. I'm having him flown in now. I know you're familiar with his work."

"I have no doubt." Carlos took a breath and lengthened his stride in an attempt to match the general's gait. "My colleagues and I travel in quite a small circle. So small, that Samuel's loss...his loss will be monumental. Who is it?"

"Dr. Felix Paul," Sinclair said over his shoulder. "He should be landing at the airfield any minute."

Carlos smiled. "Ah, Felix. Yes, he is a good man—I know him well. We worked closely together years ago. But, Payton, if I may, his specialty is not at all suited for—"

"I need all the sharp minds I can get."

They rounded a corner, and Sinclair quickened his gait. *Were they going in circles?*

"Yes, Dr. Paul possesses a sharp mind." Carlos spoke two or three words between breaths. He needed bigger lungs. Or legs. The general glanced back.

"Don't worry, we're almost there." After a few more steps, the general smiled. "Look over there, Carlos. We call it Mojave Park."

The beauty of the greenery before him made Carlos stop. An underground park, complete with shrubs, trees, and bar-b-que pits. Men and women sat on benches, lay in the grass, and cooled their feet in a lazy river. *"Que bonita."*

"The park provides everyone with a respite—the illusion of spending time in the great outdoors. Off duty personnel are encouraged to relax and recharge their batteries. Please feel free to take advantage of its restorative qualities. It really helps."

Strolling to the edge of the river, Carlos bent over and stuck his finger in the rushing water. He smiled and turned to the general. "It's cold. I like the soothing sound."

"I'm glad it meets with your approval. It cost the taxpayers millions."

"Worth every penny."

"Down the way a bit is our commissary. We offer cuisines from around the world."

"An underground food court."

The general chuckled. "On a much grander scale. Are you hungry?"

"No, *gracias*."

"Very well, follow me." The general led Carlos down a few more passageways. He stopped and opened a door. "This is my office. My door is open to you anytime—day or night."

It took Carlos a few moments to catch his breath before crossing the threshold. A desk cluttered with files and stacks of paperwork caught his attention. "Payton, your desk is…is a bit disorganized, yes?"

"That monstrosity belongs to my assistant. He has his own filing system." Sinclair glanced at his watch. "He must be getting a bite to eat. Follow me." He crossed the length of the vestibule and opened another door leading to his private office.

The word minimalist came to mind. No pictures on the walls, only a map of the underground facility hanging behind the general's desk. A near empty bookcase stood against the far wall—the Bible, two binders, and something called a U. S. Military Justice Handbook. No personal items adorned the desk, not even a picture of his daughter. Carlos could not help but think the man had already packed his belongings, determined to leave in disgrace. The leather chairs in front of the desk were a welcome sight. Sinclair stood behind his desk, slid open a drawer, and brought out a gold lighter. He lit another cigarette, inhaling long and deep. Carlos eased his aching bones in a plush chair.

"*Señor*, tell me more about the aliens, these people you call ENOs."

Sinclair blew out a stream of smoke and eased into the leather chair behind his desk. "My men do their best to take care of their needs, but it's not an easy task. I told you about the catatonic state they're in when they arrive. It's so severe that some of the men refer to them as Cats. A word I discourage, but there you have it. I'm desperate for answers. If I don't get any—and fast—Operation Zero will begin."

"Ay, Dios mio."

"Carlos, I'll be direct." He stubbed out the cigarette. "Even though Gatekeeper is a defense contractor and not part of the government, I report directly to the Joint Chiefs. They gave Gatekeeper full operational command of this project over a decade ago. I've been tasked with three objectives. First, to reverse engineer the Tombstone. Second, to ascertain who the ENOs are, and where they come from. Third, to establish some form of communication with these extraterrestrials."

"I understand, but I still don't—"

"When I first took command, I contacted Donaldson, Polansky, and at least half a dozen others. Of course, I thought of you first, but...you were dealing with your own issues."

Dark images filled Carlos's thoughts—MIT, Lilly's death, his own terrible breakdown and addiction to drugs.

"The point is," Sinclair said, "most of the people I called were enthusiastic—at first. They offered advice, some suggested possible theories. Polansky even stayed for a week."

"A week? No more than that?"

"Eventually, they all deserted the project—some lasting no more than a few hours. Now, with the knowledge of what they've seen, the government is wary of what they might say."

"But the non-disclosure agreements, surely—"

"NDAs have been broken before. You know the government can't afford to have any of this wind up in a court of law, or worse, on the six o'clock news."

"But what are you saying? I signed the contract and I don't plan on telling anyone what I've seen. You know you can trust me, Payton."

"Of course. I just want to be up front with you. Being part of this project is something that will follow you—follow us all—for the rest of our lives. Do you understand?"

Carlos nodded. "Of course."

"This is too important to jump into casually. Something I may not have impressed on the physicists I first brought on board."

"Don't blame yourself, Payton. I understand. But listen, we need a team working on this. Dr. Paul is brilliant, yes, but he and I alone can hardly—"

"Leave that to me." The general offered a smile. "I'm still

34

waiting on more call backs. Others will come, I'm sure of it. I'm going to contact the Joint Chiefs and tell them about my progress in obtaining your services. If I'm right about Dr. Paul, he'll certainly jump at the chance to work with you. That might be enough to put Operation Zero on hold—at least for a while. In the meantime, you must be exhausted. I've assigned Sergeant Sandoval as your liaison officer. I'll have him escort you to your quarters, where you can get some rest—unless you remember how to get back to your room without help."

"*Ay, Dios mio*. A mouse in a maze would have more success in retracing his steps than I would in this underground puzzle. The sergeant's help is more than welcome." Besides, he did not want to think about anything. His head ached with visions of aliens, the Tombstone, and concentration camps. Thoughts of Lilly and MIT also screamed for attention. He had to decide whether to take another vitamin and chance passing out, or a Xanax and be certain of it.

"I'll call the sergeant." Sinclair lifted the telephone, but a loud knock on the door stopped him. "Enter."

A thin black-shirted guard stepped in. "Sir. Sorry to interrupt, sir, but there's been a development. A big one, sir."

"Yes, go on."

"There's a situation with the Tombstone...er, uh, I mean the TDS." The man glanced away, his hands trembling, his breath irregular.

"Get ahold of yourself." Then, in a softer tone, Sinclair said, "What's the problem, son?"

"Sir, the Tombstone...well...uh—"

"Out with it." Sinclair stood up.

"Well, sir, it sort of duplicated itself."

"You can't be serious."

"I am, sir. There's another Tombstone. Now there's two of them, and some Cats...err...uh, ENOs are walking out of that one, too."

"Shit." Sinclair rushed out of the office. Carlos did his best to keep up.

The news of a second Tombstone producing more aliens made him forget all about his own needs. He also forgot about the paperback book Dr. Turnbride placed in his pocket.

35

CHAPTER 6

Carlos raced down the hallway after General Sinclair. He found it impossible to keep up with the younger man but managed to catch fleeting glimpses of the back of his uniform. They hurried down long stretches of hallway, negotiating several sharp turns. After a few minutes, he reached The Shelter, out of breath, and witnessing complete pandemonium.

The ice-cold temperature bit at his face. He leaned against a wall, thankful for his heavy wool peacoat. He caught sight of the general standing near the Tombstone. A second monolith, an exact replica of the first, stood at an angle to the original. The duplicate straddled the yellow and black marking-tape outlining the position of the first.

A bright flash lit up the cavern. Carlos raised his arm, protecting his eyes from the intense illumination. Thunder rumbled throughout the cave. Two females and two males emerged from the original Tombstone. Moments later, sparks of brilliant light accompanied the arrival of three more beings from the duplicate.

Carlos ignored his fear, venturing further into The Shelter until he stood only a few feet behind Sinclair.

"General." A robust man in black uniform saluted.

Returning the salute, the general said, "Major Bay, what's the situation?"

A flash of light surged through the cave causing the major to turn away. Thunder rumbled overhead, then faded.

"Major Bay, " the general yelled, "sitrep."

"At sixteen-thirty-four, a second TSD, an exact replica of the original, materialized. It began emitting ENOs at once."

"It *materialized?*" the general said, leaning in. "From what? From where?"

"Sir, it divided from the first Tombstone and seems just as active, maybe more so."

Several flashes of light appeared. More than two dozen beings emerged from the duplicate Tombstone's luminescent depths. Black Shirts scrambled to corral the new arrivals.

"Mobilize all off-duty personnel," General Sinclair shouted. "I want them down here on the double. We've got to stay ahead of this."

"Yes, sir."

The spectacle of guards and new arrivals passed before Carlos like a curious parade. Realizing he stood only an arm's length from actual extraterrestrials made him shudder. Their wide eyes stared straight ahead. The aliens' white hair and smooth skin startled him at first. As he grew accustomed to their appearance, he became fascinated by the minor differences to human beings.

Everything at the outer edges of the main cave blended together, presenting itself in a dark palette of shadows. More new arrivals emerged from the Tombstones, heralded by sparks of bright light and thunder. They placed the creatures in two long and winding lines that lead away from the center of the cave. The respective lines vanished through tunnels at opposite ends of the main cavern. Immense banners hung over both openings, identifying them as the Southern Tunnel System and Northern Tunnel System. Only the faint flickering of bare light bulbs hanging from electrical cords illuminated the rows of bodies disappearing into the tunnels.

Carlos grew accustomed to the drama of activity, unease, and bravery. A grand opera. Orders were shouted, alarm bells echoed, and red lights flashed. Guards in black shirts ran, some at full speed, in all directions. They worked together as a team—well trained, well prepared. They remained professional, whether securing new arrivals, moving equipment out of the way to make room for the new Tombstone, or directing traffic through the underground chamber. The pandemonium had a certain purpose. A choreographed chaos.

Bolts of white light struck at irregular intervals. It brought the shadows at the edges of the cave into clear focus, revealing the immense size of the facility. A crack of thunder accompanying the lighting forced Carlos to duck and back away from the Tombstones.

He caught sight of an elevator door sliding open. A tall man, with a gray beard and thick glasses, emerged. The man wore a black suit and a dark gray newsboy hat turned backward. Taking tentative steps across the threshold of the elevator, his eyes widened. Flashes of intense light illuminated his rugged face.

"Felix," Carlos shouted. "Over here."

It took a full minute for Dr. Felix Paul to weave his way through the commotion. He reached out his hand, hesitated, then withdrew the offer to shake. "So glad to see you," he shouted in his southern drawl above the uproar. "What the hell's going on? What in Gawd's name? This is insane."

"You wouldn't believe me if I told you," Carlos said. "Suffice it to say, we are witnessing the miracle you and I so often discussed. Dare I say it? This appears to be the Grand Design in action—something from nothing."

Dr. Paul's eyes grew wide. He mumbled, "I don't understand... what is this madness?"

"I'm not supposed to tell, it's a classified secret. Where is your escort?"

"Oh! Uh...they were dickin' around with something up top, so I just got on the elevator and pressed a button. I didn't expect any of this."

"Ah, the same old Felix. So anxious to attack a problem."

"Who in the hell are all those naked people, and what in the hell are those two giant boxes they're stepping out of? We're underground, right? What's with all that thunder and lightning? What the hell's—"

"Dr. Paul," General Sinclair said. "I need you to follow me, please."

"Felix," Carlos said, bragging like a proud papa, "this is my good friend Payton Sinclair—a student of mine at MIT. He's in charge of everything you see here."

Felix snorted but held out his hand. "Good to meet you in person, general. You sounded awfully desperate on the phone. Now I can see why. Would you be so kind as to tell me exactly what in the hell I'm looking at?"

"In due time, doctor. Please follow me." Sinclair motioned toward the metal stairs leading to the second-floor offices.

Seeing Dr. Paul's hesitation, Carlos said, "It'll be okay, my friend. Just some paperwork. You know how the government is, you can't even pee without getting shot."

"What did you say?" Sinclair frowned.

"Oh, just something I overheard. I'll wait for you here."

"Are you sure, Carlos?" Sinclair said.

"*Si*, I'm okay. Besides, it will allow me time to observe the Tombstones and perhaps form a theory."

"Fine, but don't move. I'll get Sergeant Sandoval down here to keep you company. Dr. Paul and I will be right back."

Carlos watched the general usher Dr. Paul up the metal stairs to the small conference room, the same room where he'd signed the non-disclosure papers. His attention turned back to the Tombstones. If the situation weren't so serious, it might have been amusing.

Captain Bay growled orders over his radio, shouting commands to the uniformed men scrambling to gain the upper hand over a growing number of extraterrestrials. So many Keystone Cops chasing after naked criminals. A great wave of new black-shirted personnel arrived on the scene. Wearing white gloves, they took two or three unclothed beings at a time, placing them in either the north or south tunnel lines. Still more aliens emerged from the Tombstones. The tide of the altercation could go either way.

"You there!"

Carlos turned. "Ah, Capitan Bay. What may I do for you?"

"It's *Major* Bay. Here, take this one and follow me." The major shoved a naked woman toward Carlos.

Taller by at least six inches, she leaned against him. The warmth of her breath felt good on his face. He steadied himself and held her at arms' length, his hands on her shoulders. The sight of her body made him uncomfortable. Lifting his gaze from her bare breasts, he backed away, trying his best to ignore her nudity. Her violet eyes seemed to stare straight through him, as if she were focused on some distant point behind him. He turned around, glancing back at a wall of granite. "Miss, what are you looking for?"

She remained silent. From the details of her face she appeared to be in her early twenties, but her weary eyes conveyed the impression of an old soul. Locks of close-cropped, white hair, firm shoulders,

40

and an athletic build gave her a boyish look. However, her smooth, unblemished skin, and feminine curves put a lie to that idea.

"C'mon," Major Bay said, "grab her and follow me."

Carlos's heart thumped when he took a quick peek at the mayhem surrounding them. Lightning flashed time and again, signaling a steady stream of new arrivals. The drumbeat of thunder filled his ears like cannon fire. An incessant alarm hee-hawed in the distance, like a braying mule, echoing throughout the cave.

The girl with the violet eyes collided against Carlos, like a wind-up toy forever bumping against him. She moved forward seeming to follow an unseen path running through him—advancing ever forward.

"What is your name, young lady?"

She ignored the question, ignored him altogether.

"Excuse me, miss, please follow me." Being a modest man, Carlos tried to keep his eyes above her neckline, but being a man nonetheless, they darted across her soft skin from top to bottom. Strikingly beautiful. She advanced again, oblivious to the commotion surrounding them. "No, miss, you must turn around. There's nothing behind me, just a wall. Please, turn around." He reached for the bottle of vitamins in his pocket and unscrewed the lid.

The woman bumped against him, knocking the vial from his hand. It fell to the floor, its contents clattering across the concrete in every direction.

"C'mon, what are you waiting for?" Major Bay shouted over his shoulder. "Just take her elbow and let's go."

"But I'm supposed to stay here."

"Looks like that ain't gonna happen. C'mon. Now remember, she can't hear you, so just grab her by the arm and redirect her. Don't be afraid of her. The Cats are as harmless as newborn puppies. Just stay behind me and don't get lost. Let's move."

Carlos put his hand on her elbow. The gentle pressure he applied made her change course with ease. He ushered her behind Major Bay who led two beings of his own toward an enormous archway a few yards ahead.

Despite the major's words, Carlos refused to treat this woman like an inanimate object. Somewhere, deep inside, she possessed a soul. He believed that with all his heart.

41

"Follow me, please," he whispered. "Excellent, right this way. Stay close and watch your step. *Muy bien.*"

The line of Black Shirts guiding new arrivals bottlenecked a few yards ahead. Bodies pressed against him on all sides entering the dark passage under a large banner.

Southern Tunnel System.

CHAPTER 7

Beyond the threshold of the Southern Tunnel entrance lay a myriad of smaller corridors, doorways, and side tunnels reminding Carlos of a human-sized ant farm.

"Remember, stay close or you *will* get lost," Major Bay said, glancing over his shoulder.

At the admonition Carlos hesitated, wanting to turn back at once. The girl with the violet eyes shuffled forward and remained in line. He stayed by her side. They travelled several more yards, making a series of sharp turns—right, left, right, then right again. Bare light bulbs spaced about ten feet apart hung from cords, offering the only illumination. The smell of moist soil, body odor, and raw sewage filled his nostrils.

The grade beneath his feet dipped, sending him farther into the depths of the earth. He shivered. His breath, like puffs of fog, came quicker with each step. Carlos attempted to keep up with the endless procession of guards and aliens, but countless men in black shirts escorting new arrivals rushed past him, clogging the narrow tunnel.

Goosebumps covered the girl's smooth skin. He thought about throwing his coat over her shoulders, but reasoned chivalry would have to wait. The act would only delay the march to their final destination.

"You're Professor Huerta," Major Bay said over his shoulder.

Another fan? Carlos smiled. "I am."

"It's about time one of you eggheads got your hands dirty."

Not a fan.

The ground became rough and uneven, nothing more than jagged rock and loose pebbles. It must have been uncomfortable on the girl's bare feet, but she did not complain. Her face remained steadfast, head held high, eyes staring straight ahead. She seemed determined, but to what end?

His legs cramped, screaming for relief. He found it difficult to match Major Bay's pace in the crowded tunnel. The younger man trudged ahead like a machine. Carlos focused on his hand touching the girl's smooth elbow. *Alien contact.* The thought produced adrenalin, giving him the much-needed strength to keep plodding forward.

They turned into a passageway that seemed to run on without end. Hundreds, perhaps thousands, of metal doors lined both sides of the tunnel. Each door displayed a number. Attached to the doors were small chalkboards. A piece of chalk, secured by twine, hung from each board. The boards were marked with hash marks. Major Bay studied each board they passed. Dozens of soldiers marched by, their eyes also studying the tiny chalkboards. Carlos, sweating and out of breath, finally caught up to the major. "How much farther must we—"

"Stand by." Major Bay stopped at door number 722 and lifted its chalkboard to the light. "Here, there's only three in here." He released the two beings he had shepherded through the tunnel system and lifted the latch of the metal door. After re-securing his charges, he steered them inside the dark room and nodded for Carlos to do the same with the girl. "Hurry."

"This way, miss," Carlos said, guiding her across the threshold. "*Cuidado.* Please watch your step."

The existing occupants of the room did nothing to acknowledge them. Instead, they kept to themselves, huddling together, no doubt for warmth. Carlos shivered. He blew a breath into his cupped hands and glanced at the girl.

"*Pobrecita.*" The time for chivalry had arrived. He took off his peacoat and draped it over her shoulders. "This should help keep the chill off, miss," he said with a smile. "Don't worry, everything will be alright."

"You've got a lot to learn about the Cats." Major Bay backed out of the room and into the narrow passageway. "The government may have fancy names for them—ENOs, or new arrivals—but most of us just call 'em Cats—short for catatonic." He rubbed the chalkboard with his palm and used the small piece of chalk to scribble three additional hash marks, bringing the total to six for the already crowded chamber.

Carlos stopped to survey the living quarters. General Sinclair did not exaggerate. The conditions were appalling. No furniture, one bare light bulb, and nothing but hard, cold rock—floor to ceiling. He explored the stark area trying to find another door, one that might lead to a restroom. He saw none. Instead, he spied a jagged hole cut into the ground, and assumed it led to an open sewer system. That accounted for the stench.

"Let's go," Major Bay said from the passageway. "The less time we have to spend down here, the better."

Carlos stepped into the crowded tunnel. Everywhere people pushed and shoved, trying to be first in either direction. It reminded Carlos of his time spent in Boston and rush hour on the T. Every Black Shirt ushered one or two new arrivals through the darkened passageway. Every so often a guard tripped and tumbled to the ground, dragging their impassive burdens down with them. They soon scrambled to their feet and continued the march.

He scanned the endless tunnel. New arrivals were piloted through corridors, steered around corners, and shoved into rooms. In sharp contrast to their blank stares, the young Black Shirts wore anxious expressions, a few were excited, some even laughed. Even though they were surprised by the sudden appearance of a second Tombstone, they seemed prepared, answering the challenge with grit and determination.

Major Bay hurried along, plowing his way back through the narrow tunnel. Carlos hurried to catch up.

"Excuse me," he said, gasping for air. "How many souls can this underground boarding house accommodate?"

"Boarding house?" The major chuckled. "This place was overcrowded even before the second Tombstone appeared, but now…" His words hung in the frigid air. With a shake of his head, he quick-marched to the right, then made a sharp left turn.

A bulky guard shoved his way through the tunnel. Carlos avoided a face plant by reaching out and steadying himself against the solid rock wall. Like a fish fighting his way upstream, he struggled against the push and pull of soldiers with their charges. Dozens of the new arrivals were ushered past him. He had become immune to their nakedness. It no longer mattered whether they were clothed or not. Instead, he focused on the repulsive, almost inhuman way they were herded along, like so many sheep—sheep to the slaughter.

The scene sickened him. He hugged the wall, an image of death camps coming to mind. It unsettled him. He had just guided someone down here with his own hands. He had imprisoned her in a cold, dark cell. His only defense, like the monsters from another time and another place—he was just following orders.

His stomach soured. Bile sent him reeling to his knees. He glanced up and shuddered. Major Bay had vanished. Steadying himself against the wall, he searched his pocket for a vitamin, then gagged. They had fallen on the floor in The Shelter. Panic crept through his gut like a slow-acting poison.

A strange symbol on the rock wall caught his eye. A zero with a slash. The symbol had been written in dark-blue paint. He glanced at the opposite wall. The same symbol.

He shivered, his joints aching. No matter. He knew he had to continue the journey against the crush of people, if he had any hope of making it back to The Shelter. *But which way to go? How many tunnels had they traversed?* Thoughts of being lost filled him with fear. His feet, as heavy as the granite surrounding him, would not move.

"Does anybody know which way to go? Please. I need to go back."

The boots tramping across the gravel floor buried his appeal. His mind turned to the implications of remaining behind. He hated the thought of dying two thousand feet below the surface of the earth, in a cold, dark tunnel. Or of starving to death in a foul-smelling pit, or worse, to be left alone—the one lone human—in a cavern packed with aliens. The anxiety threatened to overwhelm him. "Cathedral. Bell. Chimney. Steamboat. Devil's Bridge." The mantra came in a rush. He closed his eyes and shouted. "Cathedral. Bell. Chimney. Steamboat. Devil's Bridge." With hands covering his ears, he whispered. "Cathedral. Bell. Chimney. Steamboat. Devil's Bridge."

He became aware of a change in the acoustics of the underground corridor. The congestion had thinned, the clamor of footsteps subsided. Carlos wiped at his eyes then peered left and right. Like the thunderous crash of ocean waves followed by an almost eerie silence, he found himself in still waters. *Had he blacked out? Fainted?* In either case, the passageway lay deserted.

A lone, naked alien marched by him in silence. The extraterrestrial stopped, turned, crouched, and put his face inches from his. The alien raised a finger and drew a circle in the air. He ran his finger through it, a slash through the zero. The alien's lips were blue, his eyes black. He rose and rushed away, his feet slapping the hard, granite floor. In a moment, the creature disappeared in the shadows.

Icy air burned the inside of Carlos's throat, causing him to take short, rasping breaths. His thoughts bounced between the horror of being surrounded by people and the panic of being alone. The appearance of the alien disturbed him as well. Deep down, he knew something catastrophic would happen to him in this desert—a plane crash, a sandstorm, something terrible. This place, evil, forbidding, and so close to Area 51, held no Vortex for protection. The guardians could not hear his cries. He took a few steps to the right, climbing toward The Shelter. It would be a long and arduous journey.

Without warning, without understanding, he stopped, turned, and continued in the opposite direction, deeper into the cave. After a while, he happened upon the endless tunnel of metal doors with painted numbers.

Room 698...Carlos trudged, step by step, rubbing his fingers across each door. He examined the numbers on the chalkboards representing the number of residents jammed inside the chambers.

Room 703...Frosty mist accompanied his every breath. His body ached.

Room 714...The phrase "died of frostbite" swam through his head, repeating over and over, like a eulogy.

Room 718...Without the warmth of other bodies in the narrow corridor, he imagined a slow and chilling death—painful, terrifying.

"Cállate!" **Shut up,** he scolded himself. He imagined his body being cremated, if just for the warmth.

Room 722...A glimmer of hope. A chance at survival. Behind this door lie a small room housing six beings. They were extraterrestrials but warm bodies nonetheless. Hopefully, they would accept him. She would be there—the girl with the violet eyes.

He took hold of the chalkboard with quivering fingers and added a hashmark—himself—bringing the total number of occupants in room 722 to seven. Carlos raised the latch and pried open the metal door. He scanned the room. She stood in the shadows against the far wall, alone, away from the light. After closing the door, he strolled to the middle of the room, stopping under the bare light bulb. The girl wearing his coat stepped away from the shadows and ambled toward him. She stopped by his side, so close he felt her breath on his face. He appreciated the back of her hand against his.

"What is your name?" Carlos managed. No response. He turned his wrist and held her hand. *"Lo siento.* I'm sorry to be so forward, but I am freezing." Silence. Her eyes remained fixed, staring straight ahead.

Carlos longed for a Quaalude, an Ativan—he would even settle for a Valium, but the bag containing his vitamins lay upstairs. It may as well have been on Mars.

It didn't take long for him to come to terms with this new reality. He had experienced it before. Bitter cold, aching joints, and loneliness, the same kind of isolation he had faced when Lilly passed. How he longed for a sign, a tiny signal he had not been abandoned in this wretched cave. The slightest hint of hope. *Por favor. Anything.*

The girl with the violet eyes squeezed his hand.

CHAPTER
8

"Where am I?" Prudence Wellman said, her voice bouncing against the tile walls of the small exam room. "Who are you?" The two guards wearing black shirts, standing near the door, ignored her but not for long.

The guards unbuckled the restraints securing her to the exam table. Each man, standing on either side of the bed, reached down and grabbed an elbow. They lifted her off the bed. She did her best to resist but to no avail. They escorted her out of the room without a word and released her in the middle of a long white hallway. The polished linoleum floor cooled the soles of her bare feet. The guards backed away from her.

"What do you want? Why won't you answer me?" The two men remained silent, never taking their gaze from her.

"You're scaring me," she whispered. Tears rolled down her cheeks. Her breathing shallowed. She teetered down the hall, risking a glance back at the two soldiers. They stood their ground, studying her.

Keeping her eyes trained on them, she noticed a sudden change in their behavior. Their shoulders slouched. They bowed their heads and turned away, as if afraid of being seen. In an instant, they had gone from confident, in control, to timid and fearful.

One of the men fell to his knees, sobbing. He wiped tears from his eyes with the back of his hand. "I need to get out of here." His words echoed off the bone-white walls. "Where am I? What am I doing here?"

Prudence turned away and hurried to the other end of the corridor. A solid green door blocked her way. She took hold of the latch. It wouldn't budge. She focused again on the two guards standing at the other end of the hall. One of them stared back. She ambled toward him, taking small steps at first, then marching with more confidence.

He cowered away from her and backed against the wall.

"Look at me," she said, standing over him. When he raised his head, Prudence recognized the emotion in his eyes. Fear. The same sensation that had frightened her, now spooked him. Prudence breathed just a little easier. Like a lion tamer testing her abilities, she turned her back on the guard, but glanced over her shoulder just in case. He remained on the ground.

She scanned the hallway. Several dark glass domes hung from the ceiling. Security cameras. The doors lining the long white corridor reminded her of a hospital ward. Engraved brass plaques adorned each door. She read a plaque on one of the doors. Gamble the Empath. It didn't make any sense. She turned the latch and entered. It appeared to be an exam room. An exact duplicate of the one she had occupied. Against the far wall, a patient lay on the table. A sheet partially covered the man's face. His wrists and ankles were strapped securely to the table. The sheet lay over his right eye, leaving his left one free to follow her every move.

"You're in an underground research facility," the man said in a calm and measured tone. The sheet billowed when he spoke. "You're new. I've been here for a couple of weeks. My name is Gamble. I'd shake your hand, but…" He wiggled his fingers.

"Why—?"

"Why are you here?" Gamble finished her sentence. "Why are any of us here? The answer is simple. Experimentations, my dear girl—secret government experimentations. Real MK Ultra type stuff."

"MK…uh, what?"

"They say we're special. Ha." He wiggled his fingers again. "Yeah, I feel pretty special right now. How about you? You see, they're testing us, like lab rats. Looking for a way to communicate with the people who really aren't people."

"How…how do you know what I'm thinking?" An alarm bell

50

rang once, a harsh and sudden sound. When it stopped, the silence frightened her almost as much as the sound of the bell. She turned her attention back to the man on the table.

"I'm an empath," Gamble said. "One of several specials they have locked up on this ward. They've also got telepaths, mind readers, psychics. Oh, and rumor has it, we've even got a ghost somewhere in the—"

"What's an empath?" She took a step toward the exam table.

"Would you mind removing the sheet from my face? I'd like to take a proper look at you." She leaned forward and did as instructed. "There, that's better." Gamble smiled, keeping both eyes on her. "An empath is someone who feels what someone else feels. For instance, I feel you're frightened. No, not just frightened." He wrinkled his brow. "Young lady, you're scared to death. You'd better calm down. It isn't good for you to feel like that, believe me, it really isn't."

"Anyone can see I'm scared. You don't need a special gift to—"

"Okay, how's this? You have no idea where you are or why you're here. You think you've been drugged. You have. You want revenge on the people who did this to you. So, do I. And you think whoever is holding you here are sick bastards, who deserve to be punished by having their heads set on fire. Is that a little more specific for you, or can *anyone* see that?"

Prudence backed away from the exam table. "Well, except for the part about setting their heads on fire. I'm not that vindictive. Why are we locked up, and who are *they*?"

"The government. Our government. They're holding us because of our special abilities...and because no one will ever report us missing."

"Excuse me? What do you mean no one will ever report—"

"Do you have any living relatives?" Gamble twitched his nose. Prudence shook her head. "Neither do I. Tell me where they found you? What do you recall before being here?"

"I...I remember being in a hospital," Prudence said. "But not a regular hospital for sick people, a special hospital for—"

"Special people," Gamble said with a smile. "Relax, you're doing fine." Again, he twitched his nose. "Listen, would you mind untying my restraints? I've got the most annoying itch on my nose that needs immediate attention."

She moved forward meaning to untie him, then stopped. "How

can I be sure you won't hurt me? I don't even know you."

"You can't be certain of anything down here. Then again, you can't be certain of most things up there, can you?"

"Down here, up there. Where are we? What is this place?"

He scrunched his nose then snorted. "My dear Alice, you've tumbled down a very deep rabbit hole, indeed. We're two thousand feet underground. This is a secret site, and we're here because of our powers—the abilities that ruined our otherwise normal lives."

"My name isn't Alice. It's Prudence, and I don't have any special powers."

"Oh, but you do." Gamble chuckled. "Listen, the rest of us had no idea why we were brought here either—not at first, anyway. We soon discovered the common denominator, our special powers. Most of us were forgotten, neatly tucked away in psych wards. That's when your tax dollars went to work for evil purposes. The government stole us in the middle of the night, and we were brought here. At least, I like to think it happened in the middle of the night. It's the romantic in me. So, tell me, my dear—think hard. What's your special ability? What can *you* do that almost nobody else in the whole wide world can do?"

After a short pause, she shrugged. "You're the psychic, you tell me."

"I told you, I'm an empath. That means I can read your emotions, your feelings but not your thoughts. Alas, if only I could."

Prudence lowered her head, making direct eye contact. "Well, at one time, I thought I could see into the future." She let out a laugh. "But I never saw *this*."

"Don't worry, Pru, none of us did. Not even the psychics."

"How do you know so much about me?" She leaned against the edge of the bed. "About the others in this place?"

"The scientists can keep us separated—the guards can keep us tied up..." Chuckling, he wiggled his fingers again, like a magician proving to the audience he could not move. "...but nothing can stop us from talking, especially at night. I can feel what the psychics think, and the telepaths can get so loud sometimes, I feel like telling them to shut up. Oh, sorry."

"Sorry about what?"

"Not you, my dear, I'm talking with Clarissa. She's a telepath in the next room. She told me not to be so rude." Gamble raised his voice. "Sorry, Clarissa. Anyway, a few of us have even gotten into some of the researcher's heads. We have a pretty good idea of what they're up to, for the most part." He twitched his nose again. "For God's sake, woman, either scratch my nose yourself or cut it off. I can't stand it."

She reached out, then hesitated. "Where exactly are we?"

"Like I said, we're over two thousand feet underground—that's about two hundred stories. And we're...uh oh."

"What? What's *uh-oh*?" Prudence trembled. She withdrew her hand, just inches from the tip of Gamble's nose.

"Someone's at the door." He mirrored her terror. "The Black Shirts are here for you. What's happening? I feel a...a panic attack coming on. I never get panic attacks—ever. It must be you. What the hell's going on?" Sweat streamed across his brow. He struggled against the restraints, wagging his hands about like they were flippers, then arching his back. "My God, Pru, I think I know what your ability is."

The door swung open, and three Black Shirts rushed in. They were followed by a woman in a white lab coat, her brown hair tied back in a messy bun. Before Prudence took another breath, the guards grabbed her and forced her to the floor. The woman stepped forward, crouched, and with uncanny speed, pushed a needle deep into Prudence's neck. It stung like the bite of a wasp. In a few seconds, Prudence gave up her struggle, and the soldiers eased their hold. Her limbs grew weak, darkness filling her head. Before she passed out, she glanced up at Gamble. He twitched his nose.

Waking with a start, Prudence's breath caught in the back of her throat. She sucked in a lungful of air like she had been held under water for some time. The restraints on her wrists and ankles were tight, keeping her stuck to the cold exam table as if she were a used stick of gum. She tested the strength of the leather straps. No movement.

"Ah, *fräulein*, you're awake." The deep-throated voice startled her. "Let's hope you're more cooperative than earlier, *ja*?" A big bear of a man in a white lab coat came into focus. He smiled down at her, not the kind of smile a reasonable person might mistake for affection. Prudence swallowed hard, shut her eyes, and turned away.

"I'm freezing," she whispered. Conditioned air poured from the vents in the ceiling, filling the exam room with a biting chill. She glanced over the big man's shoulders at monitors stacked against the far wall. More than the frosty temperature, the beeps and whirs of machines created an extra icy feel of clinical sterility.

The big bear rubbed his hands together. His chin and lower lip trembled. "Oh my, it *is* cold in here," he said, reaching for an exam tray. He took hold of a rather large hypodermic. "Not to worry Miss Wellman, this is only a simple dye." He held the needle high in the air and flicked at the murky orange liquid in the syringe. He pushed the plunger, sending a few drops squirting out. With a broad smile he approached her, aiming the business end of the needle at her chest. "Not to worry, this will not hurt a bit. You should hardly even feel it. Trust me, *ja*?"

"No." Tears fell from the corners of Prudence's eyes. "Why are you doing this to me?"

"*Nien*, it is not me. It is Colonel Bloodstone. He is the one you can blame."

"Who?" She pictured the big, burly man turning the needle on himself, plunging the orange liquid into *his* chest. No sooner had she given birth to the thought than the man's meaty paw twisted around, the hypodermic now facing him.

"*Mein Gott*, but it *does* hurt," he whispered, injecting the orange liquid into his chest. His hands dropped to his sides. The oversized hypodermic stuck out of his chest like a misguided lawn dart. He fell, face first on the floor.

Prudence shut her eyes, thinking over and over, *let me go. Someone get me out of here. Let me go, let me go!*

The door slammed open. The woman in the white lab coat entered the room. Using quick, authoritative steps, she moved around the big bear's body and marched toward the exam table. With practiced hands, she unbuckled the straps holding Prudence to the exam table.

At that moment, Prudence knew. She understood why Gamble asked about her special ability. The answer materialized. She could control the actions of others with her thoughts—no, much simpler than that, more organic. She need only *feel* what she wanted, and it manifested. The explanation lifted her spirits, bringing a smile to her lips. The rules to whatever game the government might be playing had just changed.

CHAPTER 9

Carlos woke, sandwiched between the cold, hard floor of the chamber and the soft, warm body of the girl with the violet eyes. She rested her head on his chest. He rubbed the sleep from his eyes and glanced about.

The extraterrestrials lay in various positions around the room, some motionless and snoring, others restless and fidgety. The dark chamber held no clues as to the time of day. Morning? Noon? Time stood still. He broke the silence with a whisper. "How long have we been asleep?" She did not respond, so he placed his hand on her back. "Excuse me, miss. Are you awake? I think it's time we leave this chamber."

She roused, yawning much like anybody would, then stared at him with unseeing eyes, unlike anyone he had ever met. He shuddered. *Who is this woman?*

He continued his hushed tone, so as to not wake the others. "Where do you come from, miss?" Her lips parted for a moment, then shut tight. "What is your name? What do I call you?"

Again, no answer. She propped up on one elbow, then rose to her feet. Effortless. Graceful. Carlos, on the other hand, labored to rise, assisted by grunts and groans along the way. The aliens stirred, stretching and yawning.

"Forgive me," he said. "I'm sorry to have disturbed you, but with great age comes great pain."

A familiar noise sounded from the other side of the metal door.

Hee-haw…hee-haw…hee-haw. The aliens found their feet at once.

"No." His heart sank. *Had the Tombstone multiplied yet again?* If another multitude of new arrivals needed shelter it would be a tragedy. The chambers were already so crowded. He took the girl by the hand and hurried to the door. The latch would not budge. When he entered last night, he must have locked it behind him.

"We must escape this underground prison." He tried to break the door down by banging against it with his shoulder. "*Ay, no me digas.*" He rubbed at the new ache he had created. "Let's hope they try to place another new arrival…er, that is, another guest such as yourself, in this room. When they open the door, we will leave." He put his ear to the cold metal.

Voices echoed through the passageway, boots tramped along the hard ground, and the alarm blared.

"Be patient, the door will open," he said, more to ease his own anxiety than anything else. "Once we get out of here, I'm going to settle you in my room. You'll be safe there—warmer at least. Or so I hope. I have yet to see my room, but they tell me it's nice. Perhaps we should—"

The door burst open. A young, wide-eyed Black Shirt guard holding two new arrivals inspected the room. Somebody rushed through the passageway behind him, pushing him into the chamber. He tumbled to the ground. Carlos stepped over the stunned guard and helped the girl do the same.

Once in the passageway, they were jostled and shoved. Carlos felt their momentum shift, sending them deeper into the tunnel. "No, no, no. Miss, put your back against the wall, and let them pass. Like this." He held her hand and demonstrated.

Hundreds of guards escorting new arrivals stormed by in a rolling stampede, brushing past Carlos and the girl. It would have been easier to stop hugging the rock wall and go with the flow, but Carlos pressed deeper into the crevices of the hard granite, holding his ground. The girl did the same. Together they stood firm against the steady crush of bodies.

After several moments, the surge of guards and new arrivals dissipated. Like the cycle of the ocean, the passageway calmed—an interval of quiet following the thunderous commotion.

Without warning, a wave of Black Shirts, minus new arrivals, rushed back through the tunnel. Carlos pulled the girl away from the wall, and together, they joined the swell of retreating bodies marching away from the chambers.

"Stay close. We'll soon be out of this nightmare." He plodded over loose rocks and gravel, managing to keep his balance by holding the girl's hand.

His heart sank at the sight of four Tombstones emitting a constant stream of new arrivals. Bright flashes lit up the subterranean chamber in a relentless light show. Black Shirts scrambled to control the situation. In the melee, nobody gave Carlos or the girl a second glance. He noticed her interest in the Tombstones.

"Do you remember anything about your journey here?" Maybe the sight of the monoliths had jarred a memory.

He placed his hand on her back, guiding her away from the madness. "This way, miss." Even though exhausted, craving his pills, and shaking from the cold, Carlos continued his reassuring tone. "We're almost there, just a little further. You're doing so good. That's it."

They entered the tiled hallway leading to the main complex of offices and suites. He hesitated, trying to remember the way to his room. *Left, left, right, left? Right, right, left, right?* He let out a false chuckle, hoping to put the girl at ease. "Don't worry, miss. I believe we go left, left, right, then left. *Si,* I'm sure of it." He took her hand. "Left, left, right, left."

It took no time at all to realize he had chosen the wrong way. He turned the girl around and guided her back to The Shelter. "I apologize, miss. It must be right, left, left, right. Yes, that's it. Shall we try again?"

After negotiating the new path through the maze, he beamed. "*Si, señorita.* This is it." He ran his fingers over the gold plaque just outside his door. "This is me. I mean, this is my name on a plaque—Dr. Carlos Huerta." He touched the inscription again and patted his chest. "Carlos. My name is Carlos." He touched her shoulder. "What is your name, miss? ¿Como *te llamas?*"

Footsteps sounded from around the corner. He hurried her inside, eased the door shut, and put his ear to the faux wood. The footfalls swept past his room and faded away.

"*Muy bien,*" he said, motioning to the room he had never seen. "*Mi casa es tu casa.* Please, feel free to relax, have a drink, or go to the restroom." She did not move. "Anything you need is yours." He eyed the suitcase on the bed. "Well, almost anything."

The girl stood motionless, uninterested in the new surroundings. Neither the soft carpet, the gentle heat wafting in from the ceiling register, nor the brightly colored walls elicited a reaction. Her gaze remained fixed—straight ahead.

Carlos traipsed to the bed and opened his suitcase. He pulled out shirts, pants, and underwear, tossing them willy-nilly across the floor. "Ah-ha!" He held up a small, black toiletry bag. Unzipping it, he picked through the contents and pulled out a prescription vial containing an assortment of his little "helpers."

A knock on the door startled him. He froze, not knowing what to do first—hide the girl, answer the door, or swallow a pill. He decided on all three. Steering the girl to the side of the door, he unscrewed the lid of the vial and tapped out a small, round, capsule into his palm. *Maldito*—just a Valium. It would have to do.

Another knock on the door. "Dr. Huerta?" The voice sounded familiar. Sergeant Sandoval. Carlos popped the pill in his mouth, worked it to the back of his throat, and swallowed. He closed his eyes, mentally guiding the capsule down his gullet.

Another knock. "Dr. Huerta."

"Coming," he said, hoping to sound casual, even relaxed.

"You okay in there, doc? You sound upset."

Carlos pulled the door open, making certain it shielded the girl. "Sergeant Sandoval. So good to see you. How are you doing?"

"Me? You're the one who's been missing for a day and a half. Where have you been?" The young man advanced, placing a foot on the threshold. "We got people out looking for you."

"*Lo siento*, young man." Carlos blocked the sergeant's path. "I'm so sorry, but I'm not ready to receive guests."

"Receive guests? Listen, Dr. Huerta, the general's hoppin' mad, and he's blaming me. Said he'd have my head if I couldn't find you."

"I, uh, I lost my way in all the confusion yesterday, that's all. But I'm back now, and everything is good. Please give my apologies to the general." He pushed at the door.

It closed halfway before connecting with Sandoval's shoe. "The general's waiting."

"Ah, yes. Please tell him I'll be there in a few moments." He tried to close the door again.

"Now, doctor," Sandoval said in a sober tone. "He needs to see you now."

"Yes, well, I'll be with you shortly."

"No, not shortly—now."

The Valium had begun its magic. With nothing in his stomach save the Valium, he grew lightheaded and a bit nauseous. "Very well," he said, giving in. "After you."

Sandoval held the door ajar for Carlos. The moment he stepped into the hallway, the sergeant shut the door and waved the professor forward.

After a few steps, Carlos turned back to the room. "Oh, I forgot my coat."

"Sir." Sandoval stuck out his arm, stopping Carlos. "The general's waiting for you."

Carlos backpedaled. "Please, do not touch me."

"Sorry, I forgot." The young man dropped his arm at once. "Let's go...after you."

Carlos nodded. They made a right turn followed by a quick left. Carlos mouthed the directions in silence, trying to commit them to memory. After a few more turns, he found himself confused and disoriented. He needed food.

"Carlos," the general said, greeting him in the hallway just outside the door to his office. "We were worried. What happened? Please, come in, tell me all about it." The general ushered Carlos through the outer vestibule and into his private office. He motioned to the soft leather chairs facing his desk. "Have a seat. Where have you been?"

Carlos eased into a chair, all the while thinking of the girl. "I'm fine. Can I go back to my room now?"

"Nonsense. Tell me what happened."

"I got lost, fell asleep, and found my way back to my room this morning."

"That's it? You got lost?" The general cocked his head. "Carlos, thank you for assisting us with our overflow problem yesterday. Major Bay told me how you volunteered to help. I appreciate it, I truly do, but you do realize we have cameras in every tunnel. We actually perform a physical sweep of the tunnel system every two hours. Forgive me for saying this, but you couldn't have gotten lost, unless you wanted to get lost. Is that what really happened, my friend? Did you *want* to be lost? I know what kind of pressure you've been under since…well, since everything. Do you have second thoughts about being here?"

"I want to go back to my room."

General Sinclair moved behind his desk and sat in the massive executive chair. He let out a long breath. "Carlos, is there something you're not telling me? Have you decided not to work on this project? Perhaps our visit to Dr. Hasting has upset you."

"Payton, the aliens—"

"ENOs."

"Yes, the ENOs, they are being kept…how shall I say? They are being held like prisoners. Surely there is something that can be done about—"

"What do you suggest, Carlos?"

He sat, his mouth open, unable to answer the question.

"No, I'm curious," the general said, "because if you know the answer, I'd love to hear it. We're out of room. Nobody expected the Tombstone to duplicate—not just once, but twice. God help us if it happens again. Let's just pray that—"

Hee-haw…hee-haw. The general's face paled.

Sergeant Sandoval burst into the room, holding a two-way radio. "Sir, the Tombstones have duplicated again."

CHAPTER 10

Carlos kept an eye on Sergeant Sandoval and General Sinclair as they raced out of the office and down the hallway. They were joined by several Black Shirts. He trudged in the opposite direction, fighting the urge to scream at the deafening noise of the constant alarm. Security forces filled the hallway, rushing past him on their way to The Shelter.

A familiar and wonderful aroma drifted through the hall, catching his interest. Carlos followed his nose and discovered an enormous cafeteria. An assortment of breakfast dishes lay abandoned on dozens of tables. He trekked to the buffet and grabbed a clean plate. *Perhaps a glazed bear claw—no, two—one for the girl*—assuming aliens enjoyed sweet morning treats—*a peeled, hardboiled egg and a large glass of orange juice.* He took a few bites of the bear claw and sipped his juice. *Delicious.* Just what he needed.

The annoying klaxon alarm brought his attention back to the challenges at hand. Find his room, feed the girl, and then...what? He had hidden an extraterrestrial in his room. If one needed a written note to urinate in this government facility, what would they do to him for that?

He juggled the plate and glass of juice while negotiating his way back to his quarters. The hardboiled egg rolled to the rim of the plate, threatening to fall to the ground. He raised the plate and let the egg roll into his mouth. It tasted fresh. Perhaps, an on-site farm kept the pantries fully stocked in this underground complex.

He grinned, at long last, spying the familiar light blue color scheme of the hallway leading to his room.

His heart double thumped. He let go of the plate and glass of juice. They crashed on the tiled floor. The door to his room lay wide open.

Carlos dashed into the suite. "Hello?" he shouted over the braying of the never-ending alarm. "Are you still here, miss?" He checked the restroom, then rushed to the edge of the bed. Thank God for little victories. The black toiletry bag appeared untouched.

In a frantic search, he rummaged through the leather bag until he found a vial marked Methaqualone. In one deft motion, he popped off the lid, tilted his head back, and shook a pill into his mouth. Soon, the klaxon would no longer matter—not much would.

"Miss, where have you gone?" he whispered. After a few moments, the early effects of the hypnotic drug forced him to consider, "Did you even exist at all?"

Turning on weak legs, he exited the suite and wandered through the maze of hallways, passages, and corridors, until he happened upon the opening to The Shelter.

Carlos observed the chaos in the enormous cavern through an altered imagination. Black Shirts. New arrivals. Lightning storms. Everything—people, walls, equipment—moved toward him, in a slow, choreographed dance, making him smile.

Just beyond the Tombstones, he spotted the girl. She still wore his dark coat, making her easy to see. Black Shirts guided hundreds of new arrivals through both the northern and southern archways. A brawny-shouldered guard escorted her toward the Northern Tunnel System.

"Miss. Wait for me." *Were the words a thought? A whisper?* He glanced up at the ceiling of the underground cavern in an attempt to discover their source. *What did they mean?* "Wait for me." *Wait for whom? Wait for what?* His stomach churned again. The sweet bear claw may have been a sour mistake. He glanced back at the entrance to the Northern Tunnel System, the girl had vanished, swallowed whole by the darkness of the passageway.

He drifted into The Shelter assisted by a wave of bodies, both uniformed human and unclothed alien. The tide carried him past the Tombstones toward the shadows at the edge of the cavern.

He closed his eyes, allowing destiny to choose his path. When he opened his eyes, he glanced up and read the banner. Northern Tunnel System.

Chilled sweat beaded on his forehead. His stomach roiled, bile snaking up his throat—a reaction to too many pills. He knew the nausea would soon fade—it almost always did. Still, he'd have to be extra vigilant if he had any hope of tracking down the girl with the violet eyes.

The passageway narrowed, the cement floor giving way to an uneven foundation of rock and loose gravel. After several turns, an endless tunnel loomed before him like the inside of a never-ending snake. Black Shirts ushered new arrivals into rooms on either side of the corridor. The girl had disappeared.

Carlos glanced at the numbers on the doors. They were identical to the room numbers of the Southern Tunnel System. Small chalkboards hung from the doors. The numbers on many of the boards were so smudged, only a gritty white haze remained.

His hopes lowered of ever finding the girl. Black Shirts bumped past him, leading new arrivals through the passageway. Other uniformed personnel swept by him in the opposite direction on their way back to The Shelter. Carlos leaned against the solid security of the rock wall—out of the way. The longer he remained motionless, the more his reason for being here faded. *Did a girl truly exist? What girl?*

Time crawled. The alarm ceased its wailing. Fewer Black Shirts marched through the tunnel in either direction. Bare light bulbs provided just enough illumination to convince him of his worst fear. Everyone had faded away. Everyone except for the thousands of poor souls deposited in the cold chambers. He pictured them huddled behind locked doors. Afraid. Alone. Carlos wrapped his arms around himself and shivered. *How long would it take to die of exposure?* He imagined the experience to be a painful one.

"So be it," he whispered.

A shape emerged from the shadows. He squinted, trying to make out the lone figure, so many yards away. *An illusion?* On several occasions, after ingesting more of the soft, pink pills than he should have, his imagination offered a companion. A friend to discuss his latest theories, ideas, or—his follies. That friend never materialized like this hallway apparition. It never took such clear shape and form. Curiosity pulled him away from the wall, and he walked toward the figure. "Are you my guide to the other side? Have I died?" Carlos took off his glasses, wiping them with a handkerchief. When he put them back on, the form in the hallway came into focus. He delighted at the sight of the girl with the violet eyes. She sauntered down the passageway, drawing nearer with each silent step.

"Miss, you worried me. Why didn't you stay in my room? Where have you been?"

Remaining silent, she stopped just a few feet from him. Her violet eyes scanned across his face. A grin appeared, an awkward expression with depressions on either side of her mouth. Dimples. The cold, robotic expression of before had disappeared.

"Are you trying to smile? If I didn't know any better, it would appear you're glad to see me." His mood improved at once. He no longer contemplated death, pain, or being alone. A definite change for the better.

She remained silent.

A gruff voice echoed from the depths of the endless passageway behind her. "They're just about gone," the voice said. "We should still give it a little bit more time, maybe a half hour, at least."

Carlos peered over her shoulder trying to catch a glimpse of the speaker. Darkness masked his view. The bare light bulbs hanging from electric cord spaced every ten feet, emitted no more illumination than dime store flashlights. He placed his hand on her elbow, guiding her back against the wall, lest they be seen. He whispered, "I don't know who belongs to that voice, but I have a bad feeling. Call it my scientist's intuition."

Her grin vanished, but she still said nothing.

"Are you ever going to speak to me?" He kept his voice low.

The dimples appeared again, another quiet smile. At that moment, Carlos understood his attraction to her. She reminded him of a young Lilly, the first time he had seen her, all those many years ago, the innocence, the sparkle in her eyes. The thought filled him with both hope and despair. "Come. Let's find our way back through this labyrinth to my room. I hope you can remember which way to go. You know I—"

In a rapid movement her hand covered his mouth—a soft, soothing touch. One he hadn't expected. Still, he did not recoil from the action. In fact, like yesterday in the chamber, he welcomed the contact. She kept her hand in place and glanced over her shoulder.

"They're gone," the harsh voice said. "We gotta be a little more careful in the future. Do you think they know what we're doing?"

"Well, we just gotta make sure nobody finds out." A second voice, this one more serene and confident. "Keep your mind on the money. We just gotta be a little more careful now that there's four Tombstones...or is it eight? Who knows? It just means more talent for us, right?"

"I guess. I just wish they kept us in the loop. They treat us like mushrooms down here."

The girl lowered her hand, took Carlos by the elbow, and ushered him deeper into the dark passageway toward the voices. He hesitated at first, then gave in to her direction, taking measured steps by her side, proceeding with caution.

The gruff voices grew louder. Step by step, Carlos's heart sped up to a troubling pace. *An arrhythmia caused by the drugs?* He had received that diagnosis in the past, too many times. No, he opted on a sudden and extreme case of fear. A reaction to the anxiety of being lost in a maze of underground passageways and, of course, to the sound of the ominous voices.

Carlos stopped. The girl gazed at him, not forcing him to advance, but waiting for him to join her. Her patience seemed to transfer to him, soothing him. He took a step forward, then another. She nodded, smiling at his slow but sure progress.

The ill-tempered voice said, "We should call it quits, you know? Just take the money and git while the gittin's good."

In a tranquil response, the calmer of the two answered. "Naw, not yet, killer. Not yet."

Killer? Carlos stopped, his heart racing.

CHAPTER
11

"You're not going to get away with this."

"I'm not trying to get away with anything," Prudence Wellman said. "I just want to get away." *Help me to the door,* she projected her "wants" onto the woman in the lab coat, *and let me know if any guards are nearby.*

The woman took Prudence by the elbow, helping her from the exam table. "There are two armed guards in the hallway. Our movements are being monitored. There are cameras everywhere. Why are you making me do this?"

"What's your name?" Prudence stared into the woman's hazel eyes.

"Doctor Janet Shelly."

"Well, Janet, you're doing this because I want you to."

"But, I, uh...but I don't—"

"Relax, Janet, you have no choice in the matter. Now tell me, other than those guards, is there anybody else waiting for us on the other side of the door?"

"No." Doctor Shelly shook her head and opened the door.

Two Black Shirts bolted into the room. Prudence filled their minds with anxiety, nightmares, and terror. Their fear seemed more intense, more consuming, even than her own. She forced herself to relax but continued to send the concentrated emotions of panic to the guards. They crumpled to their knees, covered their heads, and cowered. Doctor Shelly did the same, tears spilling down her cheeks.

"You have no idea the trouble you're in." She sobbed.

You lied to me. Don't do it again…uh…or else. Get up and come with me, Janet. I need your help. Prudence visualized the actions she required of the woman. Dr. Shelly obeyed, like a puppet being controlled by invisible strings. Prudence strolled into the hallway, the doctor following with trance-like steps.

Open the doors on that side of the hallway. Release anyone bound to their beds. Do it now, quietly, and quickly.

"I want you to know," Dr. Shelly said before opening the first door, "I don't agree with their methods. I never will."

"What do you mean by their methods?"

"I mean holding you specials here against your will. It's wrong."

"Yeah, it's called kidnapping. C'mon. Hurry up. We've got a lot of doors to open, a lot of *special* people to free." Prudence glanced at the plaque on the first door—Jedediah the Ghost.

"What the…?" She turned the knob and took a tentative step into the darkened room. The shadowy figure of a patient on the exam table stirred, a soft moan escaping its lips. Prudence stepped back in the hall and reexamined the plaque. Yup, no mistake. Jedediah the Ghost. She reentered the room. The figure of the patient had vanished, only a sheet and pillow remained.

Her heart drummed. She exited the room and moved to the next door—Marissa the Psychic.

With trembling fingers, she grabbed the knob and opened the door.

"Well, it's about time. I've been expecting you all day." A woman's voice, cheerful and excited, came from the patient strapped to the exam table. "Are you alone? Where are the heavenly angels, as I predicted?"

"You're a psychic?" Prudence said.

"Of course." The woman huffed and raised her eyebrows. "Hurry up, I've been waiting long enough. Where's the Archangel Michael? Where's Gabriel?"

Prudence worked on the woman's leather restraints. "Sorry to disappoint. I'm afraid I've come alone. No heavenly angels."

"Dammit all to Hell."

"I guess that's one reaction to being rescued." Prudence unbuckled the bonds. "And your name is—"

"Marissa, of course. It's on the door." The woman rubbed her wrists, then held out a hand. "Where are my sisters? Are they okay?"

"I don't know anything about...uh, tell me, your neighbor, Jedediah, is he really—"

"Hush now, you'll meet everyone soon enough," Marissa said, ignoring the question about the ghost. "My sisters are being held here, a few rooms down the hall." She slid off the exam table and followed Prudence into the hallway.

Dr. Shelly emerged from a room on her side of the hallway accompanied by an ancient man dressed in a white gown. He had a decided limp, wincing with each step, but smiled when he caught sight of Prudence.

"It is so good to finally meet you in the flesh, young lady. I've been waiting ever so long for you. We all have."

"You have? What's your name?"

"Willie," the old man said, "Willie T. Smith."

"It's good you meet you, Mr. Smith—"

"Willie T., please."

"Willie T. it is. Tell me, what's your particular skill?"

"Me, young lady?" He bowed. "I'm known as a Remote Viewer, one in a long, proud line of Remote Viewers. I saw you coming days ago."

"Do you need a wheelchair?"

"Oh, my goodness no—the leg acts up is all. Lack of use, I guess. I'll be right as rain in a few minutes. Just gotta get the old circulation going."

Prudence closed her eyes, projecting thoughts to them. *Listen to me, all of you. Let everyone else out of their rooms. Hurry now, I expect we don't have much time.* "The hallway is filled with cameras."

"Great," Gamble said, emerging from a room, Dr. Shelly by his side. "I hope they get a good look at me—at us all. I want them to know who's got the better of them." He faced the nearest camera and raised a middle finger.

Everybody worked as a team, throwing open doors, ducking into rooms, and releasing patients. In minutes, the hallway filled with people, voices, and smiles. Like a family reunion, animated figures greeted each other, laughing and joking. Prudence overheard excited "hellos," especially between Marissa and two other women.

Gamble leaned in toward Prudence and whispered, "That's the

triplets—Clarissa, Marissa, and Tarissa—a psychic, clairvoyant, and self-proclaimed mystic. Can you imagine the conversations they had around their dinner table growing up?" He pointed out others. "That black man over there, that's Willie T. Smith the Remote Viewer. And there's Bruce the Dowser—whatever that is—I still can't get a straight answer from anyone about it. There's Mindy the Prophet, Gregory the Confabulator—again, whatever *that* is—and Darrah the Conjuror. Uh, I'm pretty sure that means magician. Oh, there's Patricia the Witch. Keep your distance from her. She claims she doesn't dabble in the dark arts, but you can't be too careful. There's Chase the Mage, Skye the Telepath—but everybody calls her Skype—get it? And somewhere around here is Jedidiah, the uh..." Gamble cleared his throat. "You're not going to believe this, but he's the ghost."

"I've already met him...I think."

"Quiet. Quiet everyone," Clarissa said. She stood hand in hand with her sisters, Marissa and Tarissa. People in the hallway hushed, giving their complete attention.

Marissa closed her eyes and cocked her head. "They're coming."

"I knew it," Dr. Shelly said. "They'll never let us waltz out of here."

"Us?" Prudence said.

Dr. Janet Shelly nodded. "None of you are the monsters they warned us about. What they're doing to you is wrong—immoral."

Prudence smiled. "Welcome aboard, Janet. Get your keys. Let's move." With her declaration, joyful cheers erupted in the hallway.

"Dear Prudence," Gamble said, putting his hand on her shoulders, "I knew you were the one that would help us escape. When I first saw you, I knew it. I can only assume you've figured out your special ability."

"I'll tell you all about it after we *waltz* out of here." Prudence winked.

The *hee-haw* braying of an alarm filled the hallway. Most of the patients, including Prudence, covered their ears against the awful noise. They huddled together, thirteen in all, along with Dr. Shelly, in the middle of the hallway.

"You're the medium, right?" Prudence said, turning to Clarissa.

The petite woman nodded. "Clairvoyant, please."

"What's behind the green door up ahead?"

Clarissa closed her eyes. "I see guards holding guns and doctors with hypodermic needles. They're waiting well beyond the door, maybe fifty, a hundred yards back."

"They'll kill us all," Marissa said. "I feel it. We don't stand a chance."

"You were wrong about the heavenly angels, remember?" Prudence put an arm over the psychic's shoulder to calm her. "You're wrong about this, too."

Marissa peered into Prudence's eyes, then chuckled. "Well, like I often tell my clients, seeing into the future is not an exact séance."

The play on words made Prudence giggle. "Listen, everyone. The odds may be against us, but don't be afraid. The guards will be armed, but we've got weapons, too. More powerful than anything they've ever faced. We're the ones with the advantage. Keep your wits about you, use your abilities, and we'll come out on top."

"I hope you're right, young lady." Clarissa gave Prudence a sideways glance.

"You *know* I am. Follow me." Prudence led them to the green door. "Listen up. Once we get past this door, does anybody know which way to go?"

Gamble stepped forward. "There should be an elevator at the end of the next hallway that leads to The Shelter, but we have to get past this God-awful green door first."

"The Shelter...? Never mind." Prudence turned to Dr. Shelly. "Get your keys and unlock this door." She leaned in to Gamble and whispered, "What's The Shelter?"

"That's where they keep the people who aren't really people."

"Oh, well, that clears everything up."

Dr. Shelley dropped her key ring twice before finally selecting the correct key and opening the green door.

"Right," Prudence yelled over her shoulder, "let's go. They can't stop us. Trust me. Trust in your abilities."

The scene played out like a theater of the macabre. Guards raised their weapons, taking aim at the patients. The patients stood their ground, shooting wild stares at the guards. Prudence fired off emotions of anxiety and panic. Tarissa, Bruce, and Patricia wailed, waving their arms in the air. The guards dropped their weapons, and the doctors let go of their needles. All those in black shirts and white coats fell to the floor in tears. Prudence and the patients marched through the ranks of the enemy like conquering heroes.

"Let's keep moving," Prudence said, still sending malicious thoughts toward the guards. "Great job everyone."

Dr. Shelly unlocked the next door. No guards awaited them in this hallway. She shouted at the group, "To the elevator."

They cheered and followed. At the elevator lobby, Prudence turned to Dr. Shelly.

"Janet, which way, up or down?"

"There's only one way. Up."

"Great, how many floors does this elevator go?"

"One."

"One floor? But we're—what—two hundred floors underground?"

"Yes, this elevator only goes to The Shelter."

"Okay," Prudence said, "one floor at a time then. C'mon, everybody on board."

The patients crowded into the elevator.

"There's no room for me," Doctor Janet Shelly said.

"Sure there is—c'mon everybody, squeeze in."

"No," Gamble said, "she's right. There's too many of us as it is."

Prudence forced a smile. "When we get to The Shelter, I'll send the elevator back for you. It won't be long. Okay, Janet?"

Doctor Janet Shelly nodded. "Good luck." The doors slid shut.

"Listen up." Prudence raised her hand, calling for quiet inside the confined space. "We've got to be smart here."

"Hey, I've never been accused of that," Gamble said. A few chuckles filled the air.

Ding. The elevator came to a stop and the doors slid open. An enormous cavern greeted them. The area bustled with an assortment of soldiers and several hundred naked people. None of them gave the elevator a second glance.

"We should go to the left," Gamble said. "That way."

"C'mon," Prudence said. "Follow me."

Stepping off the elevator, they tip-toed to the left, backs against the wall. Prudence pressed the elevator button sending the car back for Janet. She crept toward an opening in the smooth, granite wall. Beyond the opening lay a well-lit hallway. Empty.

"Quiet, now. Baby steps."

The group slipped into the hallway. Prudence allowed a smile to work its way across her lips. They had been unnoticed by anyone behind them. The escape proceeded as if she had a plan. She didn't. A hand fell on her shoulder making her jump. "What is it, Clarissa?"

"I don't see that doctor lady, Doctor Shelly."

"I'm sure she'll be fine. We have to keep moving."

Clarissa held onto Prudence's arm. "The name Carlos keeps walking through my mind. I don't know why, but if I had to guess I'd say it's some sort of sign. A safe harbor—Carlos."

"That doesn't make any sense." Prudence wrinkled her brow. "Carlos doesn't sound like the name of a safe harbor."

Clarissa smiled. "Honey, I don't write 'em, I just read 'em."

"C'mon, everybody," Prudence said, "let's see where this hallway goes. We need to find another elevator. We're still a couple hundred stories underground."

"That's *my* job," Bruce the Dowser said. He touched his temple with an index finger. "I see an elevator about forty yards ahead. I think it goes all the way to the top."

Prudence beamed. "So, we're on the right track. Just a little way to go."

Those around her smiled and nodded at each other. The mood remained upbeat and light—optimism the order of the day. Boots stomping on the tile floor echoed ahead, shifting the feeling. Prudence froze, her heart sinking. She glanced about. A door across the hall stood ajar. The placard next to the door read Dr. Carlos Huerta.

"Quick," she whisper-shouted. "Everybody, follow me." Prudence darted across the hall and into the room. When they were all inside, she eased the door shut and put her ear against it. The sound of the boots grew louder, marched by, and faded into nothing.

"Carlos..." Clarissa whispered, "a safe harbor."

CHAPTER 12

His legs turned to stone. Carlos could not move. *A reaction to the drugs? Perhaps. Maybe the thought of never again seeing the light of day?* No. That ominous name stopped him.

Killer.

What parent in their right mind would name their little bundle of joy Killer? Sure, the extremely wealthy rock stars, and rich celebrities tended to name their offspring a variety of unusual names. The well-to-do might get away with Sunflower or Venus. *But Killer? Did the father deal drugs? And what of the mother?*

"Perhaps, we should turn around and go the other way," Carlos said.

The girl with the violet eyes did not move. She tugged at his elbow, coaxing him farther into the tunnel. He judged the gesture neither calculating, nor malicious. Somehow, he knew she would never draw him deeper into the abyss against his will. She stood by his side, waiting in complete silence, not even a blink. He sensed a fundamental honesty in her expression, truth in her eyes.

Ouch. The girl pinched his elbow. Apparently, honesty and truth were in a hurry. He submitted to her will. They advanced through the shadows, the voices growing louder.

"Listen," the gruff one said. "Someone's coming. Close that door and be quiet."

"Watch it, Jake. There's been too many alarms today. Find out who they are."

Carlos glanced about. "Who could be coming? Somebody behind us?" The girl cocked her head, staring deep into his eyes. "Oh, right," Carlos whispered. "He means us. In that case, we should be quiet, or he'll—"

"Hey." The man stood a few feet from them.

Carlos squinted, doing his best to peer through the darkness. "Who is there?"

"Who are you?"

"Who are *you*?"

The gruff voice yelled, "Shut up, and don't play stupid. Stop where you are or I'll shoot. Now answer me. Who are you?"

"Please don't shoot. My name is Carlos Huerta." He raised both hands high in the air. "Dr. Carlos Huerta. I have no weapon. It is just me and the girl."

"Girl? Did the colonel send you?"

"The colonel? *Sí, sí*, the colonel." He thought of backing away from the voice, hoping to escape under the cover of darkness, but the girl kept her hand on his back, holding him in place. "The colonel is a very good friend of mine. As a matter of fact, just the other day, we were talking, like we do, and I told him, colonel—"

"Shut yer yap."

Carlos trembled but still stood his ground. The man with the scary voice drew closer. His breath reeked. Rancid. Body odor wafted from him as if he were a human landfill. What had once been a clean black uniform hung on the man like a Halloween costume—filthy and soiled with muck. Carlos shrank away. Had the lie he told about knowing someone named the colonel been his undoing? The girl put her arm around his shoulder. He calmed at once.

The stinky man turned his attention to her. "Okay, so who's this fine, young thing? Come toward me and move slow. Remember, I got a gun pointed at you."

"She doesn't understand you, sir. You see she's an alien."

"Hey. You think I'm stupid? I know what the hell she is." He stroked the side of her face with the back of his hand. "Why the hell is she wearing a coat?"

"Oh," Carlos said, "that's mine. She looked terribly cold, and I—"

"Cold? Boy, you're an idiot. Cats don't wear nothin', 'cause

Cats don't feel nothin'. 'Sides, it's better for business, if they don't wear anything. You *sure* you know the colonel?"

The girl took a tentative step forward. Carlos stuck his hand into his pocket searching for a vitamin—force of habit.

The foul man smirked and cocked the hammer of his pistol. "Hang on there, little man. Take that hand out of your pocket nice and slow. What you got in there?"

Carlos obeyed the order, raising his trembling hand in such a measured motion it could have been timed by an hourglass.

"C'mon, c'mon, pal. Hurry it up."

"But you said nice and slow."

"Don't smart mouth me."

"Hey, Jake." The other voice came from farther down the tunnel. A door along the way cracked open just a notch, allowing a sliver of light to paint its way across the tunnel floor. "Who you talking to?"

"Hell if I know. He says he knows the colonel, which I doubt, but he's got a real money maker with him." Jake turned to the girl. "Best one I've seen in a long time."

"Really?" the invisible voice said. "Where'd he come from?"

"How the hell should I know. Maybe he's the new guy we were told to expect. Said his name's *doctor* something." He gave Carlos his full attention. "Where'd you find her?"

Carlos swallowed hard.

"You best tell me. I still don't buy that shit about you and the colonel." Jake raised his firearm, pointing it at Carlos.

"Cathedral. Bell. Chimney. Steamboat. Devil's Bridge." He closed his eyes. Mouthing the words of protection.

"What's that? Stop with the gibberish and tell me where you found her."

"I uh...that is...the colonel wanted me to be sure to—"

"I found *him*," the girl with the violet eyes said in a calm and clear voice.

Bad Breath Jake did a double take and stared at her. "You...you talked. Wait a minute, Cats don't talk."

"Quiet, little man." She reached out and touched his forehead. His firearm dropped to the ground. He soon followed, laying on the tunnel floor, still and quiet.

The door opened wider, and a thick man wearing a white

lab coat stepped into the hallway. "What'd you say, Jake? Hey, Killer?" He stepped forward, using baby steps in the dark tunnel. After staring at Jake lying flat on the ground, he turned his gaze to the girl. "What the hell's going on?"

She approached him. "Who are you?"

"Uh…uh, the name's Dunleavy. *Doctor* Dunleavy. Whoa. You can't talk, you're a—"

"I know. I'm a Cat." She touched Dunleavy's face. He collapsed in a heap.

"I don't understand," Carlos said. "What's going on?"

The girl turned to him, and he cowered back.

"Don't worry, Carlos. I would never hurt you. You're safe."

"Safe," he said, mimicking the word. "Safe from what? From you? How are you able to talk? Where do you come from? Why are you here? How did—"

Her finger covered his lips. She smiled, turned away from him, and marched with cool confidence toward the opened door used by Dr. Dunleavy.

Carlos hesitated before following her. He whispered, "*Ay, Dios mio*. Cathedral. Bell. Chimney. Steamboat. Devil's Bridge." He stepped forward on shaky legs and entered the room after her.

Two bright light bulbs illuminated the area. Unlike the chamber they had slept in the night before, this room seemed much bigger and appeared to be part of a larger complex. Three closed doors, spaced a few feet apart along the far wall, piqued his interest. He glanced at the girl—more for permission to move than anything else. She nodded. He took hold of the knob to door number one and pulled it open, hoping for a proper restroom.

The absence of light filling the room made it darker even than the tunnel. Carlos stuck his hands out in front of him and ventured inside. At the touch of flesh, he squawked and backpedaled. His shoe caught on a jagged rock, sending him off balance. The girl with the violet eyes caught him before he fell.

A woman ambled into the light. She stood shorter than Carlos, naked and shivering. Another female toddled out of the room behind her. They stopped and stared, unblinking, at the girl with the violet eyes.

The next door Carlos opened held one woman who exited. The third room held two more females. The chamber grew quite congested. Carlos moved closer to the girl wearing his coat. "Who are these people? Why are they here?"

"They were being used for sex. There." She pointed to a bed tucked away in the corner. "Sex for money. The *colonel* is Colonel Bloodstone, someone you have never met."

"Ah, Bloodstone, I see. But how did you know I have never met him?"

Moving away from him, the girl stared at the women, then closed her eyes. After a moment she turned for the main door leading back to the tunnel. The girls followed her in a single file. Carlos cut into the line, exiting the room with them. He passed one girl, then another, and another until he stood behind the girl with the violet eyes.

"Should we report this to the general?"

At the prone body of Dr. Dunleavy, she stopped and glared. A concentrated expression of disgust covered her face. She straightened and turned back toward the dark passageway. "There are more of my kind, more females in the rooms beyond. There are at least fifteen rooms used for sex. I will get them. You wait here."

"Ay, dios mio," Carlos said. "Yes, I will wait."

She wandered away, deeper into the shadows of the long tunnel. Carlos could no longer see her, instead, he listened for the clues of where she might be. He heard doors opening and bare feet slapping the cold granite floor. In a few moments the girl with the violet eyes appeared, leading a long parade of females in her wake. Passing him, she continued her journey back up the tunnel toward The Shelter. The line of girls followed her like baby ducks after their mother. Carlos did not stop them. He needed a vitamin, maybe two. He needed to find General Sinclair and report this disgusting business. Most of all, he needed this to somehow make sense.

The events of the past two days wore on him. His eyes lingered over the still body of the man called Killer. *Had she killed him?* The thought made him nauseous. He took a deep, cleansing breath, then hurried after the procession of women. Finally, he caught up to the girl with the violet eyes at the head of the line and followed her in silence.

At the archway leading into The Shelter, the girl stopped and faced her ducklings. Without speaking, they dispersed, wandering off toward the Tombstones. Black Shirts caught them one by one, turned them back to the tunnels, and lead them away from The Shelter.

A young fresh-faced guard stepped forward, taking hold of the girl with the violet eyes. She turned to Carlos.

"No. Let this one go. My name is Dr. Carlos Huerta, and the general, uh...that is, General Sinclair wants to see this...this, *cómo se dice*...ENO. I am taking her to his office. So please, let her go."

The young guard released his grip and disappeared. Carlos delighted in his own persuasion until he realized why the soldier obeyed so quickly. There were hundreds of unescorted new arrivals wandering about The Shelter. The hapless guard had more on his plate than just this one girl. No matter. Carlos had taken charge of the situation, a thing he hadn't done in quite some time. It brought a smile to his face.

He gazed into the girl's violet eyes, seeking any clue—a hint of her intentions. He found none. Securing her elbow with a weak grip, he turned her toward the white hallway leading to his room. "Do you want to see the general?"

No response.

The endless commotion in The Shelter covered them from unwanted attention. He relaxed his hold. They kept close to the side of the cavern and made slow but steady progress toward the hallway.

"Then, is it okay if we go to my room?"

No answer.

"You were there once already. You must remember, but for some reason you wandered away. Is there somewhere else you want me to take you? Perhaps to the cafeteria, or—"

"No. Your room will be fine."

"*Muy bien.* I'm glad we got that straightened out." He guided her into the hallway and through a maze of corridors, finally stopping at his room. "At last, we will truly be able to relax and have a chance to talk alone, without interruption." He pushed the door open.

Inside, a woman's voice said, "It's okay, everybody. This is Carlos."

"Is it a surprise party?" he said, staggering into the room. He acknowledged the group of people inside then glanced at the bed. The small black bag still lay on the bedspread. He took a step toward

80

the precious cargo, but the girl with the violet eyes held him back.

"You don't need that," she said.

"*Perdoname,* but I do. Believe me, it is for the best."

She closed the door with one hand and put the other on the back of his neck. "No, believe *me. This* is for the best." The girl with the violet eyes squeezed his neck.

CHAPTER 13

Like a cool washcloth on a warm summer night, her touch soothed him.

His mind flooded with memories of the remarkable feelings he had experienced in the airplane just two days prior. The thrill of it all. The illusion of control. He remembered glancing down at the white sands of the endless desert rolling by in a silent fantasy. How in control he had been then—how confident.

Those feelings paled in comparison to the way her touch filled him now with an unparalleled energy. The minutiae of his problems carried no weight. The way he had been treated by MIT evaporated. Memories of Lilly's passing no longer brought anxiety. His mind, his soul, soared above the common troubles of the world, untethered.

He faced the girl with the short red hair. "Who are you?"

"My name is Prudence. Prudence Wellman."

"I am Dr. Carlos Huerta."

"Carlos…our safe harbor, so nice to meet you." She turned to the alien. "And you?"

Gamble leaned in toward Prudence and whispered, "That's a person who isn't really a person. I told you about them, remember?"

The girl with the violet eyes bowed her head. "Just so." She glanced about, focusing on each individual, all the while keeping her hand in contact with Carlos's neck. Their names and abilities entered his mind, as if channeled through her touch.

"And a ghost?" Carlos laughed. "Really?"

"Allegedly," someone said from the back of the room. "At least that's what they say he is."

"*Dios mio.*" Carlos turned back to the girl with the violet eyes. "I now know who everybody is, all the people in my formerly empty room. Everyone except you. *¿Cómo se llama?*"

"I am The Sundarian."

He tried it out in silence, then mouthed the word. "Sundarian—*que bonita.*"

"*Gracias,*" she said. She addressed the room. "You all have many questions, chief among them, why are the aliens here? We were invited to come, many, many years ago. Trust me, we are here to help."

"Aren't you part of the nudist camp wandering around out there?" Darrah the Conjuror said. "Why should we trust you?"

Patricia the Witch stepped forward. "Are you part of the government?"

Carlos faced The Sundarian, raising his voice over the others. "You say you are here to help—help with what? Who are you? Where do you come from?"

"We deserve the truth," Gamble said, his tone demanding.

Clarissa stared at The Sundarian. "We deserve a hell of a lot more than that."

Questions rose, each spoken louder than the last.

"Silence." The word rumbled through the room. "I will speak with Carlos," The Sundarian said. She took him by the hand and led him to the restroom. She turned to the others. "Excuse us." With that, she pulled Carlos into the small room and closed the door.

"Carlos Huerta," The Sundarian said, her cool voice echoing off the bathroom tiles. "I place my hand upon your heart, that you may know the truth. What do you wish to know?"

He stared at the floor, then the ceiling. Finally, he cleared his throat, his eyes resting on hers. "Being a man of science, I need to know…everything."

"Ask."

"How did you get here?"

"Through the use of Pillars, what you call Tombstones. It is science beyond your time."

"Where do you come from?"

"Through the vast configuration. We come from the planet Areth, on the outer reaches of the galaxy. It's a terrestrial world, much like your own."

"*Muy bien*," he said. "Thank you for the honesty. And why are you here?"

"The critical juncture. In your need to advance, you have lost your way—lost yourselves. Your world is saturated with deadly chemicals. You inhale toxins, ingest plasticides. This must stop—at once."

"Ah, I see. You are here to help us with climate change."

"Just so."

"But how? A solution will take decades, centuries even to—"

"The Collective Harmony—Aretheans hold the science within us."

"How does it work?"

"There is no time to explain."

"No time?" What a ridiculous explanation. "You've been here for years—decades. Why are you now in such a rush to fix things?"

The Sundarian drew in a deep breath. "Because of you. The day you arrived, everything changed. My people came to help mankind, but there are some Aretheans who would have the Earth continue on its destructive path. Their numbers are small, yet they are determined."

"Who are they?"

"They infiltrated our stream to your world and now threaten to stop us. You have seen their cyphers."

"The symbols in the tunnels," Carlos said. "The slashed zero?"

"Just so." The Sundarian nodded. "Events have unfolded. The council sent me to awaken the others of my kind. To begin the process of renewal before we cannot."

"You can do that? Awaken the million?"

"I am The Sundarian."

Carlos closed his eyes, scratching his head. "So, the Slash Zero people—"

"They are known as Believers."

"*Bien.* These Believers are trying to stop you from helping us. Why?"

"It is their faith. They judge your world unworthy. The Council judges otherwise. We are certain your people represent one hope for the future of the universe."

"Such differing points of view."

"The Believers have faith in their prophecies. They judge you for your transgressions—your wars, hate, and pollution. Therefore, it is their duty to stop you. The Council considers only your virtues— peace, love, and understanding."

"Science versus religion."

"Just so."

"But how can the Believers stop us?"

"At this very moment, they control the mind of the general, Payton Sinclair."

"Ai, no me digas."

"They plan to force him to begin what you call, Operation Zero."

"No, no, no, no." Carlos paced the small space. "This he will never do."

"He has no choice. He is controlled by the Believers."

"But where is your proof?"

"Look in your pocket."

"My pocket?" Carlos shoved a hand in his pants pocket and came out empty.

"Your coat pocket."

He pulled out the paperback Dr. Turnbride had placed there. "I'd forgotten about this." He turned to The Sundarian. "But how did you—"

"Open it. Note the remarks."

Carlos turned to the page, just before the copyright information and studied the scribbles. "A doctor's handwriting to be sure."

> *Hasting knows why the aliens are here.*
> *He told Sinclair, then fell ill.*
> *Radiation poisoning.*
> *Keep your wits about you.*
> *Watch Sinclair.*

Carlos read the passage again.

"The general poisoned Samuel Hasting," The Sundarian said, "the most brilliant mind of your world. At the same time, he commissioned you and Dr. Felix Paul."

"What are you saying?"

"He is harming this program. You and Dr. Paul are gifted, to be sure, but not on the level of a Samuel Hasting."

"Enough." Carlos felt his face flush.

"Don't let your vanity turn you from—"

"Vanity?" He forced a quick laugh. "I'm not vain. Maybe Dr. Paul—"

"Carlos," The Sundarian said, "you must do everything in your power to help me. Fate has put us together. I cannot do this alone. You are a good man. Help me save your world."

"Well..." Carlos stiffened, shoring up his wounded ego. "...if you put it like that—"

"I do." She opened the door and they stepped out.

"It's about time," Patricia the Witch said.

Darrah put his hands on his hips. "We were beginning to wonder."

"What in the world were you doing in there?" Prudence raised her eyebrows.

"Listen to me," The Sundarian said, "all of you. You are all test subjects, imprisoned here because of my people. I am sorry. You were taken against your will. Your government put together a list of those whom they believed held special abilities—those who might communicate with us. For whatever reason, your names appeared on that list.

"But now we must work together to escape this underground prison."

"Hell, yeah," Willie T. said.

Carlos weighed his friendship with General Sinclair against all the noise in the room. He refused to give up on his student. "Surely, once the government knows why you are here, they will help you."

"No," Prudence said, "we have to keep the Black Shirts out of this. They're the reason we're in this mess in the first place."

"Just so," The Sundarian said.

"Poor Payton." Carlos hung his head.

"You must do as I ask, Carlos, or the Believers will prevail. Your world will be lost. I need you to go to the general. Tell him nothing of our planned escape or of the test subjects in your room. I will duplicate the Tombstones once more. You must keep his mind occupied until the chaos in The Shelter overwhelms him. Only he can order an evacuation. There are several means of egress from this underground prison. I will lead the test subjects—"

"Would you stop calling us test subjects?" Gregory the Confabulator shouted.

In a cool and unsympathetic voice, The Sundarian turned to him and said, "Tell me what it is you wish to be called?"

"How 'bout Specialists?" He looked about the room as if expecting applause for this simple declaration. "Don't you see? *Special*, for our special abilities, and *List*, because our names wound up on that damned government watch list of theirs. Get it? Special-lists."

A murmur rose from the room. Words of encouragement rang out.

"Just so," The Sundarian said. She turned back to Carlos. "I will lead the *Specialists* out of this underground site and send word to my people. We escape today."

"You want me to stay behind and keep the general busy with other matters." Carlos spoke in a calm, even voice, seeking assurance of what his assignment would be. She did not answer. "Despite the danger I will be in, you want me to distract him so he will not warn the Believers." Again, The Sundarian did not speak. "Because if the general warned them about the escape, something terrible would happen, yes?"

Silence.

Just to be sure, he spoke even louder. "Is that what you wish? For me to stay behind and keep the general occupied in conversation?"

Nothing.

"Very well, then. I will stay behind and divert the general's attention."

She smiled. "Specialists, please follow me." The Sundarian turned to Carlos, running a finger along his cheek. "Good luck."

CHAPTER 14

"**Nice meeting you, professor.**" Prudence reached out, placing her hand on his forearm. Carlos offered a quick smile in return. She tightened her grip. "And thank you for providing us with a safe harbor, even if only for a little while."

"Come along," Mindy the Prophet said, taking hold of Prudence's elbow. "You'll see each other again soon. I promise."

Marissa the Psychic followed. "Right, what Mindy said. And when a prophet and psychic agree," she said with a wink, "it's bound to happen. Normal folk call it destiny."

"I see..." Carlos nodded. "And what do *you* call it?"

"Er, uh...destiny."

The rest of the Specialists filed out, thanking Carlos and wishing him well. Carlos stopped the final Specialist. "Excuse me, Gregory, but can you tell me what a Confabulator is?"

Gregory chuckled. "Why, my dear sir, it simply means one who speaks—one who chats. The art of confabulation is something nearly everyone dabbles in on a daily basis. In fact, we're confabulating even now, as we speak...uh, so to speak. Face to face conversation is one of the last true pleasures of life, especially in the age of social media, don't you find?"

"*Si*, but tell me, why would someone who speaks, or, um, confabulates, find themselves placed on a government watchlist?"

"I don't know for sure, but I have given it some thought." Gregory narrowed his eyes and put a hand to his chin. "Perhaps, they sought someone who would be skilled at communicating, yes? Or maybe the powers-that-be threw a much wider net than necessary and happened to scoop me up with the others, hm? Or, and this is my personal favorite, it might have been the bureaucrat in charge of compiling the list of people with special abilities had absolutely no idea what confabulation meant. He simply placed my name on the list to cover his ass." He laughed—a contagious noise filling the room. "Although, I must admit, confabulation is somewhat mystical, is it not? I mean, verbal articulation is the one true form of magic we all share, yes?"

"*Si*," Carlos said. "But I'm so sorry your love of communicating brought you here."

"You know, my dear husband, God rest his soul, often said confabulation would someday be my undoing, but I never listened to his warning. Ironic, wouldn't you say?" Chuckling, Gregory the Confabulator hurried to join the other Specialists.

Carlos closed the door. He rushed across the carpet to the bed and stared down at the dozens of small vials, packets of powders, and various items of drug paraphernalia. It took a while to gather it up, but no time at all to dump it into the toilet. The tablets, pills, and powders swirled around the commode, begging to be rescued. *Save us*, they whimpered, *we helped you when you were scared, when you were hurting. Help us—stop this madness.* He answered their pleas, his voice echoing off the tiled walls of the restroom.

"I should have done this years ago. Now be quiet before I change my mind...or before somebody hears me talking to my toilet." He pulled the paperback from his coat pocket and tossed it on the bed. It landed upright, facing him.

How he disliked the cover of that book. Plain white background with bold black lettering. *Law and Disorder: Physics on Trial by Dr. Carlos Huerta.* The publishing house had designed the artwork and the title. His name appeared much too small, and the colors suggested that physics could only ever be black and white. Nonsense. If anything, the cover should have been gray, with a variety of shades for the title. He would have liked a larger font for his name. His ego at work? Perhaps. Maybe not. Didn't having the courage to see the world in a way others could not *require* an enormous ego? Surely.

He cracked the door open and surveyed the hallway. *Empty.* In one slow, calculating move, he exited the room. In one slow, calculating move, he exited the room and stole his way toward the general's office. After negotiating several hallways, he found himself lost. *So much for that enormous ego.*

Reversing his direction, he retraced the path back to his room. He set out in a new direction, past the cafeteria, the shops, and the park with its fake grass and artificial flowers. This time, he not only found the general's office, he found the man himself. Sinclair stood in the hallway speaking with Dr. Felix Paul. He approached them and nodded.

"Have you had a change of heart, Carlos?" Sinclair said.

Felix beamed. "Well, look who finally decided to make an appearance. Gawd, I thought you'd flown the roost."

Stepping forward, Carlos stuck out his hand. "Felix, so glad to see you decided to stay. I believe it's *flown the coop*, not roost."

"Ah, so it is. One flies the coop and comes home to roost. Isn't that right, general?"

Sinclair cocked his head, a look of annoyance covering his face.

"Well, whichever it is..." Felix shook Carlos's hand. "...yes, I decided to stay. How could I not? What a mystery we've got on our hands, eh my friend? Let's see, there's extraterrestrials, the laws of physics—not just being broken, but totally obliterated. To top it all off, we're actually getting a possible glimpse at The Grand Design."

"Why don't we continue this conversation in my office?" Sinclair said. They walked through the empty vestibule and into the general's private office. He shut the door.

"What did you mean, Payton?" Carlos declined the offer to sit. "Earlier, when you asked if I had a change of heart?"

"I thought you decided against joining the project. I mean you literally disappeared. What were you up to, and who were you with? Where did you go?"

"In this underground maze, *señor*, where could I have gone?"

"When I invited you to become a member of our scientific team, you were nervous—an insecure little shell of a man. You did not know up from down, but you've changed. You seem more confident now, more—"

"General Sinclair," Felix said, "that's quite a harsh evaluation. You know what the man's been through."

"Still, the Carlos Huerta I knew would have crumbled at my assessment or reached into his pocket for one of his little pills. Am

91

I right?"

"Well..." Carlos could feel his face flushing. "...you're not wrong." He had to remind himself, over and over, *this is not Payton Sinclair. He is controlled by aliens—the Believers.* "And it's true, I may well have crumbled at being called a little shell of a man. My breakdown at MIT...the way they let me go, so embarrassing. And Lilly—*pobrecita*—dying so young... Her loss destroyed me. I turned to pills. But now—"

"Yes," Sinclair said, "now, what? Why the sudden change?"

"It may be sudden to you—"

"Me, too," Felix said. "You have to admit, the general's appraisal, harsh as it is, seems to be on the mark. No offense, professor."

"None taken. I guess I've had time to think about my life— living in a fog, a dream, ever since Lilly died. But I have thought, for the longest time, about changing my ways—of finding a new path. In fact, I've been thinking about a great many things, lately. And thanks to you, Payton, I've met someone who helped me discover that new path."

Sinclair sat behind his desk and hammered at the computer keyboard. "I believe I mentioned this to you before, Carlos. There're security cameras in every tunnel. We caught an interesting clip the night you disappeared." He banged a few more keys, then swiveled the monitor around so it faced Carlos.

The screen revealed a video of two people trudging through a darkened tunnel. The figures passed under a light bulb, their faces coming into focus. Sinclair pressed a button, freezing the frame, and enlarged the image.

Felix Paul slid his glasses down the bridge of his nose. "Who is that woman with you?"

"Yes, Carlos," General Sinclair said, "who is that *ENO* with you?"

"She is not an ENO," Carlos said. "She is a person. She has a name."

"Oh, you're naming them now—like pets." Sinclair bolted out of his chair. "This is bullshit. She must have put some kind of spell on you—messed with your head. Believe me, Carlos, those things are far from human, and they certainly don't dabble in psychotherapy. Hell, they don't even talk."

"No?" Carlos eased into one of the red leather chairs facing the general's desk. "Then, tell me, what do they do? If anyone should know, my friend, it is you."

Felix shook his head "What do you mean by that? What do you mean he should know?"

"I find it so very strange," Carlos said, "why you invited Dr. Paul to be a part of this scientific team. His specialty is Engineering—hardly the area of expertise used in explaining how matter materializes from nothing." Carlos turned to Felix Paul. "No offense."

"None taken, Carlos. In fact, I thought about that myself."

"Felix and I worked together, years ago, on a project requiring many disciplines." Carlos stood and approached the desk. "We became close. When you first mentioned he would join us, I approved, happy for the opportunity to work alongside a friend—the only one I've seen here besides you."

"What about Hasting?"

"I'll get to Samuel in a moment. You invited Felix to join in on this project, but he is not a good fit, is he Payton?"

"What are you getting at?" Sinclair moved out from behind his desk and stared down at Carlos.

"Dr. Paul should not be on this team—nor should I, for that matter. What did you say, *señor?* Ah yes, you called me a nervous, insecure little shell of a man. That I didn't know my ups from my downs." He furrowed his brow. "And now, we come to poor Dr. Hasting. The perfect choice for this project. His doctors declared the cancer in remission months ago. Yet after signing on here, he fell ill almost at once. However, it is not the cancer. A reliable source tells me Samuel has radiation poisoning."

"Radiation?" Felix sat in the chair nearest him. "What's going on?"

"I may be wrong but if I had to guess," Carlos said, "I would say the general is making it look like he is doing everything in his power to assemble a scientific team to solve the mystery of why the aliens are here, when in fact, he is doing the exact opposite."

"To what end?" Sinclair leaned in.

"You know very well—so you will be held blameless when Operation Zero is activated. You want the aliens euthanized because you, yourself, are a—"

Hee-haw, hee-haw.

The office door crashed open. Sinclair straightened. "What is it, sergeant?"

A disheveled and out of breath Sergeant Sandoval shouted above the alarm. "Sir, the Tombstones have duplicated again. There's eight of 'em now. The whole thing's out of control. The men are panicked."

"Get Major Bay—"

"He's the one who sent me to get you. We need you in The Shelter. The situation's critical."

Black Shirts raced by, their boots drumming out a cadence on the hallway floor.

Sinclair stared at Carlos. "This isn't over, Huerta. Report to your quarters. Now." With that, the general and Sergeant Sandoval rushed out of the office.

"Radiation sickness?" Felix said. "Where did that come from?"

"Oh uh, just a shot in the dark. Did you see his face? He *is* hiding something."

"He's not the only one, Carlos. Spill it."

"I don't think I can spill anything, my friend, not just yet." Two days ago, Carlos would have been reduced to an unresponsive wreck by the confrontation in this office—a little shell of a man. But two days ago, he had not met The Sundarian. "Do what you can to get out of this underground tomb, Felix. It's not safe."

"No shit."

"I'll talk to you soon."

"But—"

Carlos raced out of the office and into the hallway. The blaring alarm clawed at his concentration, yet he became aware of the lack of pain in his movements. He jogged along the passageway with no difficulty at all. The clatter coming from The Shelter grew louder with each step. He dove into the chaos of the underground cavern and his eyes widened. Eight Tombstones spewed forth hundreds, perhaps thousands, of catatonic beings. The Black Shirts were no longer in control.

In the middle of the turmoil stood Sinclair, shouting orders, directing traffic. Finally, in a bold and deafening voice, he yelled, "Evacuate!" He rushed toward the Southern Tunnel Archway. "Open the chambers and release the ENOs."

Carlos had to push his way through the crush of bodies. A constant series of brilliant flashes streamed above the cavern floor like strobe lights. New arrivals poured from the Tombstones, a virtual rush-hour two thousand feet beneath the surface of the earth. Thunder crashed without pause. He kept his eyes fixed on the opening of the Southern Tunnel System. Recognizing Sinclair just a few feet away, Carlos rushed after the general only to be thrown off course by two burly Black Shirts.

"Payton!" His cries came too little, too late. Sinclair vanished into the mouth of the Southern Tunnel System without ever looking back.

Carlos fought his way through the lines of both humans and aliens. Finally entering the tunnel, out of breath but upright. Being pushed, pulled, and elbowed, only strengthened his resolve to find the general.

Two Black Shirts ran over him like linebackers sacking a quarterback. He found himself on the ground, a large knot on the back of his head. Fearing he might be trampled, he scrambled to the wall and sat against the damp rock. He tried to stand but could not. Rubbing his eyes, Carlos leaned back and passed out.

CHAPTER 15

Prudence peered around the corner of the hallway leading to The Shelter. They'd wasted an enormous amount of time following a maze of hallways and passages. They had gotten lost twice, winding up at dead ends, and needed to double back. The Specialists waited behind her for a signal to proceed. At the end of the line stood The Sundarian.

"What's the hold up?" Gamble said.

"It's chaos," Prudence whispered. "Which is good, since I don't think we'll get noticed."

"Great. So why don't we get going?"

"Because it's *total* chaos, which is bad, since I think we'll get separated."

"Right." Bruce the Dowser stepped forward, surveying the pandemonium over Prudence's shoulder. He smiled. "You're in my wheelhouse now. This is exactly where my skills come in to play."

"What do you mean?" Prudence wrinkled her brow.

"Young lady, you do know what dowsing is, don't you?"

She had no idea but still nodded, then thought better of it and shook her head.

His smile grew, revealing a missing front tooth, giving him the appearance of a mischievous third grader. "It means I can divine my way through most situations like this, chaotic or otherwise. Not only that, my skill set is especially suited for use in caves."

He searched the ground and shrugged his shoulders. "Although it's easier with a divining rod—a stick or whatnot—I think I can handle this situation minus any props."

"But how—"

"Watch." Bruce raised a hand over his head and shook it. He yelled over his shoulder, "Look sharp now Specialists. Follow me and stick together." Without delay, he stepped into the mayhem of The Shelter.

The Specialists followed suit, forming a sort of quick-step conga line. Bruce darted around the confusion, past the disorder, and through the turmoil. In a few short minutes, he led them, without incident, to the other side of the cavern.

"Well done." Prudence bent over to catch her breath. "But where do we go from here?"

"There," said the calm voice of The Sundarian. She pointed toward the entrance of the Southern Tunnel System. Crowds of new arrivals being led by soldiers clogged the entryway.

"Are you sure?" Prudence said. "We need to get to the surface, not farther down into this underground prison."

"Prudence is right," Bruce the Dowser said. "If we go in any deeper, we might never climb our way out."

"Carlos needs our help." The Sundarian turned and strode toward the Southern Tunnel archway. A sea of Black Shirts and new arrivals blocked her path. She gained little ground—like wading through waves of maple syrup. Still, she persevered, eyes straight ahead, progress slow but steady.

"In that case, count me in." Bruce pulled away from the group and trailed after the alien.

"We need to render aid as best we can," Mindy the Prophet said. "Trust me, good things will come of this."

"If we don't help Carlos, we'll regret it." Patricia the Witch trailed after Mindy.

Jedediah the Ghost, released an audible moan and swept over Prudence, tousling her crimson hair. He chased after The Sundarian, diving through the bodies of all those who happened to stand in his way, slipping in and around them like smoke.

Prudence trained her eyes on him. He turned back for a moment, then continued toward the Southern Tunnel System. "Did he just shake his head at me? Am I being scolded?"

"Perhaps a supernatural comment on your reluctance to put our escape at risk," Gregory the Confabulator said. "I suppose it's a clear sign. We must follow the alien."

"I concur." Darrah the Conjuror nodded. "It's absolutely the right thing to do, yes?"

Though Prudence stood her ground, one by one, the Specialists broke ranks and followed after The Sundarian.

"C'mon, Pru." Skye the Telepath took her by the hand. "We were meant for this." Her high pitched, childlike voice seemed out of place in the chaos.

"What do you mean we were meant for this?"

"The universe has a reason for everything—you'll see. Stay close and we'll find a way through this. There's always a way through." She pulled Prudence forward.

They were no longer being hunted. Nobody seemed the least bit concerned about who they were or where they might be going— least of all the Black Shirts.

"Very well." Prudence projected signals of unease and apprehension to anyone who happened to be in their way. Black Shirts lost interest in their duties, fell to their knees, and wept. The extraterrestrials moved aside, opening up a path for them. Skye and Prudence dashed through the commotion catching up with the others.

Bruce, once again, showcased his gap-toothed smile. "I'm impressed, Pru. Your powers are truly impressive."

The small band of Specialists at the entrance of the Southern Tunnel System found their way past the logjam of humans and aliens with the help of Prudence's special powers, and Bruce's deft dowsing.

"Where's The Sundarian?" Prudence said.

Chase the Mage grabbed her hand. "She went on ahead."

"Well, that's just great. How are we supposed to know where to go?"

"You're kidding, right?" Willie T. Smith, the Remote Viewer, shook his head. "I've had her in my sights since we left Carlos's room. I'm watching her even now with my mind's eye. Follow me."

"How does *your* ability work?" Prudence said.

"Once again, you're joking, right? I can no more explain how my power allows me to see beyond the here and now, than you can explain your ability. Am I right?"

Totally. No matter how much she wanted to understand her power, she couldn't. End of story. She moved aside. "Please, lead the way, Mr. Smith."

"I will. But listen here, girl, it's Willie T.—got it?" He took a step toward the Southern Tunnel System and shouted back to the Specialists, "Everybody fall in line behind me. No lollygagging, now. I'll get us where we got to go."

"How can you be so sure?" Gamble called out.

Willie T. Smith glared at Gamble, then grinned. "Like the Reverend Dr. Martin Luther King Jr. once said, 'If you're waiting for the right time to do the right thing, then you're just wasting time.' Don't waste my time, Gamble. Let's get going."

"My mistake." Gamble gave a rueful smile. "Lead the way."

Willie T. found room to move forward at the side of the tunnel, against the rock wall. He matched the main flow of traffic, journeying farther into the depths of the earth. Prudence opened her mouth in a wide yawn, easing the pressure on her ears. The deeper they ventured, the more she yawned.

"We're getting closer," Willie T. said.

"How do you know?" she said. "Have you been here before?"

Stopping, he glanced about, then continued in another direction. "Let's try this way for a bit."

"Are you sure you know where you're going?"

"Listen." He stopped again and turned to her. "Stumbling is not falling."

"Dr. King?"

"Nope. Malcom X. Now follow me." He hurried along then stopped once more.

"Now what is it?" Prudence had just about run out of patience.

"Listen here." He turned to her and frowned. "Trust me. Your gray matter got to have a little more faith in me than your pie hole."

"Malcom X?"

"Naw, that's pure Willie T. Now let's go." He guided them deeper into the tunnel system. They passed several Black Shirts leading aliens through dark passageways and damp cavities. "Look over yonder. There she is."

Twenty yards ahead of them, The Sundarian strolled forward at a steady pace. Prudence reached out and put her hand on the

Remote Viewer's elbow. "Great job. I knew you could do it."

Willie T's eyebrows rose. "Yeah, uh, right."

Unsure of The Sundarian's motive, Prudence hesitated. "We should hang back, just a little, maybe. Don't you think?"

"Why?"

"Let's just see where she's going first. Perhaps, there's a reason she didn't want us tagging along, but, then again, she might need our help."

"Like back-up. Good idea."

Prudence fell in line behind Willie T. but keeping The Sundarian in sight proved more difficult than she imagined. Not only did the guards and new arrivals block her view, the single string of light bulbs running the length of the tunnel cast a confusing mix of silhouettes and shadows on the rock walls.

"I lost her," Prudence said. "How could that happen?"

"Don't worry," Tarissa the Mystic said. She tilted her head up and closed her eyes. "I've got her locked in. She's about forty feet ahead of us on the right."

"Nice, Tarissa," Prudence said. "How is it you can see her with your eyes closed?"

The question pried the Mystic's eyes open. She cocked her head. "Why, my dear, with my eyes shut is really the only way I *can* see her."

"Oh, uh...sorry. I didn't mean to ask a stupid question."

"Nonsense, Pru," Clarissa said. "There are no stupid questions." She whispered to Marissa and Tarissa but loud enough to be heard. "Except that one."

The three sisters covered their mouths and snickered. Tarissa stepped forward and placed her hand on Willie T's shoulder.

"Hush now," Willie T. said. "Hang on and mind your step."

The Specialists crept along to the side of the tunnel. The crush of Black Shirts and new arrivals swept them along over gravel and loose rocks. Tarissa gave Willie T. directions with her eyes shut tight.

"Slow down. Good, now move ahead. Slowly. She's stopped, and we're gaining on her. What do you want to do, Prudence?"

"Give her some ground. Why did she stop?"

"She's looking for something," Mindy the Prophet said. "It's not Carlos...it's another tunnel. She's looking for the entrance to a secret tunnel."

"How is that even possible?" Prudence shook her head. "With thousands of people trudging up and down this tunnel for decades... how can a thing like a secret tunnel even exist?"

"*Si*, Mindy's right," Chase the Mage said. "There is definitely a hidden tunnel up ahead. About twenty yards away. *Allí*. Just over there." She pointed ahead.

"We'd better get a move on then or we'll lose her for sure," Willie T. said.

"How could we possibly lose her," Mindy the Prophet said, "with all of us using our abilities to track her every move? No, that is simply out of the question."

Prudence edged her way alongside the rock wall, doing her best to keep a low profile. With her back pressed against the sharp edges of the tunnel, she crept along, feeling her way forward. The others did the same.

Tarissa stopped. "Whoa."

"What is it, sweetie?" Prudence put a hand on her arm. "Is something wrong?"

"Wait. This can't be."

Gamble stepped to the head of the line. "What can't be?"

"I've lost her." Tarissa opened her eyes and glanced at the others. "I have no idea where she's gone."

"What do you mean by that, sister?" Marissa put a hand to the side of her head and closed her eyes. "My God, you're right. The Sundarian has vanished."

"It's true." Clarissa nodded. "She's disappeared. But how could that be? Our abilities, especially when working together, should be invincible."

"Maybe we just passed by her—like ships in the night." Prudence needed to stem the growing panic in their voices. She sent forth feelings of calm and confidence. "If The Sundarian did find an entrance to a secret tunnel, especially in this darkness and with this many people rushing around, it would have been easy for us to miss. We've got to retrace our steps and keep our eyes open, or closed—whichever works." She glanced over her shoulder at the oncoming swarms of humans and aliens trudging toward them.

"And we'll be fighting that lot all the way back," Gamble said.

"I can do something about that." Prudence closed her eyes and concentrated. She thought about sharp knives protruding from the walls of the tunnel. Pain. Cuts. Agony.

Black Shirts guided new arrivals away from the sides of the passageway and elbowed for room near the center of the tunnel. Prudence glanced back at the Specialists. They too had stepped away from the pain of the knives.

"No," she yelled. "I'm making the *guards* think there are knives on the walls. There really aren't any knives. It's perfectly safe."

The Black Shirts and new arrivals fanned out to clog the tunnel opening once again.

"Skye," Prudence said, "come here, please. Can you send a message to just our group, telling them the walls of the tunnel are safe? It's going to be tricky, but I've got to direct everyone else to the center of the tunnel except for us. We need to double back, and we need to do it now."

Skye brightened. "I've never sent a party line message before, but I'll give it a try."

"You can do it, Skype," Gamble said.

"By the way, I hate it when you guys call me that. My name is Skye."

"Skye it is." Prudence turned back to face the oncoming horde of marching bodies. She sent out another message of knives protruding from the tunnel walls. Once again, the multitude crowded into the center of the passageway, moving away from the walls. In the back of her mind, she heard Skye's thoughts, loud and clear.

"Take heed, Specialists. There's no danger of knives poking out of the walls. It's just a trick to fool the oncoming Black Shirts and get them out of our way."

"It's working," Prudence said to Skye while still sending out the message of knives protruding from the tunnel walls. She marveled at the control she had over her ability.

"Practice makes perfect, my dear," Darrah the Conjurer said with a little chuckle. He slid past her, his back against the wall.

Jedediah the Ghost flew overhead. The whoosh of air in his wake felt good against Prudence's skin. Despite the nearly freezing temperature in the tunnel, beads of sweat had formed on her brow. "Keep your eyes open for some kind of entrance to a side tunnel. Use your hands to feel for it."

The group heeded her words and inched their way back up the tunnel, their hands probing along the rock wall for some kind of opening.

"If we missed it the first time around," Chase the Mage said, "what makes you think we can find it this—"

"Got it!" Gregory shouted as if he'd won a prize. "Look, it's right here, behind this boulder. It's camouflaged, we all just missed it at first—at least I did."

Prudence rushed toward him and examined his find. The boulder jutted out from the wall just enough to blend in with the tunnel. An entryway hidden in plain sight.

"You'd never see it unless you knew where to look," Gregory said.

A new voice entered the conversation. "Knew where to look for what?" A cold hand touched Prudence's shoulder.

She jumped. "Who are you? What do you want?"

"Whoa, calm down. I've been following you for a while. My name is Sergeant Sandoval. Why are you trying to track down the professor, and how come you're not afraid of those knives?"

"There are no knives."

"What do you mean? They're right...hey, where'd they go?"

Prudence leaned forward, inches from the man's face. "How do you know Carlos?"

"I'm his liaison. He's my only job."

"Typical of you bastards." Gamble scowled.

Sandoval cocked his head. "What do you mean by that?"

"You had *one* job, and you blew it."

CHAPTER 16

Tick-tock—Tick-tock.

Colonel Andrew Bloodstone left nothing to chance, and he would have it no other way. Sitting behind his desk, observing the turmoil in The Shelter on a multi-screen monitor, brought a smile to his face. The smile widened when he saw General Sinclair mouth the word "Evacuate!"

He knew where General Sinclair would go after giving the orders to evacuate. Bloodstone kept eyes on every watcher, ears on every listener. The dark suits on the edge of The Shelter were his, along with the cameras throughout the facility. Nothing happened at the top-secret site that Bloodstone did not know about, did not control...or cause to happen.

The government needed to curtail Operation Joshua, calling it too expensive, too controversial. Bloodstone could not agree more. He would see to its demise, personally. Extraterrestrial close encounters held no interest for him. The search for alien life, are we alone in the universe, ancient astronauts—these were mere distractions. Only one thing mattered—Prudence Wellman. The girl who could defeat an army with her mind. The man who controlled *that* weapon could rule the world—and he was determined to be that man.

Cameras captured her power over the Black Shirts—toying with them—a lion tamer and her prey. Pitted against one unassuming, nondescript girl, they cried and ran away like cowards. It did not matter how many men she faced, they all backed down.

"Colonel Bloodstone." A young voice broke his concentration. How disrespectful. He spun and faced the Black Shirt standing at the door to his office. "Lieutenant?"

"Sir, the Cats are leaving their cells, in mass."

Bloodstone knew the young man meant "en masse." He did not correct him but made a mental note to deal with the boy at a later time. Ignorance had no place in his world. Likewise, impudence. "What's their target?"

"Uh, sir?"

"What is their objective—where are they going?"

"Well, uh, here. The aliens are heading here, to The Shelter."

Bloodstone read the lieutenant's nametape. "Lieutenant Houser, you are now assigned to me. Let's move."

"Yes, sir." Houser saluted, possibly assuming the reassignment to be an honor.

Pushing past the lieutenant, Bloodstone ventured into the hall just outside his office. He flagged down three other Gatekeepers. "You men, follow me. Let's move."

They quick-marched down the hallway and entered The Shelter. He led his makeshift detail toward the nearest elevator. A column of Black Shirts waited in line to evacuate. Colonel Bloodstone and his men cut to the front of the queue. The elevator doors slid open, and the colonel stepped aboard. He waved his men in with one hand while holding the other up like a traffic cop, keeping out the unwanted Black Shirts. The elevator doors closed.

"Lieutenant Houser."

"Yes, sir," the boy said.

"When we reach the surface, commandeer a vehicle. I need to get to the airfield. Do you understand?"

"A vehicle. Yes, sir."

He turned to another man and raised his voice, "I need a Command-and-Control facility set up ASAFP. Is that clear?"

"Yes, sir," the man said.

Bloodstone took note of the quick response. The young man might have been Hispanic—brown skin and black hair. In any case, he seemed to be on the ball.

The moment the elevator doors opened. Lieutenant Houser sprinted off in search of transport.

The colonel's face reddened. "Why is there no security at this door?" He waited for an answer. The Black Shirts glanced at the floor, at each other, anywhere but at him. "I want armed security at each elevator exit. Is that understood?"

"Yes, sir," the brown-skinned man answered.

"General Sinclair is MIA." The sooner these boys understood the severity of the situation, the better. The salad days of General Payton Sinclair had come to an abrupt end. "I'm in command now."

Gatekeepers scrambled in the garage bay near the elevators. Motors rumbled and tires screeched. The stench of diesel fumes filled the air. Bloodstone stepped out of the elevator and shouted above the din of the full-scale retreat, "I need technical, tactical, and recon units ready when we hit the airfield. Timing's everything. Tick-tock."

"Yes, sir." The Hispanic pulled a two-way radio from his belt and barked out orders. "Colonel Bloodstone needs the airfield command office ready in five minutes. Route all eyes and ears to that office. This is priority one. The colonel needs secure lines open to Washington and Nellis at once. Tactical, technical, and recon report on the double."

Colonel Bloodstone raised his eyebrows. "Well done. What's your name?"

The man lowered the radio and furrowed his brow. "Uh, De La Cuesta, sir. Corporal Benjamin De La Cuesta."

"You just got bumped up. It's now Staff Sergeant De La Cuesta."

"Thank you, sir. I'm so glad you—"

"Can the speech. Where's my ride?"

An SUV raced toward them and screeched to a halt, Lieutenant Houser at the wheel. Colonel Bloodstone and the three Black Shirts jumped in. The vehicle raced away from the elevator atrium, speeding past several slow-rolling military vehicles. It swept under the rising gate arm at the exit of the parking facility. The tires bit into stark desert sand with a vengeance, while the occupants bounced up and down as if in a blender. Lieutenant Houser did not back off the gas.

A swirling dust devil followed the speeding vehicle, rising up into the night sky, leaving a trail from the mouth of The Shelter's entrance to the edge of the airfield. Once on the smooth tarmac, the passengers straightened ties and smoothed back unruly hair. Still, the lieutenant pressed on the accelerator.

Other vehicles joined them on the airfield, forming a convoy heading for the cluster of buildings south of the runway. One cinder block building in particular stood out. Colonel Bloodstone's Command and Control center, his strategic operations post—his last stand.

The vehicle stopped, with tires screeching, in front of the block building. A large tent had been erected to the left of the building. The new infirmary.

"Lieutenant," Bloodstone said, "let me out here then park around back. The rest of you help with the landlines and security. I want this building to be a fortress. If the ENOs attack...well, then this will be the end of the ENOs."

"Yes, sir," they said, in unison.

"I'll meet you inside," Lieutenant Houser said.

"Negative." Bloodstone turned to De La Cuesta. "Staff Sergeant, with me. Let's roll."

The colonel jumped out of the SUV, giving Lieutenant Houser a quick glance. The man sat behind the wheel, confused. Lost. The colonel and De La Cuesta raced up the stairs and entered the stronghold.

Odors of rotting wood and disinfectant assaulted Bloodstone's senses. On the positive side, computers, landlines, monitors, and miles of wire were being tended to. Clatter filled the large complex— duct tape tearing, boots stamping on wooden floorboards, boxes being stacked, paper shuffling, and voices shouting. The nerve center took shape, breathing its first breath in the wee hours of a new day. Before his very eyes, Bloodstone's vision, his purpose, came to life. If the ENOs wanted a fight—and any reasonable man would assume they did—then, by God, that is what they would get. But only after securing the girl.

A young (wmsateren't they all?) man with the insignia of master sergeant saluted and stepped in front of the colonel, interrupting his trek to the back of the room. "Excuse me, sir, but your desk is this way."

"They're all my desks, son. Out of the way." Bloodstone brushed past the man and continued his quick march. He sat behind a large table at the rear of the room, examining the four monitors stacked on top of each other. He grunted his approval. "This will do. Get these computers up and running. I need eyes—now."

"Sir, yes, sir," a master sergeant said before setting two

technicians to the task of making it happen. Within minutes the monitors sprang to life. A keyboard, joystick, and headset were placed on the desk, along with a red folder. "Uh, sir, every camera in The Shelter is at your command. The joystick operates the feed to the monitors. Just press this button, here, and you can display any zone at all." He flipped open the folder. "This data sheet shows the corresponding codes and locations of all cameras inside the facility."

"And the direct line to Nellis?"

"Uh, we're still patching that through. It's hard-wired and runs under the—"

"I don't need to know how it works, just tell me when it does. Same thing for that line to the Joint Chiefs."

"Sir, yes, sir."

"Staff Sergeant De La Cuesta. Find the master sergeant a rifle and station him outside—Guard duty. On the double. This center needs full security."

"Sir, yes, sir." De La Cuesta escorted the master sergeant to the exit. "Get a squad together and watch this door. Nobody in or out without my okay."

"Hey...uh, I don't...I don't answer to you. I report directly to General—"

"Things have changed. Colonel Bloodstone's in charge now."

"We didn't get the word. When did—"

De La Cuesta slammed the door shut.

"Good man," Bloodstone yelled from the back of the room. "Come back here and run through the elevator cameras."

De La Cuesta rushed to the colonel's side. He picked up the joystick, pressed a numbered code on the keyboard and toggled through the elevator cams.

The colonel leaned back, keeping his eyes fixed on the monitors. "Go a little faster."

"Yes, sir." De La Cuesta pushed his thumb against the toggle, a rapid clicking noise sounded as the monitors flickered. The elevators were empty.

"Shit." Colonel Bloodstone dismissed a hovering technician with a wave of his hand and turned to De La Cuesta. "Find a camera with a wide-scan view of The Shelter."

The staff sergeant checked the data sheet and hit a few keys on the keyboard. All four monitors displayed different angles of The Shelter.

"Zoom in on that man," Bloodstone ordered.

"What man?"

Bloodstone grabbed the remote. With skilled fingers, he maneuvered the joystick, zooming in on a man wearing a brown suit laying on the ground. Dr. Carlos Huerta. Bloodstone used the toggle to pull back and scan the full Shelter. Across the cavern stood the group of patients he'd been monitoring from his office. Their pink scrubs and white slippers made them easy to find. Prudence Wellman stood at the head of this small group—her bright ginger hair perhaps easier to spot than the colorful scrubs.

He panned the camera back across The Shelter. Huerta stood and ducked under the archway into the Southern Tunnel System. Bloodstone pressed a few keys and located Huerta on another camera. The professor stumbled through the main passageway toward the endless row of alien chambers.

"And where are you going?" Bloodstone murmured. He scanned back to the tunnel entrance. The group of patients crossed under the Southern Tunnel archway. The colonel mumbled, "The professor's following the general, and the patients are following the professor. Where the hell is everyone going?"

"Say again, sir?"

"Nothing, De La Cuesta. Get me a cup of coffee. It's gonna be a long night."

Tick-tock—Tick-tock.

CHAPTER 17

Confronting Sergeant Sandoval, Prudence put her nose inches from his face and whisper-shouted, "Are you saying, you have no idea who we are?"

"No, ma'am." Sandoval backed up. "I followed ya'll 'cause I heard you talking about the professor...uh, Carlos Huerta."

"How do you know we're all together?" Gamble said.

"Well, just look at you." Sandoval snorted. "Pink scrubs, white slippers—the lot of you. Shoot, you're easy to spot."

Gamble turned to Prudence. "Why don't you just put a whammy on him?"

"Whammy? Is that what you think of my ability? A Whammy?"

"C'mon, Pru, you know what I mean. He's a Black Shirt."

Prudence turned to the sergeant. "You said the professor's your only job. What do you mean by that?"

"I'm assigned to him, to make sure he comes to no harm."

Gamble shook his head. "Like I said before, son, you sure do suck at your job."

"Excuse me," Clarissa said, "but while we're standing here arguing, The Sundarian is getting away."

"The Sundarian?" Sandoval wrinkled his brow.

"You're right, Clarissa. Listen," Prudence said to the sergeant, "Carlos may be in trouble. So, if it's your job to keep him safe... come with us, but keep your yap shut. You have no idea what we're capable of. Do you understand?"

"Yes, ma'am."

Gamble shook his head. "Are you sure, Pru?"

She turned to face the Specialists. "I've got a feeling about this one. Let's go. We need to hurry."

She could have easily brought the sergeant to his knees with a mental message of dread and panic, as Gamble had suggested, but she heard something in the sergeant's voice. Compassion—a genuine concern for the professor's well-being. She let the others pass, then stopped Sandoval. "Don't make me regret this."

He nodded. They ducked behind the boulder together and stepped through the entrance of the secret tunnel.

The noise of the Southern Tunnel System soon faded. Darkness, darker than anything Prudence had ever known, surrounded them. Instead of freezing, the temperature in this black chamber climbed, feeling balmy, almost tropical.

"C'mon, gang." Bruce the Dowser's disembodied voice echoed through the shadows. "Let's form a line, this time with that Black Shirt fellow at the rear. Hold hands, and I'll try to lead us through."

Prudence heard doubt, maybe fear in the man's voice. Even though she didn't have an empathetic bone in her body, she sensed Bruce's uncertainty. "Are you sure?"

"It's pretty dark. Like I said, I'll do my best."

They inched their way through the nothingness. Prudence took baby steps, hoping to avoid an imagined cliff waiting to swallow her whole. She squeezed the young sergeant's hand.

Bruce hesitated several times, skirting along at a turtle's pace. "I'm not sure." Two more steps. "I don't know." One-half step. "Maybe not."

The frigid air of the Southern Tunnel System whistled at their backs. They progressed through the darkness at a slow, laborious pace—and then not at all.

Blinking, Prudence focused on her breathing, on her heartbeat, on anything but the darkness. The absence of light led her to the brink of despair. The lack of movement pushed her to the edge. "Anybody getting any readings?" She could not stop her voice from stammering. "Are we in another cave? Is it manmade? Can anybody hear me? Hello?"

"Calm down, Pru," Tarissa said, "my third eye needs time to adjust."

"Third eye?"

"You bet. It's how I see the world. After all, we mystics are aware of everything."

"Great. So, can you clue the rest of us in?"

"I'm afraid it doesn't work that way, my dear." Raising her voice, she said, "Bruce, I'm quite adept at seeing through darkness. So, if you don't mind, I'll come to the front of the line and take over."

"Ah, sweet lady," Bruce said, "with pleasure."

Prudence held her ground while Tarissa took the lead, stirring the air around her. A sudden chill ran through her blood, making her shiver. Thoughts of being separated from the group and wandering off alone sent fear coursing through her body. She had never experienced claustrophobia, but she imagined it felt a lot like this.

Apparently, the Specialists were picking up on the vibe. "We've got to get out of here," Bruce said.

"This place is cursed," Willie T. said.

Moans and cries filled the dark space.

Darrah shouted, "C'mon, everybody, have courage. Trust in your powers. Believe in your abilities."

"Who in the heck *are* you people?" Sandoval whispered.

"Sergeant," Prudence muttered, "don't you dare let go of my hand...please."

He tightened his grip. She drew in a deep, quiet breath. The sergeant's firm touch stilled her anxiety. In a moment, the rhythm of her heartbeat calmed.

"Thank you," she said, sensing an invisible peace settle over the group. She reached up and pulled the sergeant's head down to whisper, "I mean it. Panic would have led to disaster."

"It often does."

"Right," Tarissa said, her voice filling the void. "I've got a bead on The Sundarian. Hold tight to one another." With that, she quick-marched through the blackness.

They travelled along in this fashion for several minutes, the sound of their feet crunching over loose gravel echoing against unseen objects.

"Look," Sandoval said from the back of the line. "Does anybody else see that?"

Prudence squinted, trying her best to see through the darkness.

113

She could not be sure of anything. "Are you pointing in any particular direction?" The absence of light had thrown her off her game. Her confidence wavered.

"Stop it, Pru," Darrah said. "You're bringing the rest of us down again."

She wanted to challenge him, to argue his anxiety had nothing to do with her, but she could not. "I'm sorry." In the pitch-black surroundings, she closed her eyes and concentrated on happy things—birthdays, holidays, family. In an instant, her mood soared. Cheerful memories filled her mind, leaving no room for despair.

"A light," Gamble called out. "Just over there."

"I see it, too," Tarrissa said, "and with my physical eyes."

The light grew brighter. The ground became visible—a mixture of stones, dirt, and gravel.

"I see the light," Willie T. said, his tone almost sing-songy.

Chase the Mage joined in. "There it is, over there."

At last, a faint glow caught Prudence's attention. "C'mon, let's pick up the pace. We're almost there."

Tarissa marched straight for the light, everyone else following close behind in single file. More of the chamber revealed itself. They soon broke the conga-line protocol and strolled forward in clusters of twos and threes. Marissa, Tarissa, and Clarissa. Chase Rodriquez and Willie T. Smith. Gregory and Darrah. Bruce the Dowser, Gamble, and Patricia the Witch. Skye and Mindy marched side by side. Prudence and Sergeant Sandoval, still holding hands, brought up the rear.

Tarissa finally reached the small opening to an illuminated space. She waited for the others to catch up before stooping down and lumbering through the small crevice. Prudence let go of the sergeant's hand and entered the illuminated chamber. Her hand went up, shielding her eyes against the brilliance. She glanced down and shrieked.

Chase leaned in. "What is it, Pru?"

"Look down. Look at what we're standing on." A surface of pure gold, polished and smooth, stretched out before them. Mountains of the precious metal surrounded the cave.

"*La casa de los Dioses,*" Chase said, falling to her knees. "The house of the gods."

"What the hell did we stumble into?" Patricia spun in circles,

114

taking it all in.

The contrast between the pitch-black chamber they'd just wandered through, and the luster of this underground treasure trove played tricks on Prudence's mind. She sucked in a deep lungful of tropical air. *Had they somehow found their way to the surface? No. Impossible.*

Gamble bent over and picked up a golden rock. "It's heavy—the real deal." He snickered. "We're rich."

Triumphant shouts arose from the group, euphoria gripping the Specialists. Jedediah the Ghost floated overhead, performing lazy circles in a sort of otherworldly happy dance. Marissa, Tarissa, and Clarissa held hands, twirling about in joyous abandon. Willie T. and Bruce the Dowser filled their pockets with golden gravel.

"Everybody, stop," Prudence shouted. "Look."

Several yards in the distance, a lone figure marched on. The Sundarian. Her black peacoat stood out against the golden backdrop.

"Where's she going?" Darrah the Conjurer said.

Prudence shrugged. "I don't see Carlos. Do you?"

Tarissa closed her eyes and tilted her head back. She massaged her temples and sucked in a deep breath. "Gotcha. The professor's close by, Pru. I feel his presence."

"Can you narrow it down a little?"

"Yes. He's here, somewhere in this golden shrine."

The Sundarian stopped and glanced back at the Specialists.

"Hey," Sergeant Sandoval said. "Isn't that the professor's coat?"

Jedediah flew overhead toward The Sundarian, his form taking on the shape of white smoke. He turned back to Prudence, signaling her to follow.

"Once again," the sergeant whispered, his eyes locked on Jedediah the Ghost, "who *are* you people?"

CHAPTER 18

Carlos had never imagined such a place—mountains of gold, valleys of the precious metal. Rivers, lakes, and meadows bordered the shiny, yellow element. Large palm trees and waist-high shrubs softened the metallic scene. *A dream perhaps? No.* He touched the gold, ran his hand across its inviting surface. He could smell it. The farther he trudged into this vast storehouse of underground treasure, the more enthralled he became. But still, for the life of him, he could not recall how he had gotten here.

He closed his eyes and concentrated on the entrance to the Southern Tunnel System. Snippets of memory, like a movie trailer, played in his mind—being knocked down by two broad-shouldered Black Shirts, spotting General Sinclair march under the archway. He remembered following the general to the opening of a secret passageway, hidden from view by murky shadows and an enormous stone. He squeezed behind the boulder, crossed a threshold, and entered a black void, so dark at first, he thought he had lost his sight.

"Take your time, the memories will come."

Carlos spun around at the voice of The Sundarian. "What are you doing here? No. What am *I* doing here? No. Where *are* we?"

"Close your eyes again."

He did as he was told, following visual clues to piece together his journey through the darkness. He had stilled his breath and listened for the general's footsteps ahead of him, crunching over the loose gravel. Navigating the black chamber like a bat, he followed Sinclair by sound alone. Soon, without hesitation, he found himself leaping over obstacles, climbing unseen ridges, jumping across crevices.

His eyes shot open. "But how can that be?" He turned to The Sundarian. "I'm not an athlete. I have never taken a hike in my life. How could I have done those things—the running, the jumping—all without seeing? It is impossible."

"Nothing is impossible. Your senses are heightened," she said. "The medications you took for so many years masked your true self."

"*No me degas*. Are you telling me my true self runs parkour?"

"No." The Sundarian smiled. "Your true self finds a way to do what must be done. You followed the general with confidence—with purpose."

"*Si*, you're right. I feel...different. I don't hurt anymore." He rubbed his shoulder and chuckled. "I ran after Payton. Me...I ran, didn't I?"

"You did, but we must leave now."

"No, I must find Payton. He needs my help."

"There is no time for the general. The Believers are transporting gold to Areth as we speak. Once they have finished the task, they will—"

"*Espera me*. Wait. What are you saying?"

They stood on a slight rise, with a view of the entire underground valley of gold. The Sundarian pointed in the distance. "Behold."

A towering monolith stood at least a mile away. Carlos squinted, trying to make sense of the activity taking place near the bottom of the Tombstone. "Are those Believers?"

"Just so. The general is being used to extend the life of Operation Joshua, allowing Believers time to take the gold."

"Stealing gold? How very human."

"The precious metal is stored in vast mines on Areth. It is atomized, saturating the atmosphere, protecting our ozone from the ravages of the sun. The Believers intentions are noble, but only when it suits their doctrine. They seek gold throughout the galaxy. In their pursuit of the treasure to save Areth, they have become destroyers of worlds."

"Payton Sinclair is an innocent in all of this."

"The general cannot be saved. His mind has been taken."

"No." Carlos turned away, refusing to listen. "You said yourself, nothing is impossible."

"Carlos, wait." A new voice called out, female, familiar.

He stopped and glanced back. The Specialists marched up the path led by the red-haired girl. They stopped next to The Sundarian.

"Where are you going?" Prudence Wellman shouted. "Wait for us."

"Prudence..." Carlos squinted, taking in the man next to her. "... and Sergeant Sandoval. Where have *you* been hiding?"

"I've been looking for you," the sergeant said.

"And so, here I am. Now, if you'll excuse me, I must find my friend." He turned around and continued his march down the golden trail toward the monolith. In a few moments, he heard footsteps on the trail behind him. He turned. The Specialists tramped along the path in his wake.

"So, what's our plan?" Prudence grinned.

"The general is my friend. I mean to rescue him from this rogue group of aliens, find my way back to The Shelter, and then escape this underground facility."

"And after that?"

"Something compels me to lead the extraterrestrials to the ocean. They have come to save our world. The ocean seems to be the most logical place to begin."

"Wait," Sandoval said. "The ENOs are here to save our world? Did I hear you right?"

"Just so," The Sundarian said.

Sandoval turned back to Carlos. "Then why do you want them to leave The Shelter?"

"Listen." Carlos glared at the sergeant. "The government means to kill them all by lethal injection. It's a long story. Suffice it to say, we need to save them, so that they may save us."

"What have they done to General Sinclair?"

"Enough. There is no time for questions. Follow me or go back."

"You have to have faith." Prudence put a hand on the sergeant's shoulder. "Please."

Carlos tramped down the rise toward the towering monolith. The others, including Sergeant Sandoval, followed. The closer they got the more details became clear. They witnessed aliens at the base of the structure depositing boxes, bags, and handfuls of gold into a container. Every few seconds, the box would vanish and be replaced by another. A continuous column of aliens moved forward, taking turns depositing gold into the vessel. Beyond the monolith, in all directions, aliens marched forward carrying the precious metal.

Carlos raised his hand, signaling the others to slow. He pressed a finger to his lips, asking for quiet. They crept forward, concealed by thick shrubs, and neared the Tombstone.

Where is the general? The Sundarian projected her words to Carlos. Glancing at her, he shrugged his shoulders and shook his head.

A hand took hold of his arm. Chase. She pointed to the right and whispered, "There."

Not more than twenty yards away, Carlos spied Payton Sinclair standing in the queue of aliens. The general struggled with a heavy bag. The veins in his neck bulged.

"He's carrying gold," Chase said, keeping her tone soft.

But not soft enough. The line of aliens dropped their treasures to the ground, their heads jerking in her direction. High pitched noises shot from their mouths.

The Sundarian turned to Prudence. "Direct your powers at The Believers."

With eyes wide, she glared at the base of the monolith and raised her arms above her head. The noise of the extraterrestrials ceased. All of them—those in line, the ones standing at the base of the monolith, and the aliens in the distance gathering treasure—fell to their knees. Only Payton Sinclair remained standing, still wrestling with the weight of the bag he carried.

Carlos rushed forward, taking Sinclair by the arm. "Payton, let go of the bag. Drop it and come with me."

The bag fell to the ground. Carlos smiled, but the general shoved him. "No. We need gold." He punched Carlos in the mouth.

The Sundarian advanced, catching Carlos before he fell. She reached over him, placing her hand on the general's neck.

Sinclair groaned and stared at Carlos. "Oh my God. Where are we?"

"You're safe." Carlos wiped at the blood on his lip. "Let's go."

"We'd better hurry," The Sundarian said. "I don't think Prudence can hold them back much longer."

"Then go," Tarissa shouted, "and we'll meet you at the entrance."

The Sundarian hesitated. "But I can't let you try and—"

"I said go." Tarissa scowled. "We've got this."

Carlos took Sinclair by the arm and led him up the path. The Sundarian and Sergeant Sandoval followed. They stopped at the top of the hill and turned back.

Near the bottom of the monolith, Jedediah the Ghost swirled about, stirring up clouds of golden dust, like a supernatural tornado. Patricia held her arms up sending concentrated lightning bolts toward the aliens. Chase the Mage took aim and rolled fireballs along the ground—bowling for extraterrestrials. Patricia the Witch dug her heels in and reached back. She paused at the sight of Carlos. "Get outta here. This will not be pretty."

Carlos secured his hold on the general and raced down the path toward the golden chamber's exit. A thunderous clash sounded behind him. The yellow sky lit up in a mixture of colors—copper, white, silver, and orange. Patricia's laughter travelled overhead. "Ha, got you." She sounded like someone who had just stepped on a bug. "And you, and you."

In short order, the Specialists caught up with Carlos, and together they found their way to the exit.

"What you did back there," The Sundarian said. "You were quite—"

"Think nothing of it," Carlos said. "Anyone would have done the same—"

"Foolish." The Sundarian stared over his shoulder. "You were foolish. Look behind you."

He turned around. Hundreds of aliens rushed along the path toward them.

"My God, they're fast," Clarissa said.

Carlos helped each Specialist through the tiny crevice leading to the pitch-black passageway. "Watch your head. Duck down. Let's keep going."

Sergeant Sandoval hesitated.

"C'mon." Prudence held her hand out to him. "Don't get skittish on me now."

He jerked his thumb back at the advancing aliens. "You know, they might not be the worst thing we'll face if we manage to get out of here alive."

"What do you mean?"

"Colonel Bloodstone relieved General Sinclair—about as mean a motherfu—uh, beggin' your pardon, ma'am. It's just that the colonel is one ornery cuss."

"Tell me about him," Prudence said, "and make it fast."

Gregory hurried past them. "We really don't have time for this."

"The man's got a permanent chip on his shoulder," Sandoval said, ignoring the Confabulator's warning. "Even Sinclair used to keep his distance from the man."

"Damn," Prudence said. "I've heard that name."

"Quickly." The Sundarian insisted on being the last one out. Prudence grabbed the sergeant's hand and they slipped through the small crevice together. Carlos helped the general navigate the opening.

The Sundarian bowed and exited. With a wave of her hand, the small opening closed, shutting off all light coming from the golden chamber. "There, that should slow them down—for a little while, anyway."

CHAPTER 19

His heart beat like a machine. Once again, life held meaning, real purpose. He'd joined a movement much larger than himself. Saving the planet—nothing could be more important. The thought made Carlos want to run through the shadows—to jump, to fly. Instead, he held tight to the general, trudging through the darkness with the others. He looked forward to travelling under the Southern Tunnel System archway and back to The Shelter toward freedom. He no longer questioned how to proceed, just how fast.

In short order, the group squeezed past the large boulder and entered the tunnel system. A steady stream of aliens marched up the grade toward The Shelter. Their silence uneased him. "Where are the guards?"

"The general gave the order to evacuate," Sergeant Sandoval said. He glanced at his watch. "I can't imagine Bloodstone rescinding it. So, most of the force is at the airbase, per protocol. The few guards wandering around here are probably lost or suffering from fatigue. Don't worry, nobody's gonna challenge us."

Carlos peered at the Tombstones. At their base, all alien activity had ceased. The overhead lightning show had come to an end—no more thunder, no new arrivals. "Hello," he shouted. *Hello, hello, hello...* The word echoed across the chamber, disappearing into the darkness of the Northern and Southern tunnels. He turned to the sergeant and grinned like a schoolboy. "I've wanted to do that for the longest time."

123

Sandoval faced the Specialists and started counting.

"What are you doing?" Carlos said.

"Just a quick head count. I'll check again once we're up top. Best to make sure we're all accounted for, don't you think, sir?"

"Sir? Oh, that won't do. Call me Carlos if you like, or professor if you must."

"Sure thing, doc."

"Doc. Yes, that will do nicely," Carlos said.

"It suits you," Prudence said, catching up to them. "Doc."

"Carlos," General Sinclair said, his voice scratchy and weak, "I need to sit down."

The Sundarian shook her head. "His energy has been depleted. He will not recover."

"Nonsense." Carlos placed his friend in the passenger seat of an abandoned golf cart a few feet from one of the Tombstones. "Rest here, my friend. We'll be departing in a moment." He brushed at the sleeves of his white dress shirt, straightened his tie, and turned to the sergeant. "How are we going to get out of here?"

"There's seven elevators that go all the way to the top," Sandoval said. "Three over there at the East wall, and three at the West. This one's the one we took when I first escorted you down, remember? But there's twenty-one of us, and only room for about ten—"

"Correction," Carlos said. He directed the sergeant's eyes to the gaping black mouths of the Southern and Northern tunnels. Countless aliens, timid and hesitant, marched from the shadows into The Shelter. "We are over one million strong, so we will need a much bigger elevator."

The sergeant wiped beads of sweat from his forehead. "Uh, if we climb up two stories, there's several more service elevators. Most of them take you up only a dozen or so floors. You have to get out and board another set of elevators that'll take you up to the next set, and so on and so on. It's a time-consuming journey. They're hydraulic, mainly used for heavy equipment, but eventually they get you to the top."

"Will there be any Black Shirt bastards waiting for us up top?" Willie T. grabbed a handful of Sergeant Sandoval's tie.

The sergeant pushed the remote viewer's hand away. "Of course. The general ordered an evacuation, not a retreat. Security will be stationed at every elevator door. It's procedure. More 'n likely, they'll be heavily armed."

Willie T. shook his head and turned to Carlos. "It's suicide, doc."

Mumbling, the general coughed and took a deep breath. "Stairs."

"What did you say?" Carlos turned back to Sinclair and leaned down.

"Use the stairwells."

Sergeant Sandoval nodded. "Of course, remember those old wooden hatches in the desert? There's a shit load of 'em—over a hundred. They're located around the perimeter." He pointed and said, "behind yellow doors. But it's two thousand steps to the top—more than the World Trade Center. It's gonna take some hard climbing to reach the surface. Still, I bet nobody would expect us to use them."

"Brilliant," Prudence said.

"Thank you, Payton." Carlos put his hand on the general's shoulder. "You may have just saved the world." He stood up and turned to the Specialists. "Right. We're going to be using the stairwells to get to the surface."

Willie T. leaned in. "Will there be security at the exits?"

"I doubt it," Sandoval said. "Like I said, there's hundreds of 'em. They might pick a few, you know, a small percentage, and post some sentries. But it'd be a pretty low priority. No, they'll be watching the elevators for sure."

"What about cameras?" Willie T. said, his tone persistent. "Are there cameras in the stairwells?"

"Once again, a small percentage. I've never seen anybody monitoring the stairs, 'cause nobody ever uses 'em. Listen, we're so far down underground, it's all about the elevators."

"In that case," Willie T. said, "the secret of getting started is getting started."

Prudence narrowed her eyes. "Malcom X?"

"Mark Twain. Let's go."

Carlos bowed his head. The aliens stopped in their tracks.

Prudence put a hand on Carlos's shoulder. "Are *you* communicating with them, doc?"

"Yes," Carlos said. He opened his eyes and winked. "The Sundarian taught me their language."

The extraterrestrial nodded in agreement.

"But you didn't say a word," Prudence said.

125

"Their language has no words, only clean and uncensored thought. It's much more effective than our awkward method of communication. There's no need for interpretation. You see, the fact that—"

"Doc," Gregory said, "even though I appreciate the tone of your voice, and the enlightenment you provide, I think it's wise to hurry things along. If we're going to climb out of this God-forsaken hole in the ground, we'd best begin."

"*Si,*" Carlos said. He closed his eyes once more. *My dear Aretheans, we will use stairs to exit this underground prison. There are hundreds of stairwells located throughout. Use the yellow doors. Quickly now.*

"So, doc," Sergeant Sandoval said, "what happens when we reach topside?"

"Interesting question."

"What? You don't have a plan? Listen, we're gonna have millions of aliens exiting stairwells smack dab in the middle of the desert, and you've got no plan? If I know anything about Bloodstone, he's got all the men fired up. That means a ton of itchy trigger fingers waiting for a reason to start shooting."

"Well, in that case, let's not give them a reason, eh? We'll have to play it by ear. Off we go." He glanced back at the Southern Tunnel archway and frowned. "*Ay Dios mio.* Are those..."

"Yes," The Sundarian said, "Believers."

The Believers rushed under the archway, their temperament setting them apart from the other aliens. They battled through their own kind, knocking the weaker ones to the ground. With anger in their eyes, the Believers trampled over extraterrestrials and crowded into The Shelter.

Carlos turned around. "Payton? Has anybody seen the general?"

"There," Mindy the Prophet called out.

Sinclair drove the golf cart straight at the line of Believers. Many fell to the ground—bones crunched—blood spilled. He crushed at least seven aliens before skidding across uneven terrain and flipping over. The Believers surrounded him—kicking and punching. Aretheans gathered around and joined in the conflict, attacking the Believers. A donnybrook.

Carlos's stomach roiled at the scene, but he could not save his friend this time. "We must go." He stepped in front of an alien waiting in line.

Sergeant Sandoval allowed a dozen aliens to pass before he stopped a tall, slender female. She paused, allowing him the opportunity to step in front of her. He took Prudence by the hand and together they cut in line.

"Let's go," Carlos shouted. "General Sinclair has bought us some time. Let's use it."

Jedediah the Ghost flew over the chamber, performing several loop-de-loops. In one quick motion, he streaked toward a solid rock wall and disappeared inside.

Carlos glanced back at the mouths of the tunnels. Hundreds of aliens still emerged from the shadows. The mêlée had dispersed, the Believers advancing as well. Ahead, yellow doors popped open, and many thousands began their climb to the surface.

"We must make haste," The Sundarian said, "troubled waters rise against us."

Carlos furrowed his brow at the warning. He closed his eyes and sent another message to the aliens. *Faster. Do not look back. Hurry.*

He kept up with the aliens and entered the stairwell. Jumping onto the first metal step, he chanced a quick glance up. A never-ending line of aliens clambered up the countless flights of stairs, their forms disappearing in the shadows.

To take his mind off the Believers, General Sinclair, and the repetition of climbing one step after the next, he turned his thoughts to the unknown variables of the Continuum Hypothesis. He had studied the theory, with its maze-like twists and turns, as a sort of hobby while teaching at MIT.

Accompanied by the thump-thump-thumping of the aliens on the stairs, he allowed his mind the pleasure of considering an almost incomprehensible puzzle. The unique idea that infinity could be quantified. He had a firm grasp of the points on the number line, collectively called a "continuum." He also knew there were more points than numbers with which to count them. Beyond the continuum lay larger infinities still—an endless progression of even more entities. According to the Continuum Hypothesis, there is no infinity between the smallest kind—the set of counting numbers and the second smallest—the continuum itself.

"In other words," he mumbled as he glanced up at endless steps, "everything, no matter how small, or how large, can be counted.

Infinity is a known equation. All things can be calculated. Even these stairs. Step, by step, by step—"

A sickening noise jarred him back to reality. He glanced back and yelled, "Sergeant, do you hear that?"

The sergeant glanced down, then turned to Carlos with terror in his eyes. "Holy shit."

"What is it, sergeant?"

"It sounds like…like they're flooding The Shelter."

Carlos's heart sank. He glanced up at the stairwell, a never-ending tunnel of darkness. *How many landings had they climbed? Surely more than one hundred. One-fifty, perhaps?*

Would knowing there existed an equation which allowed for measuring infinity save his life? Or could his fascination with numbers, with continuums and absolutes, be the final ramblings of a troubled old physics professor? An old man about to drown. He shut his eyes and sent forth his version of an SOS to the aliens.

Faster. Faster. We must climb to the top as fast as we can.

The girl in front of him pulled away. He increased his pace to match hers. Those behind him picked up their speed. Now taking steps two at a time, their feet sent a clackity-clack echo throughout the stairwell. The sound of rushing water at the bottom of the stairs faded. A good sign, but he feared they could not keep up this tempo—his calves were already tightening. *How long could they outrun the rising water?*

"We'll never make it." Sergeant Sandoval's voice bounced off the concrete walls.

Carlos chanced another quick glimpse down and caught sight of the sergeant. The man's face dripped with sweat. He stepped aside, allowing several aliens to pass by while he caught his breath. Carlos jumped back in line in front of the sergeant. "Where does this water come from?" he said between irregular breaths.

"Diversion pipes straight from Groom Lake. It's listed as a dry lake. It's not. Reagan had the pipes installed in the eighties, a sort of contingency plan. In case things got out of control."

"A wise decision."

"Depends on your point of view."

Carlos could no longer speak. His breathing came in spurts, trying to supply his body with much needed oxygen. He knew if he kept up this pace, he would soon pass out.

"Hey, watch it," Sergeant Sandoval said.

At the man's cry, Carlos glanced back. An alien had taken the sergeant's place. The creature wrapped Carlos in a bear hug, lifted him, and increased the pace up the stairs. Carlos grinned. He relaxed in the comfortable arms of the Good Samaritan extraterrestrial, grateful for the chance to finally catch his breath.

"Wow, this is incredible," Sergeant Sandoval shouted. "They're so freakin' strong."

Carlos peeked back. An alien had picked up the sergeant. Prudence also relaxed in the arms of an extraterrestrial. In fact, he spotted other humans being whisked up the stairs by aliens, even a few Black Shirts. The aliens took the stairs three quick steps at a time, making astonishing progress.

"Have you thought about an exit strategy yet?" Sergeant Sandoval's voice sounded like he sat on top of an angry washing machine.

"We are the one million," Carlos called back over his shoulder, "and we have the unique abilities of the Specialists. How many Black Shirts will be waiting for us?"

Sergeant Sandoval took his time answering. "The base houses a defense force of one thousand—Gatekeeper's finest. Well-armed, and highly motivated. Colonel Bloodstone is ruthless. He also has Nellis Air Force Base at his beck and call. They've got jets, and those jets are fitted with weapons of war."

How many heads could young Prudence control. Her abilities against the Believers had been remarkable, to be sure. But how would she, and the Specialists, fare against a well-trained military force?

The top landing fast approached, leaving no more time for conjecture. He closed his eyes, bowed his head, and sent a message to the one million.

Welcome to Earth.

CHAPTER 20

Tick-tock—Tick-tock.

"Son of a bitch," Colonel Bloodstone whispered. "The ENOs are heading for the stairwells. Shit." He pushed away from the desk and stood. A palpable silence filled the room. Sweat dripped from the colonel's nose. He took out a handkerchief and wiped off the pasty film of perspiration. He glanced down at a bead that had fallen on his desk.

Inspiration struck. Of course, he needed to make certain Prudence had a head start, but after that...

He returned to the desk, plopped down in the leather chair, and leaned forward—the monitors an inch from his face. "Come on, honey, move your ass."

"Excuse me, sir?"

"Shut up, De La Cuesta." Bloodstone watched Huerta, two patients in pink scrubs, and Prudence Wellman sprint up the stairs. He also saw a black-shirted Gatekeeper travelling with them. He knew the man. Sergeant Henry Sandoval—traitor. "Get me the number of that stairwell," he said, pointing at the monitor.

Cameras tracked the progress of the aliens climbing the stairway. Dr. Huerta clambered up near the front of the line followed by a dozen aliens, Sergeant Sandoval, and a few steps behind him, Prudence Wellman. Colonel Bloodstone dabbed at the sweat on his brow once again. He watched Prudence climb step after step. De La Cuesta switched to a new camera every time the group rose out of frame.

"Keep this group on the monitor. Find any other stairwells with cameras."

"Sir, we're going to need a lot more monitors to—"

"Just do it. Toggle through them."

De La Cuesta kept The Shelter on one monitor, the progress of the Huerta group on another, and toggled through the stairwells with working cameras on the third and fourth screens.

A smile crawled across his lips. Colonel Bloodstone wiped at his brow again and scanned the area around his desk. Only he and Staff Sergeant De La Cuesta had full view of the monitors. Bloodstone folded the wet handkerchief and placed it on the center of the desk. He gave his new staff sergeant a hard stare.

"Pay close attention, son. I want you to keep your eyes on the group in stairwell A-22, particularly this girl right here." He pressed his finger to the monitor, on top of Prudence Wellman. "When she gets within, let's say, about thirty floors of reaching the surface, you tell me, loud and strong."

"I don't understand, sir."

"I'm going to activate Operation Red Sea."

"Sir?" De La Cuesta wrinkled his brow. "I'm afraid I'm not familiar with—"

"Of course not. The operation is a last resort measure created for this exact scenario. It calls for sealing the tunnels and flooding the facility. Now keep your eyes glued to that girl."

"Yes, sir." De La Cuesta turned to the monitor.

Time passed. Bloodstone kept his eyes on De La Cuesta—De La Cuesta on the monitor. They remained in this position, not a word spoken between them, for more than an hour. The colonel, his eyes still on his staff sergeant, barked out a word. "Coffee." A cup appeared in less than a minute. He slurped at the disgusting brew, his eyes never moving from De La Cuesta.

"Sir," De La Cuesta said, breaking the silence, "the red head has just passed floor one-fifty-three. She's within—"

"Make the call."

"Yes, sir." De La Cuesta picked up a red telephone handset. "Activate Operation Red Sea. Yes, sir, this is a direct order from Colonel Bloodstone." De La Cuesta muted the phone with his left hand and whispered, "Sir, they need your codename and day code."

The colonel snatched the phone from De La Cuesta. "This is Colonel Ulysses S. Bloodstone. Codename Rosewood. Day Code 331155. Activate Red Sea. Yes, I realize we still have men in The Shelter. I have no choice. We can't afford to let the ENOs escape. Seal the tunnel systems and open the pipelines—flood it all."

He hung up and turned his attention back to the four monitors on his desk. Enormous metal doors sealed off the Northern and Southern Tunnel Systems. Mountains of water rushed in from giant spillways, catching aliens, guards, and technicians by surprise. They scrambled like so many rats on a sinking ship. He glanced at the Wellman stairwell. They were making excellent progress in their climb toward the surface.

"Staff Sergeant, scan down this stairwell, if the cameras are still operational."

"Yes, sir." De La Cuesta hit the toggle several times, revealing the landings all the way to the bottom. Water filled the stairwell. Thousands of ENOs floated by the camera, their eyes open, their expressions at last—well and truly, catatonic.

"Get me a shot of The Shelter."

De La Cuesta consulted the log and toggled through a series of views. "Sir."

Something odd caught the colonel's eye on The Shelter monitor. The Tombstones had vanished. *A trick of the lens? Perhaps.* The Shelter, proper, lay fully submerged. Aliens, by the score, floated through the green-tinted waters. The monoliths, however, were gone.

"Staff Sergeant," Bloodstone said, matter-of-factly, "is the secure line to Nellis operational?"

De La Cuesta consulted with a technician. "Yes, sir. Just."

Reaching for the handset, Bloodstone pressed the base unit for a dial tone. He hit "speaker," placed the receiver back in its cradle, and pushed "star-nine-nine."

A gruff voice, brusque and throaty, came over the line. "Brigadier General Thomas Grant, 57th Wing Commander, Nellis Air Force Base."

"Sir, this is Colonel Ulysses S. Bloodstone at The Shelter. Codename Rosewood. Day Code 331155. Sir, General Payton Sinclair has been killed in action. I am now in charge. The ENOs are rioting. They're attempting to escape as we speak."

133

"How many?"

"All of them. They're using the stairwells."

"Have you activated Operation Red Sea?"

"Done. The pipelines are fully opened, and The Shelter is flooded. Water is rising in the stairwells, but the ENOs are exhibiting incredible speed. They will reach the surface before the water does."

"How many of them will reach topside?"

"Thousands. At their rate of speed, in ten, maybe fifteen minutes."

"What do you need, colonel?"

"A squadron of fighters should be sufficient."

"I'll clear it with DOD and the Joint Chiefs. I'll get back on the horn in thirty seconds." The line went dead.

Proper protocol for mass murder must be observed. Colonel Bloodstone turned his attention to the Prudence Wellman monitor. An ENO still carried her up and away from the fully submerged Shelter. The speed and sheer strength of the ENOs took the colonel's breath away. They would have made magnificent soldiers.

"Staff Sergeant."

"Sir, yes, sir."

"Staff Sergeant, I need to be able to control the desert halogens. I must direct the jets. Get it done."

"Yes sir—"

"And get my damn laptop up and running. I need access to the HR files."

"I don't understand. HR files, sir?"

De La Cuesta exhibited moments of intelligence, to be sure, but the man's curiosity could be a problem. On a positive note— General Sinclair had been eliminated, the jet fighters were being readied, and Prudence Wellman would soon be his.

Tick-tock—Tick-tock.

CHAPTER 21

The aliens stopped dead in their tracks.

Carlos tapped the extraterrestrial who carried him up the stairs. "Will you please put me down?"

Sergeant Sandoval wriggled free from the alien carrying him. He climbed a few steps up and faced Carlos. "What now?"

Over the railing, Carlos peered down at the endless stairwell. The noise of rushing water sounded far below. "I don't think we have a choice, sergeant. Come, let's go up to the front of the line." He rushed up the steps, Sergeant Sandoval in tow.

At the top landing, Carlos examined the creature standing at the door. "He's not even breathing heavily." He glanced back. "None of them are. They just ran up two thousand stairs in less than an hour and they—"

"Doc, now's not the time for a play by play. We gotta come up with a plan to get outta this hole in the ground."

Prudence, The Sundarian, and a few of the other Specialists joined them. Carlos faced Sergeant Sandoval.

"Why don't we simply open the door?"

"No," Sandoval whisper-shouted, "There's no way we just open this door. Who knows what's on the other side? Now, I'll admit I've seen a lot of strange things tonight, but there might be an army waiting for us."

"I won't let them hurt us," Prudence said.

Carlos reached past the sergeant and pushed the panic bar. The door sprung open. "Ahh, smell that air, sergeant. So fresh, sweet, and still warm, even at night." He turned at the faint sound of metal-on-metal clinking in the distance. The half-moon helped his vision. "You were right, Sergeant Sandoval. Those little boxes, the phone booths in the desert—they *are* exits. They're all popping open."

With tentative steps, the sergeant slipped around Carlos and set foot on the surface of the Earth for the first time. He grinned. "We made it."

Carlos followed the sergeant, his shoes crunching into the soft white sand. He turned to Sandoval and nodded. The Sundarian and Prudence followed. Carlos closed his eyes and sent a telepathic message to the aliens.

Everybody, please, exit the stairwells.

Thousands of aliens emerged from the small wooden hatches and set foot on Earth for the first time. The night sky, awash in a glittering array of stars, planets, and passing meteors, lent dramatic effect to this historic event. Carlos beamed. "One giant leap for mankind."

The extraterrestrials glanced around, curious about their new surroundings. Gone were the catatonic movements and cold expressions. These were animated beings, interested in investigating this strange new world. Carlos stepped aside as hundreds of them marched passed him into the warm desert night.

After a few minutes, Carlos glanced down. Water spilled over his shoes. He and Sergeant Sandoval hurried away from the stairwell, followed by Prudence and The Sundarian. Rising water flowed from the exit hatch as if a pipe had burst. The lifeless bodies of aliens, carried by rushing waters, floated across the desert. A heartbreaking display of death.

The Sundarian closed her eyes. "We must persist. We will endure."

Carlos heard no cries of anguish from the extraterrestrials who had managed to escape ahead of the deluge. They stepped over and around the corpses of their fallen comrades, apparently accepting the loss as part of the mission to save Earth.

"Doc." Sandoval leaned toward Carlos and whispered, "There're so many bodies. What are we supposed to do?"

"The only thing we can do. Carry on."

"But everyone's dead."

"No, my boy. Look about. There are thousands—hundreds of thousands—awaiting instructions. The loss of life is tremendous to be sure, but no one is giving up. We will journey west, across the desert to the Pacific Ocean."

Skirting away from the floating dead as if they were contagious, Sergeant Sandoval glanced at the chaos around him. "Fine, Doc," he said, panic playing in this voice. "But tell me, just where the hell is west? Which way? How do we get to the ocean?"

Prudence put a hand on the sergeants back. The Sundarian touched his shoulder.

"Calm down, son," Carlos said. "You should know how to find west. Remember your military training. All you have to do is find the North Star—"

"Sorry, Doc," Sandoval said, shivering. "I'm a soldier, not a sailor."

"Look." Carlos pointed straight up. "There's the Big Dipper, do you see it?"

"Yeah, I'm with you so far." The sergeant wiped at his eyes. "There's so many bodies. What are we gonna—"

"Listen, *mijo. Cálmate.* Look up there." He pointed to the stars. "All we have to do is draw a line from those two brilliant stars in the cup of the dipper—do you see—straight across the sky to the handle of the Little Dipper and the final star. That one. That's the North Star. Once you find true north, that's half the battle."

The sergeant chortled. "What's the other half?"

"Ah, good question." Carlos smiled, once again an educator in his element. "We know we live in the Northern Hemisphere, right? *Right*, sergeant?"

"Uh, yeah, so far, so good."

"Therefore, if we walk toward the North Star, we are travelling toward true north. That means, on our right is east, and on our left is west." He glanced up at the sky once more, swiveled just a bit, and smiled, then pointed with his left index finger. "There. That's the way to the Pacific Ocean."

"You are a patient teacher," The Sundarian said. Carlos beamed.

Halogen lamps lit up the desert, turning night into day. The bank of lights surrounding Carlos and the Specialists remained dark. Fighter jets swooped down from the night sky, their engines screaming like banshees. Vast chunks of wilderness exploded into balls of fire. Carlos shielded his face from the heat. The jets raced high into the heavens, disappearing for an instant. They circled, then began another dive. The desert blew apart again, erupting into sheets of flame. The ground beneath him rumbled.

"No, no, no, por favor, Dios mio, no."

More halogen lights illuminated other sections of the once black desert. Thousands of aliens became easy prey. Lightning tore through the heavens. Again, the desert exploded into a roiling inferno.

"Oh shit." Sandoval stepped over a body floating beneath him. A bank of lights illuminated the adjacent desert, revealing thousands of drifting corpses. "Shit, shit, shit. Doc, those jets are coming back."

And yet, somehow the fear of that fact did not register. Carlos turned to the left.

Sandoval grabbed him. "We'll never make it to the ocean. We gotta head south to Vegas. With the speed of these aliens, maybe we can outrun 'em and get lost in the darkness."

"And then what?"

"And then we don't die."

Yes, dead aliens could not save the Earth. Carlos used his mind to send out the word. The aliens turned south.

The sound of jets streaking overhead started like a distant buzzing. Again, they unleashed hell. Carlos felt the familiar hug of strong arms wrap around him. Scooped up, an alien whisked him off to the relative safety of a dark and forbidding desert. He glanced to his right. Sergeant Sandoval raced by in the same manner. Fire from the sky lit up the desert where they had stood moments before.

After several minutes, Carlos listened for the sound of jets. All quiet. He bowed his head and closed his eyes, sending a message to the aliens.

Slow down, the danger has passed.

Lowered to the ground along with the sergeant, Carlos peered to the horizon. "We've got about two hours before the sun comes up. More than enough time to make it to Las Vegas under cover of darkness."

"Sounds good." Sergeant Sandoval cleared his throat. "They wouldn't dare open fire on us in Vegas. Too much publicity."

Prudence and Skye caught up to them.

"Where are the others?" Carlos looked them over, neither

seemed injured.

"We passed Clarissa, Tarissa, and Marissa a few minutes ago," Skye said. "They should be here in a little while. Clarissa said she sent out a message to the rest of The Specialists, but she hasn't heard anything back yet."

Sandoval whispered, "If they're still in the stairwells..."

"They are not," The Sundarian said.

"And we don't have time for *ifs*." Carlos bowed his head and shut his eyes, once again transmitting to the aliens.

We must keep moving south.

Like a small tribe of wandering nomads, the aliens were on the move again, taking giant strides across the desert floor. Carlos, the sergeant, Prudence, and Skye followed on foot, losing ground with each step.

"Let me help," The Sundarian called out.

The humans were scooped up like babes in the arms of the aliens.

"This is so cool." Prudence chuckled. Her mane of short, red hair sprang up and down as the alien carrying her bounded across the desert.

Ahead, a soft glow, miles in the distance, shone on the horizon.

"That must be Las Vegas," Carlos said.

"It sure is, doc." Sergeant Sandoval's voice finally held a note of relief. "At this speed, we'll be there in no time."

An alien hurried past Carlos. In his arms he held Willie T. Smith, the remote viewer.

"Willie," Carlos shouted. "Willie!" No use. Willie's laughter consumed him.

Another alien raced by, this one carrying Gregory the Confabulator. He too cackled with carefree abandon. Mindy the Prophet flew past, followed by Patricia the Witch. In short order, the dull glow of the city shone brighter. Perhaps, too bright.

After burners lit up the sky behind them. The fighters were miles away, presumably still circling over the flooded underground facility known as The Shelter. The cover of darkness, and speed of the aliens had saved their lives. The thought filled Carlos with something he had not experienced in quite some time—hope. They had done it. Against all odds, they had escaped.

Streetlights approached at an incredible speed. A freeway cutting through the desert lay in their path. Only a few cars, trucks, and eighteen-wheelers negotiated the ribbon of highway this early in the morning. Carlos closed his eyes.

Slow down. Let's gather together to make our plans before the sun rises.

Like early westerners riding trusty steeds, Carlos and the Specialists circled up and dismounted. He scanned the small congregation. *Where were Gamble and Darrah?*

"Marissa. Send a message to Gamble and Darrah."

After a moment, Marissa closed her eyes and hung her head. "Gamble the Empath and Darrah the Conjuror are gone."

Cries overtook the group.

"Listen up," Sandoval said, "we've got to decide what we're going to do. Those jets back there aren't going to keep circling forever. Even though we've managed to escape The Shelter, we're not out of danger."

Carlos sucked in a shaky breath. "I need to find out how many we've lost."

"Didn't you hear?" Skye said, "Gamble and Darrah."

"And the aliens?" Carlos cleared his head. *How many have we lost?*

Silence covered the group. They huddled together, occupying a tiny plot of land in the vast Mojave Desert—between the raging fires of the bombing strikes behind them and the glow of Vegas ahead.

"*Ay, Dios mio.*" Carlos spoke in a hushed voice, the kind of tone reserved for somber occasions. "The aliens are decimated. Drowned in the stairwells or killed in the bombings."

Mindy the Prophet fought back tears. "In the stairwells, they grabbed hold of me and kept passing me forward. When the water nipped at their legs, they worked faster, handing me up to the next, and the next until I got out of harm's way. They saved my life."

Marissa, Clarissa, and Tarissa drew together and moaned. Prudence clung to the sergeant.

"Listen to me," Carlos said. "Listen. All of you. We must keep moving. We owe it to those we've lost. There is no other choice. We must keep going."

"Carlos is right," Prudence said. "There's been so much death and misery. The aliens paid an awful price to get us this far—so did Gamble and Chase. We need to honor their sacrifice by moving forward."

"How many," Sergeant Sandoval whispered, leaning closer to Carlos. "How many aliens are still with us?"

"Only those standing here, *mijo*." Carlos wiped a tear from his eye.

Sergeant Sandoval staggered back, his eyes widening.

Less than two dozen remained.

Tick-tock—Tick-tock.

"Damnit!" Colonel Bloodstone slammed his fist on the desk. "Who in the hell gave the order to fire on exit A-22?"

"That must have been Nellis," Staff Sergeant De La Cuesta said. His lower lip trembled.

"For Christ's sake, these creatures need to be wiped from the face of the earth with precision strikes, not carpet bombing. A-22 should have been off limits." He took a breath, composed himself, and checked his watch. "We need boots on the ground—flush 'em out, and finish 'em off. Is the special forces team assembled?"

"Are you sure?"

"Don't you ever question my authority. Is the team assembled or not?"

"They are, sir."

"One more thing. I need you to track down Major Ezekiel Bay— on the double."

Staff Sergeant De La Cuesta saluted and rushed off.

Bloodstone leaned forward, placed his stubby fingers on the laptop, and pounded at it with the same authority as he ordered his men about. He brought up the Human Resources folder, a document he had nearly memorized. After all, a superior officer—a true leader of men—needed to know everything about those serving beneath him.

Major Ezekiel Carver Bay. Age 35. Single. Service—U.S. Army.

Honorable Discharge. Combat Duty. Military Intelligence. Gate-keeper rating 99.5. Other leaders would have stopped there. Blood-stone dug deeper. He checked Facebook, Instagram, and Twitter. He searched high school records, college grades, and anything he could find on the internet. Major Bay possessed all the skills required for the next phase of this FUBAR operation. He glanced at the photo of the major. Quite rugged.

Footsteps grabbed the colonel's attention. Major Bay marched forward, stood at attention, and saluted. An impressive entrance. Effective. Professional.

Bloodstone returned the salute. He took a moment to appreciate the major's athletic build, strong jawline, and steel-gray eyes. Four years out of the Army did not show. The colonel held out his hand. "Major, how are you?" They shook. "Your middle name, Carver—is there a story that goes along with it?"

"Supposedly George Washington Carver is in the family tree—somewhere."

"Interesting." Bloodstone stood and grabbed a red file folder and his laptop. "This way." He proceeded to a quiet office near the back of the building and stationed De La Cuesta at the door. Drawn blackout shades chilled the small room. "Major, let me get right to the point. We have a situation. Professor Huerta—"

"Professor Carlos Huerta?"

"You know the man?"

"The first time the Tombstones duplicated, he helped me lead some ENOs into the Southern Tunnel System."

"Very good. Last night, sorties flown from Nellis Air Force Base succeeded in eliminating nearly every ENO."

"Nearly every ENO?"

"Despite our best efforts, a handful of them escaped." The colonel pulled a slip of paper from the red file folder and shared it with the major. "Intel shows them at five klicks north of Las Vegas. This is their last known position."

"Sir, I don't understand why you're telling me about—"

"Bottom line—I'm sending a handful of elite Gatekeepers into the field, under your command, to find those aliens—and kill them."

The major cocked his head. "Why not send the regular military?"

"Simple. I don't want the regular military to screw this operation up any more than it has been."

"Sir, if I may—"

"Of course, I can't order you to accept this mission. Gatekeeper is, after all, a civilian contractor. All I ask is that you hear me out.

"Last night, during the alien uprising, we discovered that, not only do the ENOs possess amazing speed, and are incredibly strong—they are also prone to extreme violence."

"Sir, that doesn't make any sense. They've always been quite docile—"

"Before you continue, you need to see this." Bloodstone opened his laptop, hit a few keys, and turned it toward the major.

The video showed a golf cart lying on its side. Aliens surrounded the vehicle and dragged a man out from behind the wheel.

"General Sinclair," Major Bay murmured, watching the aliens beat the general, a vicious mob thrashing without mercy. More aliens joined the fray, even attacking their own kind in order to get at the human.

"Sinclair never stood a chance." Bloodstone took the laptop back.

"I had no idea."

"And now, those aliens are poised to invade Las Vegas. Innocent lives are at risk."

"You mentioned Professor Huerta. What's the connection?"

"The aliens are holding several humans hostage, Professor Huerta among them. Your mission is threefold. First, purge any and all evidence of the aliens. I want them eradicated. The second objective is to rescue the humans they've kidnapped. Third, and most important, is to bring back this woman." Bloodstone handed the major a photograph. "Prudence Wellman must be returned alive."

"Why this woman?"

"The answer to that is above both our paygrades." The lies came easy. "Any other questions?"

"How many aliens are there, sir?"

"This is fresh intel." Bloodstone retrieved another photo from the file folder. "Thermal satellite imagery shows twenty-two aliens."

"And what of Professor Huerta and the other humans?"

"Naturally, we'd like all of them brought back alive if possible, unless that jeopardizes the recovery of Prudence Wellman. Her safe return is your number one priority."

"How many humans do the aliens hold?"

"We've counted twelve solid heat registers." Bloodstone produced another photo from the folder. "You see? There, and there, clumped together. However, there's a register, just one, mind you, fluctuating both hot *and* cold."

"That's impossible."

"It may be the register of Prudence Wellman. We won't know for sure until we get eyes on."

"Do you think that's why the brass want her so bad?"

Another lie? No, he would simply ignore the question. "Any further concerns, major?"

"Just one. If it comes down to rescuing the woman or eradicating the aliens—"

"There is no either or, major. You will do both." Bloodstone stood and exited the room, brushing past his staff sergeant. He spoke over his shoulder, "I've handpicked your squad, major. They're assembled just outside."

"You don't waste any time, do you?"

"Never." Bloodstone tapped his Omega twice and surged through the front door of the Command-and-Control Center, ordering De La Cuesta to stay behind. "This way, major. Some of the men I've chosen you may recognize, others you will not." They filed outside and marched to the side of the building.

Seven men sat around a picnic table eating plates of eggs, sausages, and bread. Steam wafted into the air from cups of coffee and hot tea.

"As you were." Colonel Bloodstone stood at the head of the table. "Gentlemen, this is Major Ezekiel Bay. He'll be in command of this mission. Major, this is your squad." Bloodstone moved his eyes around the table. "Second Lieutenant John Sullivan, expert marksman. Second Lieutenant Cory Meyer, tactical. First Lieutenant Jose Pagan, demolitions. Captain Enos Dempsey, tactical. Captain Dillon Quarrels, communications." He paused. "And here are the men you don't know." Two men, wearing civilian clothing, stood and ambled forward. "May I present Gamble and Darrah."

Gamble smiled and nodded. "What's up?"

"Hey," Darrah muttered.

"Just Gamble and Darrah?" Major Bay raised his eyebrows. "No last names, no specialties?"

"Oh, they have specialties, major. Gamble is an Empath. And Darrah is known as Darrah the Conjuror."

The Gatekeepers at the table exchanged nervous laughter.

Major Bay shook his head. "What the hell does that—"

"These two men have been embedded in the special patient's unit."

"Embedded?"

Colonel Bloodstone pursed his lips and blew out a burst of air. "They were undercover, reporting directly to me."

"Why did you need someone on the inside?"

"In case things went sideways. And, boy, did they ever go sideways."

"Sir, I'll need to talk to them before we head out."

"Oh, you'll have plenty of time for that. You see, they're going with you."

"Whoa. I assume they've had no tactical training. I think it's best if—"

"Listen up, major. Gamble tells me he's gotten very close to Prudence Wellman—they are fast friends. Remember, Wellman is the ultimate goal. His insight is crucial."

"You're an empath?" Major Bay turned to Gamble. "What does that even mean?"

Gamble chuckled. "You've never heard of empathy?"

"Yes, of course I've heard—"

"Well, empaths feel empathy in spades. But truth is, that's something I ain't got. It's just my cover story which, by the way, I have played to perfection. But Prudence, she's like the opposite of an empath. She can send out signals that make people do exactly what she wants. Once she gets inside your head, man, you're cooked."

"How do you counter a thing like that?" Major Bay addressed Bloodstone.

"Perhaps Darrah can best answer that question."

"I can," Darrah said. "You just gotta keep your wits about you. Don't let any of her tricks take you by surprise. She's gonna come at ya, come at ya hard. You just gotta ignore the signals she's sending—let 'em bounce right off you."

"And how do you do that?"

Darrah beamed. "Well, unlike my friend Gamble here, I'm not a charlatan. I *do* possess certain magical abilities. That bitch ain't never got inside my head. How? Ha, I tell you what, just keep your mind strong and get behind me when the time comes and let this little baby seal the deal." He lifted a pistol into the air and grinned. "Loaded with tranquilizers."

Major Bay turned back to the colonel. "Sir, I'm not sure if this—"

"I know it's a lot, major, but I believe a man of your capabilities will get the job done."

Major Bay remained silent.

"Now then, major, two jeeps are fueled and waiting for you out front. God speed."

"But sir—"

Turning, Colonel Bloodstone marched away, disappearing around the corner of the building. Always leave them wanting for more. *Who said that? Hitler? Tarantino? Oh well, no matter.* Bloodstone returned to his desk and watched the jeeps on the computer monitor. They flew across the runway. Two of the men he had selected wore the latest in tactical helmet cams. Bloodstone would be able to watch the mission unfold in real time.

"De La Cuesta."

"Yes, sir."

"Tell me, who said, 'always leave them wanting for more?'"

De La Cuesta pulled out his phone and typed at a furious pace. "Uh, the circus man, PT Barnum—er...according to Google, sir."

"Of course." Colonel Bloodstone leaned back in his chair and settled back. "And, staff sergeant, get me a cup of coffee, would you? It's gonna be a long day."

Tick-tock—Tick-tock.

CHAPTER 23

"It's going to be a long day," Carlos said.

"Really, doc?" Sergeant Sandoval snorted. "Is that what you're thinking?"

"I'm also thinking about twilight." Carlos searched the heavens. "The past is the beginning of the beginning, and all that is and has been is but the twilight of the dawn."

"Come again?"

"My favorite author, somebody well ahead of his time—H.G. Wells."

"War of the Worlds—I love that book."

"*Yo tambien.* A tale of conflict between mankind and an extraterrestrial race. I wonder what Wells would have thought about our Aretheans? After all, they came to save, not enslave."

"I guess it would have been a whole different book."

Carlos nodded while he yawned. He'd last slept more than a day ago on the floor of a cold dark chamber in the arms of an alien—The Sundarian.

"Doc, let me ask you…what brought you here in the first place—to America, I mean?"

Carlos closed his eyes. "I'm one of the lucky ones. My father and mother were part of the upper class in Guatemala. He, a banker—she taught school. I went to private school and excelled in the sciences, eventually attending *Universidad Nacional Autónoma de México,* studying Planetary Physics. I graduated top of my class which gave me an opportunity to come to America. MIT recruited me. I taught in the Physics Department where I met the most beautiful girl in the world. My Lilly."

"Good for you."

"Yes, but I'm still looking for the...*como se dice*, the happy ending of my story." Carlos turned back to the sky. "Lilly is in Heaven."

"I'm so sorry, doc."

"Who knows, maybe this alien encounter is just what I need, hm?" Carlos yawned again. "In any case, I think it's time we plan our next move. We need to find some clothes for the Aretheans and Specialists, or they'll certainly stand out, even in a place like Las Vegas."

"Good idea. What do you suggest?"

"Oh..." Carlos reached for his wallet. "I suppose a Goodwill store, or Salvation Army will work. I only have a few dollars. Shirts, pants, shoes for two dozen—it adds up. Oh, and we'll need hats for the Aretheans."

"Definitely hats." The sergeant checked his wallet. "Not to worry, I got a couple credit cards. But I'll need help hauling all those clothes back."

"You're a good man. We'll need to get closer to Las Vegas—near enough for you and your helpers to find a clothing store but not close enough to be seen."

"Sure, a place where you can lay low and wait for us. Sounds good on paper but the logistics might be a little tricky."

"Sergeant, this entire night has been tricky. Yet here we are." He glanced at the stars once again. "On a night such as this, nothing seems impossible."

"I hope so, doc. What do you say we get going?"

"*Bien*. Let me pass the word." Carlos closed his eyes and sent thoughts to the aliens.

They stood and fanned out, each creature positioning itself behind a human, waiting for word to move out. The Sundarian chose Carlos. He nodded.

Keep low, my friends, away from the lights of the road. We mustn't be seen. Travel fast and silent.

The aliens secured their human riders and jogged to the left toward a steady queue of lights on the highway. Rush hour had begun. They formed a convoy, following the highway at a safe distance.

The gentle rocking motion of The Sundarian lulled Carlos into a fast sleep. He woke to the noise of automobiles chugging along the highway. Signs of civilization sprang up all around them.

"Doc," Sergeant Sandoval yelled, "we'd better slow down or we'll wind up in somebody's backyard."

Carlos scanned the terrain. They were nearing cinder block walls surrounding a maze of two-story tract houses.

Slow. Slow. We must slow down.

The group of aliens reduced speed, then trotted along at an unhurried pace.

"Over there." Sergeant Sandoval pointed to a ravine near the highway, sheltered by a block wall. "Look, there's a shopping mall not too far away."

Carlos sent directions to the aliens. In a few moments, both the extraterrestrials and humans huddled together, protected behind the wall, secreted in a low-lying gulch.

"I need volunteers to help me get some clothes," Sandoval said.

Prudence raised her eyebrows. "For the aliens?"

"Yup, and you, too."

Glancing down, she rubbed at the sleeve of the pink scrubs. "Hm, good call. Okay, let's go."

"No," Carlos said. "Your abilities will be needed here if we happen to be discovered."

Sandoval nodded. "Everyone will be a whole lot safer with you around. All I need is a little help to haul back some clothes."

"Summer dresses for the girls," she said, "floral prints—that'll make it lighter."

"Uh, floral prints?"

"Oh, I'd better go along," Mindy the Prophet said. She glanced at Prudence and rolled her eyes. "Men, am I right?"

"Great," the sergeant said, "any other volunteers?"

Gregory the Confabulator, Patricia the Witch, and Willie T. all stepped forward.

"Okay. Five of us should be more than enough," Sandoval said. "The sooner we head out, the quicker we'll be back. Keep your eyes open for trouble, doc. Let's hit it."

The sky grew brighter, yet still not sunrise. Sergeant Sandoval and the small group of Specialists dashed away from the ravine and slipped along the block wall toward illuminated signs. Rising on tall posts, they announced the first traces of civilization. Target. Walmart. Kohls. JCPenney. Macy's.

It took only a few minutes for Sergeant Sandoval and his group to reach the empty parking lot of a giant mall. The shopping complex, so far removed from Las Vegas, had obviously been built for the millions of modern-day settlers who would soon migrate to the valley. The gleaming new facades of the department stores were constructed of rock, stucco, and cinder block. Light brown and dark brown color schemes, borrowed from the desert, covered the structures. The parking lot, flat, smooth, and pitch black, wore a coat of fresh white lines. The smell of new construction mixed with morning dew filled the air.

"This way," Sandoval shouted to the group.

"Slow down a little, sergeant." Gregory bent over, taking uncontrolled breaths, hands on his knees. "Remember, our specialty's up here..." He tapped his head. "...not in our feet."

Sandoval had forgotten he wore a pair of black combat boots, while the patients were struggling along in skid-resistant slippers. "Sorry." He started out again, glancing back every so often, monitoring the progress of the Specialists.

"Shit." Sandoval stopped outside the gated storefront doors.
OPEN
MON-FRI 9AM–10PM
SAT-SUN 10AM–9PM
He slammed an open hand against the gate.

"What now?" Gregory said. "We're losing precious time on a mission that appears to be doomed to failure."

"Ha," Patricia the Witch said, "nice words, Confabulator, but no match for magic." She waved her arms in the air and brought them down hard against the gates. The barriers vanished.

"Holy shit!" Sandoval stumbled back a few steps. "You really *are* magic."

"Did you have any doubt?"

"I don't get it," Gregory said, "what do you have against words, anyway?"

"Words are fine," she said, "but they don't pay the bills."

"What's that supposed to—"

"C'mon, you two, we gotta keep moving." Sandoval turned and raced for the nearest clothing store. "Damn." An iron accordion security fence blocked the way. He turned to the witch. "Do you mind?"

"Not at all." She gave Gregory a wink. Raising her arms once more, she brought them down against the obstruction. It clicked open. "Anything else, sergeant?"

"Let's get to work." He led the way deep into the store. No alarms sounded—no bells, horns, or buzzers. A good sign or bad, he couldn't tell. "Mindy, how about a dozen sun dresses?"

"Summer floral prints," she corrected. "On it."

"Alright, c'mon guys, shorts, pants, shoes, and shirts. And don't forget the hats, plenty of hats. Let's go."

The group grabbed clothing off the racks and shelves as if they were trying to beat the clock in a game show. Soon, their arms were laden with stolen goods.

"Okay," Sandoval said, "it's been about three minutes, let's skedaddle."

They ran down the main aisle. A few garments slipped from their grasp, littering the polished floor behind them.

"Hurry." Running full speed ahead, Sandoval glanced over his shoulder. "There's no alarm, but that doesn't mean—"

"Stop right there." An elderly man wearing a bright red security uniform barked out the order. He aimed a flashlight at the sergeant.

Sandoval, caught off guard by the light, barreled into the man, knocking him over. "C'mon, guys. He's unarmed. Let's go, go, go."

The group rushed to the left, right, and straight over the man. He squirmed and shielded his face. Some of the clothes they fumbled on their way past landed on the guard's face. Sandoval rushed the group through the mall and out the front entrance.

An orange and pink sky startled him. Sunrise.

A lone security vehicle, engine running, waited near the door. The old Plymouth rested half on the sidewalk, and half on the blacktop. Sandoval jumped in and popped the trunk. "C'mon, everybody, move it. Clothes in the back." He revved the engine. Mindy, Patricia, and Gregory tossed their bundles in the trunk, slammed it shut, and jumped into the rear seat. Willie T. rode shotgun. Sandoval punched the gas.

With tires screeching, he raced out of the parking lot and onto a frontage road. He followed the signs and zoomed down a ramp leading onto Highway 95 North.

"We gotta fly, the cops out here are cowboys."

Gregory leaned forward. "Do they ride horses?"

"No, they don't ride horses."

"Do they wear cowboy hats?" Mindy said.

"Let's just say it's like the wild west out here. They're a little, uh, enthusiastic."

Two patrol cars sped by on the other side of the freeway, their lights flashing, sirens blaring. They cut through traffic, flying south, toward the mall.

Sandoval, his eyes on the lookout for an exit, took deep breaths in order to counteract the adrenalin racing through his system. He signaled into the left turn lane and cut across the freeway, heading west on Kyle Canyon Road.

The wall near the ravine where Carlos and the aliens waited came up fast. Sandoval pulled off the two-lane road, navigated the vehicle across the bumpy desert, and stopped. The engine sputtered, clunked, and died. He tried to restart it, but it only shuddered, wheezing like an old chain-smoker. "The engine's shot." He cocked his head at the eerie silence.

The Specialists started for the ravine.

"Wait," Sandoval whisper-shouted. He ducked low and sped past them. Glancing into the ravine from a prone position, he spied five Black Shirts positioned across the ground in various ragdoll poses. He stood and raced down into the narrow gulley. For the first time since working for Gatekeeper, he wished he carried a firearm.

Carlos Huerta lay on his back—out cold.

The extraterrestrials and Prudence Wellman were gone.

CHAPTER 24

"Doc, wake up." Sandoval rolled the professor over and felt for a pulse. He patted the man's cheek. "You'll be okay, doc. C'mon, wake up."

Carlos groaned. His eyelids fluttered open. *"Ay, mi cabeza."*

"That's it, doc. Easy does it." Sandoval helped him sit up. "Slowly now. Take your time. I got you."

"¿Qué pasó?" Holding his head with both hands, Carlos closed his eyes and shook his head, as if dislodging cobwebs.

"You're doing good," Sandoval said. "Tell me what happened."

"Nos tomaron por sorpresa—"

"Whoa, in English, doc, please."

"We were taken by surprise." He pointed at the uniformed men on the ground. "These Black Shirts attacked us. Prudence...she... she stopped them. The aliens scattered. *Ay Dios, mio,* that's all I remember."

Sandoval surveyed the ravine. Both Specialists and Gatekeepers lay side by side, still breathing, but unconscious. Mindy the Prophet raced down into the gulley.

"They have her," she said, touching her temple and closing her eyes. "Prudence took everyone down, the Black Shirts, the doc—everybody. They drugged Pru and took her away. Somehow, they're immune to her powers."

"They who?" Sandoval said, pressing. "Who's immune?"

"No, this doesn't make any sense." Mindy opened her eyes.

155

"Darrah and Gamble."

"But that's impossible, Mindy. They're both dead."

She glared at him. "I just call 'em like I see 'em."

"I don't understand," Willie T. said. "Even if they were alive, why would they take Prudence?"

At a moan from a Black Shirt, Sandoval yelled, "Each Gatekeeper carries a set of cuffs. Gregory, Willie T. roll 'em over on their stomachs and get their hands behind them. Quick, they're coming to."

In short order, the Black Shirts were restrained. One by one, the downed Specialists regained consciousness, struggling to find their balance. They appeared a bit confused. Marissa, Clarissa, and Tarissa huddled together. Bruce the Dowser and Skye sat still for a while. Jedediah the Ghost hovered above them all.

"What the hell? What's going on?" A Gatekeeper writhed in the sand like a snake, trying to wrestle out of the handcuffs.

Sandoval approached the man. "Major Bay?"

"What the hell, sergeant? Why are me and my men in cuffs? What happened?"

"Well, sir, I'd say Prudence Wellman opened a can of whoop-ass on y'all."

Major Bay winced, a clear sign of pain still coursing through his body. "What happened to the Cats?"

"The aliens? I have no idea, sir."

The major struggled to his knees. "Get me out of these cuffs."

"Uh, no can do, sir."

"What the hell does that mean?"

"Until we can figure out what happened, and where the aliens are, I think we'd better take it one step at a time." Sergeant Sandoval spoke in an even and clear tone.

"Damnit, set me free, sergeant."

"Don't do it." Carlos Huerta stood next to Sandoval. "These men were going to kill us all. They held guns on us. If Prudence had not intervened, we might be dead."

"Nonsense." Major Bay winced.

Clarissa moved behind the major, placed a finger on her temple, and closed her eyes.

The sergeant glanced about. The Gatekeeper's holsters were empty. Handguns littered the ravine. "Looks to me like the doc's telling the truth. You guys drew down on them."

"I don't carry a sidearm," Major Bay said. "Never have. You?"

"I'm a liaison, no need to be armed. But the men you're with…" He turned to the Specialists. "Let's grab the clothes and get out of here."

"You can't leave us out here, sergeant." Major Bay fought against his restraints.

"Why not? If Prudence Wellman hadn't stopped you, you would have opened fire."

"Those were our orders. We're here to stop the aliens from attacking Las Vegas."

"What are you talking about? These gentle souls are about as dangerous as I am."

"Listen, I don't know what they did to you, but those aliens beat General Sinclair to death. And they're about to attack Vegas."

"Are you nuts? Who put that shit in your head?"

"Colonel Bloodstone," Clarissa said, her eyes shooting open. She stared at the major. "Colonel Bloodstone has filled this man's head with the most vicious lies. He is convinced the Aretheans are murderers—that they plan on destroying Earth."

Carlos stared at the major. "You know that's not true. You told me yourself, just two days ago. You said the aliens were as harmless as newborn puppies. Do you remember?"

Major Bay stared at the ground.

"*Si*, you *do* remember," Carlos said. "They have not come to harm us. They are here to save our world—to reverse our climate change. *We* are the monsters in all of this."

"But General Sinclair…" The major wrinkled his brow. "…I saw them tear him apart."

"It's true, some Aretheans are evil." The Sundarian stepped out from behind the cinderblock wall. "But evil exists in all beings, in all races. Just know, the Aretheans you saw attack General Sinclair represent a small minority of our people."

"My God, look at you," Major Bay said. "Your skin is shimmering."

"And yours is black. What is your point?"

"Come on out." Sandoval spoke to a tall alien standing behind The Sundarian. "Don't be afraid."

The extraterrestrial moved around the wall. He stood well over six-feet tall, with a bodybuilder's physique. The alien easily towered over all those in the ravine. His movements, however, belied his stature. He seemed timid, almost shy.

"I guess they kinda take on a nice glow under the sun," Mindy the Prophet said. She petted the alien's arm. "Feels silky, too."

Carlos turned to the tall male. "Where are the other Aretheans?"

"He cannot speak," The Sundarian said. "They were frightened. They ran away."

"They're headed for Vegas," the major said. "It's not too late to do the right thing, sergeant. Get us out of these cuffs."

The Sundarian approached the major. "I place my hand upon your heart, that you may understand truth. What do you wish to know?"

Major Bay bowed his head, sucked in a deep breath, and stared into her violet eyes. "What's really going on? Why does Bloodstone want Prudence Wellman?"

"For her abilities," The Sundarian answered in a calm voice. "She is the most powerful force on earth. A power for good—or evil. He means to use her as a weapon of war."

"Look into her eyes." Carlos leaned in toward the major. "You know she's telling the truth."

"I feel your fear," the alien said.

"Fear?" Major Bay shook his head. "What are you talking about?"

"Fear of the unknown is a universal emotion. Let me ease your apprehension." She reached for his forehead.

"Stop." He ducked away.

She drew closer, pressing the back of her hand to his brow. In an instant, his expression changed. Major Bay glanced about, at first disoriented, then calm, almost serene. "The aliens are here to *save* our world. And we've...we've—"

"You may have killed us all," The Sundarian said. "The girl might have provided us strength for our lack of numbers, but she is gone. Taken."

"We must get her back," Carlos shouted.

"We can help," Major Bay said, his tone pleading. "Take these handcuffs off me and my men."

"Do it, sergeant," Carlos said. "Do it now."

158

Sandoval shook his head. "It's a trick."

"No," The Sundarian said. "His words are true."

Sandoval blew out a deep breath, moved behind the major, and worked the key into the cuffs. He tossed them to the sand.

"That's what I'm talking about." One of the Black Shirts called out. "C'mon, sarge, now the rest of us." The man held up his wrists. "Let's go, buddy. Move it."

"No," Major Bay said. "They'll murder you." He turned to The Sundarian. "Can you make all of my men understand?"

She motioned to the tall alien. Together, they placed their hands on the foreheads of the Gatekeepers. One by one, the Black Shirts became calm, clear eyed, and focused. Sergeant Sandoval acknowledged the visible change in their demeanor and un-cuffed them. They reached for their firearms, picked them up, and holstered them.

"We need to find the missing extraterrestrials," Carlos said.

Major Bay nodded. "Meyer, Dempsey, Sullivan—begin a search for the aliens."

"Let us help," Bruce the Dowser said. "By now you've seen, we have special abilities. Willie T. and I can guide your men in the right direction. Trust me."

"Okay. But don't wander too far off. Captain, just get a bead on which direction they might be headed. Copy?"

"Roger that."

"Right," Sandoval said. "Let's go get Prudence."

Major Bay shook his head. "But you have no vehicle."

"Don't need one."

"I don't understand. What do you—"

The sergeant held up his hand. "Sundarian, if you don't mind."

The aliens slipped behind the sergeant and the major.

Major Bay frowned. "What are they doing?"

"You'll see."

A sudden flurry of wind descended on the ravine, blowing across the desert, producing a mini cyclone of sand and dust.

"*Mira,*" Carlos shouted, "it's Jedediah. He's showing you the way."

Sergeant Sandoval grinned. "Let's go."

The aliens scooped up the humans and raced across the desert, following the supernatural dust devil.

CHAPTER 25

The Sundarian shouted over Major Bay's shoulder. "I see the jeeps."

"Wow, fast, strong, and enhanced vision. I'm impressed," Major Bay yelled. "Are they anywhere near the base yet?"

"No. Not even close." She increased her speed. The dust swirled up, trailing in the wake of her footsteps. The tall alien carrying the sergeant pulled alongside.

"Damn." Major Bay laughed. "They sure can move."

"There," Sergeant Sandoval yelled, "straight ahead. See the dust?"

"Affirmative," the major said. "About two klicks away."

In no time, the aliens caught up to the jeeps bouncing across the desert. The tall alien bent forward and grabbed hold of a back bumper. With his heels dug into the sand, he forced the vehicle to come to a sudden halt. The other jeep slowed of its own accord.

Sandoval hopped out of the alien's arms, backed away from the spinning tires, and moved to the side of the jeep. The vehicle sank deeper into the desert sand.

A man in civilian clothes sat in the driver's seat, gripping the steering wheel with one hand and pounding on the dash with the other. "C'mon, get going, you stupid machine." Prudence Wellman lay in the backseat.

The other vehicle made a U-turn and roared back at full speed toward The Sundarian. When the vehicle reached within inches of her, the alien stepped aside, matador style, and the jeep sped past.

"*Ole*," Major Bay said.

"Who are you?" Sergeant Sandoval shouted at the man.

"Damnit." The stranger jumped out of the stalled jeep. He drew his pistol, levelling it at the sergeant. With a smirk, he said, "My name is Gamble. Gamble the Empath." In an instant, the tall alien released the bumper, sprinted to the front of the Jeep, and grabbed Gamble's arm. "Whoa, wait a minute, big fella, what are you—"

In one fluid motion the alien flung Gamble across the desert. Gamble the Empath flew toward the horizon, his screams fading in the distance.

The other driver hit the accelerator. The jeep would not move, held in place by The Sundarian. He gave up and turned toward the Black Shirt. "Major Bay," he said. "Wow, it sure is good to see you."

"Can you be sure of that, Darrah?" The Sundarian reached in and pulled the magician out of the driver's seat.

"No, no, no, no..." Darrah fumbled with a tranquilizer gun.

The Sundarian flung Darrah across the desert after Gamble. Neither Major Bay, nor Sergeant Sandoval could agree upon which man achieved the most airtime.

Sandoval climbed into the back seat alongside Prudence. She cleared her throat and opened her eyes. "What...what happened?"

"Relax. You're safe." He slipped his hand behind her, cradling her head.

She sat up. "I don't remember what happened."

He helped her into the passenger's side and then took the wheel. The engine kicked over on the first try. "I'll explain on the way back to the ravine."

The major jumped into the other abandoned jeep. He turned the key, feathered the gas, and faced The Sundarian. "Hop in. How about I give *you* a ride this time?"

At full throttle they sped across the open desert, although much slower than the aliens had run. When they reached the ravine, Professor Huerta, the Gatekeepers, and Specialists stood on the lip of the chasm, cheering them home.

"Back so soon?" Huerta said, shaking the sergeant's hand. "That didn't take long."

"That's a good thing," Sandoval said, helping Prudence from the jeep. "The sun's starting to heat up this frying pan. Where's the search party? Did they find the aliens?"

"No, but they found signs of them heading east toward the highway."

"I'm glad you didn't go after them," Major Bay said.

Captain Dempsey nodded. "Figured we better wait it out here. Don't know what Bloodstone's up to."

"Would somebody please tell me what's going on?" Prudence shouted.

"I'm so glad you're safe, *mija*." Wrapping his arms around her, Carlos caught her up on the missing aliens and how the Black Shirts had joined their cause.

"So, what's the plan, doc?" Sergeant Sandoval said.

"Plan? You know me by now, don't you? I have no plan. Perhaps we should all slip into something more comfortable. Let's see what you brought back from the mall, eh?"

The aliens and humans chose a few garments from the pile of clothes next to the Plymouth.

"Don't forget the hats." Carlos motioned to The Sundarian. "Can you recommend our next move?"

She sat in the shade of a Joshua Tree and gazed at the tall alien. Sandoval guessed they were telecommunicating. He waited in silence.

"We need them," The Sundarian said. "The other Aretheans. The task of restoring your world is complex. We need as much help as we can get."

"Shoot," Willie T. said. "You already know, finding's what I do best."

Bruce nodded. "Yup, let's get 'er done."

"Sounds like just the job for a clairvoyant, a mystic, and a psychic," Clarissa said, holding hands with her sisters.

"And if anyone gets in our way," Prudence said, giving her open palm a punch with her clenched fist. "I'll make them sorry for it."

"Dear Prudence," The Sundarian said, "you have a much greater purpose. With your abilities, our powers can be much amplified. Your talent is unequaled. What we now lack in quantity, you more than make up for in quality."

The complement made Prudence blush, mirroring the color of

the bright pink scrubs on the ground. "Gosh, nobody's ever spoken to me like that before. Most people just... Who are you again?"

The Sundarian held out her hand. Prudence stepped forward and joined the aliens in the shade of the Joshua Tree.

"Major," Sergeant Sandoval said, "I'll defer to you. We need to find the missing aliens—but remember—we have some powerful weapons in the Specialists."

"Specialists?"

"It's what we call ourselves." Gregory grinned. "Uh, for our special abilities and the fact that we were placed on a government watchlist, so..."

"I've seen them in action, sir," Sandoval said. "They make a fantastic team."

"Right," the major said, "we'd better get started. Gather round, Specialists. Let's learn each other's names and exactly what you specialize in. This is my squad." He introduced the Gatekeepers, and in return, the Specialists sounded off, giving name and specialty. "Good. Uh, you there..." He motioned toward the tall alien. "...what's your name?"

"He cannot answer you," The Sundarian said. "And his name you would be hard pressed to pronounce."

"I'll call him Bob, then. Is that alright? Okay. Bob, you handled yourself well back there. We sure could use your help again."

Bob jumped up and pranced toward the group of humans. His wide grin made it clear he looked forward to another adventure in the desert.

"Professor Huerta," the major said, "once again, I need you to remain behind with The Sundarian and Prudence. I'll leave some of my men with you for protection."

"Okay, uh, protection against what?"

The major avoided an answer. "We'll be back soon."

"*Bien, no problema.*"

"Good, there's water in the jeeps. Sergeant, leave the doc with a couple of canteens."

"Yes, sir." Sandoval scampered off to one of the vehicles and grabbed a water can. Marching back, he planted the container in the shade next to Prudence. "You'll be okay here?"

She nodded. "Thanks for the water. And, sergeant, thank you for earlier."

"Like the doc said, no problem."

The Sundarian touched his shoulder. "Please, find my people."

"Right." He straightened and turned to shake hands with the professor. "Hang in there, doc. Take care of yourself, you hear?"

"Okay," Major Bay said, "we only have two jeeps. There isn't enough room for everyone, so we'll take the clairvoyant, and the dowser, and—"

"Major," Clarissa said. "We travel together, my sisters and me. We're a packaged deal."

"Like I said, there isn't enough room for—"

"Then we'll stay behind."

The major put his hands on his hips and glared down at the much smaller woman.

"That's not going to work, young man. I do not easily intimidate."

"Damn, you're good." He let out a deep breath. "Okay, you three, the dowser, and Willie Smith, let's go. The rest of you are going to have to stay here."

An audible groan went up from those not chosen. They brooded for a moment, then turned back for the Joshua Tree. "We'll at least get some clothes for the ones you find," Skye the Telepath said. "Help me, Mindy?" Together they brought back stacks of clothes and placed them in the jeeps.

"Okay, let's head out. Clarissa," the major said, turning to the clairvoyant riding shotgun, "you're my GPS. Which way?"

She closed her eyes and put a hand to her temple. "Due east. What do you say Willie?"

"Absolutely, ma'am," Willie T. called out from the other jeep.

"Yes," Clarissa said, "I feel very confident in that choice, major."

He smiled. "Then I'm confident in your confidence."

"She's a whole lot better than GPS," Bruce said.

"Stop, both of you," she said. "You'll make me blush."

Major Bay raised a hand in the air and shouted, "We're heading east."

CHAPTER 26

Carlos watched The Sundarian lift the corners of her mouth up and down at Prudence. He didn't know what it meant, but Prudence spoke up before he could ask.

"Are you okay?"

"Forgive me," The Sundarian said. "Emotions do not come easy for us. I am trying to smile."

"Huh...a smile. Why?"

"When humans smile at one another, they seem to enjoy it. I wanted to bring you joy."

Prudence nodded. "Thank you for that. I do feel better."

"Excuse me, Miss Sundarian," Carlos said. "When you placed your hand to the major's forehead, he became a different man. What did you tell him? How does the touch work?"

Reaching forward, she placed her hand on his brow. He found himself both in the desert near the Joshua Tree, and at the same time, out of his body. A universe of worlds filled his mind. Planets, stars, moons, and suns in the vast configuration. He zoomed through a million light years, past every star in the known galaxy, then past every unknown star in the unknown galaxies. All at once, he understood the reality, the necessity, for a multiverse—the infinite system of universes. And there, on the boundary of time itself, he saw Areth, The Sundarian's home planet.

A terrestrial world with seven moons in various colors and phases, Areth shone green against the blackness of space. A huge sun attacked the Arethean atmosphere, a sky laden with gold. Large bodies of water covered the surface of the planet. Towering mountains, bottomless valleys, and pristine deserts were all part of the Areth ecosystem. The Aretheans lived in harmony, not only with each other but with their environment. A perfect world in a future time and distant place. All part of the Collective Harmony, in tune with a Communal Spirit.

He opened his eyes when she removed her hand. *"Ay, que linda.* So beautiful."

"You are such a special being, Carlos Huerta. In time you will learn how to develop the gift of communication—true communication. You will know my voice in your head, even if I am not with you."

"Where will you be?"

"Shall I tell you how I see your planet?"

Her perspective would be invaluable. He smiled and nodded.

"Earth—she called to us, and we answered her distress signals. When we arrived, we found you—a slow and backward species. Prone to outbursts of anger and hate, you picture yourselves at the top of an imagined food chain, masters of the cosmos, when, in reality, you are the cause of the problem—our very reason for coming. Is it any wonder we remained silent upon first contact? We were afraid."

"Surely, that is not an accurate assessment of humanity."

"It is. Your primitive technologies are killing your home. We offer a new way, a path to freedom. We will show you skills that will enrich your world—and your lives."

"But are we not the most intelligent creatures on Earth? Surely we can—"

"No," The Sundarian said in a hurry. "There is a certain insect— they inhabit a small island in the Pacific northwest. They more than surpass your cognitive capabilities."

Prudence laughed out loud.

"I see no humor in this," Carlos said, "not in the least."

"Well, I think it's funny. Just imagine, the world being run by bugs. They can't do any worse than we have." She turned to The Sundarian. "Tell me, why is it then, if these insects are more intelligent than humans, why aren't they in charge of everything?"

"It is simply a matter of size, you see, and numbers. Otherwise—"

"Otherwise, what?" Carlos said. "You think if they were as big as us, if they were as plentiful, that they'd—"

"So, what if these bug people happen to know a bit more than you do, professor?" Prudence giggled as she spoke. "I mean who cares if they do?"

"Everybody should. I can assure you, madam, these so-called bug people are nothing more than..." He stopped and eyed Prudence, then The Sundarian. Both avoided his gaze. "Oh, I see, you are having a joke with me. When did you two cook this up?"

"Doc," Prudence said, "you're wound up tighter than a train engineer's watch. You need to relax. The great bug debate can wait for another time, yes?"

"Forgive me." A slight grin accompanied his apology and he laughed.

"She suggested the subterfuge." The Sundarian pointed at Prudence.

"Ouch. Throw me under the bus."

"We do not have busses on Areth." The Sundarian bowed to Prudence and then turned to Carlos. "We were resolved to begin repairs of your planet when the time presented itself. Now that the time has come, much like those insects, we do not have the numbers. But we must keep trying."

"How?" Prudence said. "Without the numbers, how can you begin to save our world?"

"That depends on you."

Prudence stared at The Sundarian. "What? The joke's on me now?"

"Dear girl..." The Sundarian shook her head. "I understand you are capable of sending out a signal—a signal that can bring about change."

"A change in behavior to other people—not the planet."

"How do you know? Have you tried?"

"I can't save the world." Prudence turned away. The Sundarian reached around, placed her hand on Prudence's cheek, and turned her back.

"Why don't we try...together?"

"What? You mean now? Here?"

"I do," The Sundarian said. "I know the limits of my abilities. Do you? Who can say, but that the signals I place in your mind will awaken the entire globe? In such a case, our mission would be complete, and my people would return to Areth this very day."

"What's that?" Carlos raised his eyebrows. "You say Earth can be restored now? In one shot?"

The Sundarian met his eyes. "In theory."

"Is your theory backed by science?"

"No, good doctor. By faith."

The Specialists gathered around. Prudence and The Sundarian held hands. The Gatekeepers drew close and stood vigil. Carlos kept a keen eye on the two women.

He hoped for the best, but without the proper controls—without trials—something could go wrong. "Are you sure you want to test your idea at this moment?"

The Sundarian ignored him and shut her eyes. "Do the same Prudence. Close your eyes."

Carlos's heart rate picked up. He studied the others gathered around Prudence and The Sundarian. They wore varied expressions from excitement to fear. The Black Shirts appeared apprehensive, keeping their hands near their firearms. Prudence winced, groaned once, then stiffened, her head tilting back.

The sand beneath Carlos's feet seemed to vibrate, but only slightly, as if it were dancing over the skin of a drum. He rubbed his eyes. The sun bore down hard, making him think he had imagined the dancing sand. No. It happened again. The sand jumped up, at least an inch into the air, then settled down on the ground.

"Whoa." Prudence let go of The Sundarian's hand. "Unbelievable. I have never felt anything like that in my life."

"You imagined a journey," The Sundarian said. "I merely suggested a path."

"But what happened? I don't understand."

The Sundarian stood, helped Prudence up, and motioned to the ravine. "Observe."

Carlos also followed Prudence's gaze to the ground beneath her feet. Instead of sand, a thick blanket of mossy growth covered the ravine. Tiny buds twisted and strained, popping through the greenery in a life and death struggle to reach the sky. It reminded Carlos of a film he'd seen in college—a time-lapse video of a flower writhing about, fighting to grow. But what happened now took place before his very eyes in real time. Flowers sprouted. Here, amongst the Joshua Trees in the middle of the Mojave Desert, new

170

life appeared. His gaze turned north, following the change, visible for miles. Small trees popped up, rising from the former dust bowl. Greenery covered the desert. "How can this be?"

"Her powers are extraordinary," The Sundarian said. "She is truly unique."

"I...I never dreamed that I—"

"They're coming," Mindy the Prophet shouted. "Armed soldiers are coming. They know exactly where we are."

"How far away are they?" Captain Quarrels said.

Mindy closed her eyes and placed a hand to her forehead. Her breathing accelerated, almost uncontrolled, as if she could not catch a full breath. Fear covered her face.

"Calm down." Patricia the Witch stepped forward and stroked Mindy's forehead. She placed a hand on the girl's shoulder and leaned in. "Calm down and breath."

Opening her eyes, Mindy glanced over her shoulder and pointed. "They're one mile away and closing fast." Two drones circled overhead buzzing like a hornet's nest. Diesel engines gurgled across the desert, growing louder with each passing heartbeat. "They're right there." Mindy pointed out four columns of black exhaust rising in the distance.

"We gotta move," Captain Quarrels shouted. "Now!"

Watching The Sundarian lift Prudence and speed away, Carlos took one step after them. An explosion rocked the ground. The Plymouth blew apart, sending shards of metal, rock, and glass into the air. He fell flat on his back, a high-pitched ringing noise lodged in his ears.

Strong arms lifted him up. Captain Quarrels and First Lieutenant Jose Pagan stood on either side of him, supporting his weight and hurrying him along. They followed the group of Specialists out of the ravine toward the highway.

"C'mon, professor. We gotta move." Pagan's voice sounded muffled. Carlos opened his mouth, trying to clear his ears. Another explosion sounded. "They're firing mortars. We gotta book."

Carlos only caught every other word. The old mantra began of its own accord. *Cathedral. Bell. Chimney. Steamboat. Devil's Bridge.* One more explosion behind them. *Cathedral. Bell. Chimney. Steamboat—*

Boom. Boom. Boom. Incoming projectiles whistled overhead.

Strong arms wrapped around his waist, lifting him up. The smooth arms belonged to The Sundarian. He struggled to peek back. A mortar hit the ground sending both Captain Quarrels and Jose Pagan into the air.

"Don't look," The Sundarian said, her breath even and calm. "They were good men."

"*Ay, Dios mio.* But what of the rest? The Specialists?"

After a few seconds she set him down. He stood next to Prudence. They were only a few yards from the shoulder of the busy highway. He turned to thank the alien, but she had vanished, leaving a trail of dust in her wake.

"*Mira,*" he said, pointing to the ground, "desert sand. It's all around us."

Prudence nodded. "I'm afraid we only managed to create an oasis in a very small area. A tiny drop in the proverbial bucket."

The Sundarian came back with Mindy the Prophet and Patricia the Witch. She set them down and turned to face the ravine.

Falling to her knees, Mindy put her hands to her face and sobbed.

"What is it?" Carlos said.

She glanced up at him. "Chase and Skye...they're dead."

"*No, Dios mio, no.*"

The Sundarian raised her arms and released a piercing shriek. Dark clouds formed. Thunder rumbled across the valley. A storm broke loose, filling the sky with torrential rain.

"May their machines bog down in the muck," The Sundarian said through tight lips, "and their flying machines be blinded by the downpour. Curse their weapons of war. Since the beginning, they have done nothing but fight us. They are a backward people. Ignorant. Lost." She turned to Carlos. "Forgive me. I do not rail against the likes of you. Indeed, we came for those of your like."

Tears clouded Carlos's vision. He leaned forward and hugged The Sundarian. Not only did she accept the gesture, she hugged back.

"What do we do now?" Patricia glanced up, shading her eyes against the rising sun.

"We keep moving," Carlos said. "South into Vegas and mingle with the populace. Perhaps the soldiers will not attack us in the city."

"Good. It is settled. We move." The alien led the way, Carlos by her side. "As I carried you to safety," she said, "you repeated the same words over and over."

He nodded. "Cathedral. Bell. Chimney. Steamboat. Devil's Bridge. A little mantra of mine. It reminds me of my home in Sedona. Of the Vortex."

A bus pulled over just ahead of them. The doors opened and Major Bay stepped out.

By all means, Carlos, The Sundarian planted her thoughts in his mind, *continue this mantra of yours. It seems to be working.*

"It has yet to fail."

Tell me more of this Vortex.

Colonel Bloodstone stood behind his desk, strangling the telephone "What do you mean an *unexpected thunderstorm*?" He placed his hand over the receiver, glared at Staff Sergeant De La Cuesta and whispered, "Check the weather report." He spoke into the phone again. "Go on."

"Well, sir..." The man on the other end of the line spoke in a dramatic fashion. "What I mean is, one minute we were racing through the Mojave, and the next, we got hit by a mother of a monsoon—a real Charlie Foxtrot. See, what happened is the drones tracked the enemy's position like clockwork. So, we threw in a few rounds—mortars, you know? Nothing serious, just wanted to check range and disorient 'em. Next thing you know—bam! We couldn't see two feet in front of us. The jeeps got stuck, and the drones, well, who knows what happened to them."

"Captain Ugarte." Bloodstone's mouth lathered as he spoke, his spittle hitting the desk. "I needed Prudence Wellman taken alive. Do you understand? How do you know you didn't murder her with one of your bombs?"

"Oh, we didn't, sir. We blew the shit out of an old junker—a Plymouth, I'm told. We found four combatants tits up, but we didn't touch that girl. Redhead, right? Nah, when we swept the area, we found two Black Shirts and a couple of gals, both of 'em blonde. Didn't come across no redhead. So, you see, colonel, we didn't—"

Bloodstone banged the handset into its cradle. Incompetence, plain and simple. This would never have happened in the *real* army. The men he now commanded only played at being soldiers. No accountability, no responsibility. Even Major Bay, his number one choice, had jumped sides at the first opportunity—at least that's what Gamble the Empath claimed.

To say Gamble spilled his guts would have been redundant. The man died from countless injuries after being tossed through the air like a toy by an alien freak.

Bloodstone gave his staff sergeant another 'if looks could kill' stare. "History leaves me no alternative, De La Cuesta. I need to take charge of this situation personally, run the show like Macarthur in Korea. That's the only way to achieve success."

"But, sir, you're…uh, that is…aren't you a little—"

"Old. You think I'm too old for this."

"Sir, I never said—"

"You didn't have to. This is the first time, in the minute since I've known you, that I respect your candor and also agree with you. But my mind is resolute. Here." Bloodstone turned back to the computer and banged at the keyboard for a few moments. The printer came to life and spit out a page. "Here's a list of twenty men. Round them up and assemble them in the quad. I'll need every one of them to get the job done."

"Yes, sir. Right away."

"Also note the other things I need. I'll be at the hospital tent if you have any questions."

De La Cuesta saluted, grabbed the list, and darted out of the office. Colonel Bloodstone exited the command-and-control center, ignoring the salutes of his men with a dismissive wave of the hand. Toy soldiers—beneath his respect. He entered the medical tent, covering his nose against the smells.

Chloroform, antiseptics, disinfectants, blood, urine, feces, and bowels—he marched past a dozen gurneys before stopping at the cot holding the body of Gamble the Empath. Earlier, surgeons had poured the remains of the man into a body bag and zipped it shut. Bloodstone stared at the black plastic for a moment before turning his attention across the aisle to the motionless figure of Darrah the Conjuror.

"Dr. Turnbride," he shouted, competing with the noise of enormous swamp coolers providing the tent with a constant flow of temperate air.

Turnbride glanced up from a clipboard. He placed it down and strode toward the colonel. "Yes, sir?"

"Well?" Bloodstone put his hands on his hips. "Talk to me."

"Sir, as I said, Darrah needs to be airlifted to a real hospital." Turnbride picked up the clipboard hanging at the end of the bed and offered it to the colonel.

"That don't mean a damn thing to me. I'm not the doctor here—you are. All I need to know is when he's coming out of the coma."

"I can't say. For someone who's been thrown across the desert like a...like a piece of trash, well...all I know is he shouldn't even be alive."

"Can you wake him up?"

"Wake him up? Absolutely not. In fact—"

"Just for a little bit. I need to ask him one or two questions, that's all. Wake him up for that and then he's all yours."

"Sir, he's in extreme pain—off the charts. If I attempt to bring him back to consciousness, it would be fatal."

Colonel Bloodstone snatched the clipboard from the doctor. "Fractured neck, spinal cord injury, dislocated limbs, internal bleeding, ruptured spleen, numerous fractures, subarachnoid hemorrhage—what the hell's that?"

"It means his brain is bleeding. That almost always leads to stroke, and that stroke is almost always—"

"Fair enough. You know, think of it this way—maybe meeting his maker wouldn't be such a bad thing. For someone in his condition, it might even be a blessing."

Dr. Turnbride's mouth fell open.

Bloodstone's face grew red. "I'm not the monster here, Turnbride. Those aliens are. Hell, who knows how many more people they'll treat like garbage. Besides, you've listed him in critical condition. I mean, he's already got one foot in the grave, and—"

"Colonel, by all rights, this man should be dead."

"Exactly. Just give me a few seconds to talk to him, and then maybe he'll finally shuffle off this mortal coil. That would be for the best, right?"

"You can't be serious. I can't allow—"

A sound came from the patient—a low, almost inhuman, gurgling noise. The colonel leaned over Darrah at once. "Is he still alive?"

"Stop it, colonel," Turnbride shouted. "He isn't—"

"Quiet." He turned back to Darrah. "Is Prudence Wellman still alive?"

Blood spurted into the Conjuror's oxygen mask. The EKG monitor emitted a long, uninterrupted sound. The patient had passed.

"Bring him back," Bloodstone said. "Give him something. Adrenalin to the heart. Do it now—that's an order."

"Even you can't order the dead back to life." Doctor Turnbride took the clipboard from the colonel's hand.

The colonel narrowed his eyes at Turnbride. "And you call yourself a doctor."

Turnbride switched off the EKG machine. The ever-present whoosh of air streaming in from the swamp coolers covered the silence.

Bloodstone noticed De La Cuesta at the entrance. He checked his watch, gave Doctor Turnbride one last glare, and marched out of the tent with its loud air and horrible odors.

"Sir," Staff Sergeant De La Cuesta said, "I've gathered most of the men you asked for. If I may make a recommendation—"

"Most of the men?"

"Yes, sir. The ones I couldn't find were either KIA or MIA."

It took a moment for Colonel Bloodstone to compose himself over the news. "How many are there?"

"A dozen, sir."

Damn. He would need every one of them to get the job done. He sucked in a breath of dry desert air. "Out of my way." He pushed past the staff sergeant, then stopped and turned back. "You're not going to be a problem, are you De La Cuesta?"

"Uh, what do you mean by that?"

Narrowing his eyes, Bloodstone stared at the man. "We'll talk."

Twelve men either stood, sat, or crouched in the shade of the Command-and-Control building. Some smoked, others engaged in quiet conversation. They all stood at attention when the colonel approached.

"At ease, men. You've been through a hell of a night, so I'm not going to waste any more of your time. I handpicked each one of you based on your years of service to Gatekeeper, your years of service in the military, and your performance ratings here at The Shelter. Keep in mind, men, what I'm about to ask of you is not an order. This is strictly voluntary."

A smattering of quiet laughter arose from the group.

"I'll understand if some of you want to pack it in and call it a day. As I said, after the night you've been through—the night we've all been through—maybe we should just call it a day. This is not what you signed up for, eh? Many of your teammates lost their lives in the flood. Some died in the air raids. Countless others suffered violent deaths at the hands of the Cats." He paused for effect, exchanging a furtive glance with De La Cuesta. "In any case, here we stand. Through the flood, the fire, through it all, here we stand—together. We're just a few feet from the finish line."

"Sir?" One of the men stepped forward. A strong, thick young man of about twenty-five, his face needing a shave, eyes begging for sleep. "The finish line?"

Colonel Bloodstone approached the boy and placed a hand on his shoulder. He'd seen this gesture, this "magic touch" in a film. Patton? Braveheart? No matter. "You're, uh Sergeant Mason Whitfield, yes?"

"That's right, colonel."

"Well Mason, a short time ago, a small group of aliens were sighted just north of Las Vegas. Somehow, they managed to slip through our lines of containment. Make no mistake, they had help. A party of humans—bleeding-heart do-gooders—helped the ENOs escape.

"So, here's the deal, Mason, what I'm asking you to volunteer for is a mop-up mission. You will be well compensated for your efforts. I'll authorize bonus pay, hazard pay, whatever it takes. And here's the best part. It should only take a few hours. For that, you will be remembered for all time as someone who stepped up, stepped forward, and got the job done."

"You can count me in, colonel." Sergeant Mason Whitfield appeared to be a leader in his own right as four others gathered around him and nodded in agreement. Bloodstone had convinced five.

A seasoned black man with a salted beard and weary eyes stepped forward. "I'd like to get this over with, too. We been underground long enough. Been five years for me. It's time to end this shit."

Three men nodded in agreement. That made nine.

"And you?" The colonel directed his question to a tall, well-muscled man wearing a tattered Black Shirt. He stood next to two others, away from the rest. "Can I count on you?"

"Sir, to be honest, I've been on this project for a little more than seven years. I expect that's longer than anybody else. Now, in all that time, I always wondered one thing."

Bloodstone approached the man. "What's that?"

"Why are those aliens here? I mean, has anybody ever tried to find out why they came to our planet in the first place?"

"Does it really matter? You can see the destruction they've caused. Hell, they tried to kill us *all* last night. It's time this whole nightmare came to an end, don't you think?" He moved forward, ready to place his hand on the man's shoulder.

"Sir." The man took a step back out of his reach. "I really think we should at least try and find out why they're here. And I've said as much to my commander, and his commander, and now to you. But to be perfectly honest, sir, just like in the military, nobody ever seems to listen to the grunts. Never."

"Point well taken, uh...Lieutenant Spears, isn't it? Lieutenant Randal Spears?"

"That's right."

Of all the men he had chosen, he needed this man the most. Bloodstone cleared his throat. "Well Randall, normally I would agree with you. But listen here, those creatures overplayed their hand. I mean, they had plenty of time to tell us why they came, didn't they? Instead, they waited, built up their numbers, and then attacked. And now they're on the run. Tell me, why would they run if they've got nothing to hide?"

"Maybe they're scared, sir. After all, we're the ones who—"

"Randall, I can see you're frightened."

"No sir, I'm not—"

"It's okay to sit this one out." Time for a little reverse psychology. "It's been a long night and you've been through hell. I can understand if you want to chuck it in and head on home. Hell, everybody here will understand. But let me remind you of one thing, soldier. There are men in the hospital tent, just next door, who will never go home. They were tortured by those aliens. Tossed around like frisbees. You might even have known some of them—broke bread with them.

Listen, I don't want to see that happen to anyone else. So, I don't blame you for shying away."

"Sir, I'm not—"

"Alright," the colonel shouted, turning his back on Randall. "Let's get ready to move out. There's hot food waiting for you in the next tent. Civilian clothes, too. We'll be heading out at..." He checked the Omega. "...oh-seven-thirty. Let's go and—"

"Sir, I want in," Lieutenant Spears said. "Please."

"Are you sure?" Bloodstone placed a hand on the man's shoulder. "There's no disgrace in walking away. Like I said, everyone will understand."

"Yes, I'm sure. It's been a long haul, and there's something about seeing this thing through to the end—you understand."

Got him.

"That I do." He shook the lieutenant's hand. "All right, men, listen up. We all know what we're up against, and personally, I don't think the enemy stands a chance. Our mission is simple, but to alleviate any misunderstanding let me restate. We're going to track down and obliterate every single alien monster who dares breathe the sweet, sweet air of our blue planet Earth. In short, gentlemen, we're going to save the world."

CHAPTER 28

"How did you find this fabulous bus, major?" Carlos beamed at the man.

"Abandoned, if you can believe that. Not a soul around."

"How very fortunate." He climbed the stairs and sat in the front row.

"Not so fortunate for the group of tourists from Japan, eh, major?" Marissa the Psychic called out. She stood in the middle of the bus. "By abandoned, what he means is parked outside the Paiute Tribal Smoke Shop. As a matter of fact, fortune had nothing to do with it. Why not tell him the truth? You bus-jacked it."

"Really?" Sergeant Sandoval stepped aboard after The Sundarian.

Major Bay winked at Sandoval. "What is it the British say? **Needs must.**"

"And just how long have you actually been British?"

"Okay, listen. We tracked the aliens down to the smoke shop just off Interstate 15."

Sandoval turned to those waiting outside. "C'mon, ya'll, let's get on board. We probably only have a few minutes 'fore they put out a BOLO on this bus, just enough time to make it to The Strip. Sound like a plan, Major?"

Prudence climbed the steps followed by Mindy. Finally, the three Gatekeepers boarded, passing the major. He slapped them on the back, offering words of encouragement. "Where's Pagan and

Quarrels?"

"I'm so sorry, major." Carlos shook his head. "When the bombing started, they helped me to safety. They died saving my life."

"The bombing? What bombing?"

The Sundarian placed her hand to the major's forehead. He nodded, closed the door, and pulled out onto the freeway. Horns blared behind them. Major Bay swerved back to the shoulder and jumped on the brakes.

"Whoa." Sandoval fell into Prudence's lap. "Sorry ma'am." He stood and addressed the major. "You've never driven a bus before, have you?"

"How'd you guess?" Major Bay hit the turn signal and eased back into traffic. "Nobody else volunteered, but Bob's eager to have a go at it. He's been eyeing every move I make behind the wheel."

Sergeant Sandoval leaned in. "Speaking of which, where're the aliens?"

"Check the back of the bus." The major jerked a thumb over his shoulder.

Carlos peered toward the rear seats, allowing his eyes time to adjust to the darkness. Soon, several shapes came into focus. The aliens sat in silence, eyes forward, their heads bouncing along with the movement of the bus. The Sundarian had already joined them. Prudence navigated the center aisle, using the seat backs to keep her balance. She joined the group of aliens in the back.

"Carlos." Sergeant Sandoval motioned to the back of the bus. "Shall we?"

The two men moved down the aisle. Carlos stopped to acknowledge Marissa, Clarissa, and Tarissa. "You did great work today. Thank you."

"They sure did," Bruce the Dowser said.

"In all fairness," Willie T. said, "everybody pitched in and helped."

"I'm proud of you—all of you." Carlos nodded. "You know, none of you need to be here right now. You do know that, don't you? I wouldn't want to see anybody else hurt."

"This is exactly where we need to be—all of us." Willie T. grinned, earning and pat on the shoulder from Carlos as he continued his way down the aisle.

Finding his seat, the sergeant peered through the tinted side windows. "In this traffic, we should reach The Strip in about ten minutes."

"Good," The Sundarian said. "The restoration of Earth awaits."

Carlos nodded and closed his eyes, concentrating on a message for the aliens. *We are still in danger. The military is hunting us. But if we work together, like a team—and stay calm—we will be okay. Do you understand?* Positive emotions filled his mind. The aliens were willing to place their trust in him. He accepted their confidence. *Thank you.*

"I want to know your names," he said out loud. "Please, how about you?" He pointed at a young man wearing a blue windbreaker, black slacks, and a baseball cap.

"My name is Tintantunumareon"

"Tim-tan-tar-tum...umm?"

"Tintantunumareon," the alien said again.

"Yes, well...I like your jacket. Where did you get it?" Carlos glanced at all the aliens in the back of the bus. They wore a variety of colorful clothes and hats.

"Major Bay gave them to us," Tintantunumareon said. "Is it acceptable for your world?"

"Needs must, indeed. Uh, yes, quite acceptable, Tim—do you mind if I call you Tim?" He turned to a female sitting on his right. "And who are you?"

"My name is Pas."

"I like that name. And you?"

"I am called The Shalouin."

Carlos spoke to each alien, trying to commit their name to memory. It reminded him of the first day of school. He turned to The Sundarian.

She cocked her head. "You are forlorn for having lost the two men."

"I'm trying to reason my way through the grief of losing those two. And the awful grief of losing one million Aretheans. I tell myself that saving the world is worth the sacrifice. But it is hard."

"I understand."

"Do you?" Carlos lowered his voice. "Look at us. How can we save the world?"

"Why it's simple," the alien said. "Begin with known technologies

185

including magnetics, vibration, and synchronization to replace the constant burning of fossil fuels. Then introduce the untapped potential of light energy."

"What do you mean by—"

"Sunlight, moonlight, and starlight. Next, usher in visionary ideologies—regeneration and rejuvenation. As these mindsets take root, the Earth will, once again, be able to breathe. An atmosphere infused with gold will also help. And we now know where to acquire plenty of that mineral, don't we? That's how you save your world. Easy." Her words came fast and true. On point. She made it sound possible.

Nothing is impossible. The words resonated in his mind.

"C'mon, doc. Let's go back to the front," Sandoval said. "We really should see what the major's got planned." He stood in the aisle and waited for Carlos.

"Well, then..." Carlos rose and addressed the aliens. "It's been very pleasant talking with you. Maybe we'll have more time for confabulation later." His mood had improved.

Sergeant Sandoval, Carlos, and The Sundarian made their way up the aisle to the front of the bus, finding seats near the major.

"Sunny," Major Bay said, "glad to see you."

"Sunny?"

"I can't very well keep calling you The Sundarian now, can I? Sunny's easier."

"Just so," she said. "You are being friendly to me."

"Uh, well, yeah. Is that okay?"

"I much prefer it to the terror," she said. "Tell me, why do humans fear us?"

Carlos cleared his throat. "As a rule, we fear anything we do not understand."

"It is not a good rule. We are here to help—to replenish. We are not a threat to you."

"If you'd told us that in 1963," Major Bay said, "it would have really helped."

"We were forbidden to make contact. We were...what is the word, enchanted? No. Charmed? Forgive me, but there is no human word for it."

"We thought you all shared a medical condition—a catatonic state." Major Bay checked his side view mirror and chuckled.

"Yes, and you called us Cats," Sunny said. "A cat is an animal. You used us for sex. You locked us away in the cold. You fed us our dead."

"*¿Como se dice?*" Carlos said, grabbing the major's shoulder. "What did she say?"

Major Bay tightened his grip on the steering wheel. His voice broke. "No. The aliens were fed a diet of tofu cakes high in vitamins and minerals, Kale bars, and a generous ration of water. But...as their population increased...things went south. The bureaucrats complained about the cost." He shook his head. "They called it Project Donner. Hilarious, huh? Some *genius* in Washington had the bright idea of saving money by...by actually—"

"*Ay, no mi digas,*" Carlos said.

"That project came to an end in a hurry—long before I arrived. Believe me, if I were there then, I would have done everything I could to put an end to it." The major sucked in a deep breath and gave Sunny a quick glance. "Anyway, I can only guess that might be one reason we called you Cats. To dehumanize you."

"Yet, humans were the ones who acted like animals." Sunny eyed the major.

A tear crawled down his cheek and landed on the floorboards. The major glanced down, then up at The Sundarian. "Sunny, I'm so, so sorry for the way you've been treated."

"We are nothing like you," she said, her voice cold and deliberate. "You are a savage people, harming yourselves, destroying your world."

"I can't begin to defend the things we—"

"It is only because of Carlos Huerta you have a chance of survival."

Carlos narrowed his eyes on her. "*No entiendo.*"

"Because of your compassion. Because of the warmth."

"The warmth? Do you mean...Ah *si*, you mean the coat. Yes, you were so cold—all of you were, but, alas, I had only one coat."

"Your act of kindness became the word."

"The word?"

"To begin. To commence the restoration. Because of you, we are here."

Bob tapped Major Bay on the back and pointed out the window. Half a dozen police vehicles raced by on the other side of the

187

highway, lights flashing.

The major cleared his throat. "We gotta get off this freeway and ditch the bus. There's a place to stay up ahead." The major kept his eye on the road, on the rear-view mirror, and on Sunny. "It's on The Strip, just south of Tropicana. We'll get some rooms and decide on our next move. One step at a time, right?"

More police cruisers flew by on the northbound side of the highway.

"They'll be stopping every bus in Vegas," the major said. He gazed at The Sundarian and smiled. "Good thing there's a few thousand of those in this city. Besides, this is getaway day. Sunday. Everybody's headed back to LA, so the freeways will be jammed and the rooms empty."

"Is that good?" Sunny cocked her head.

"Sure is—it's great. In fact, traffic's starting to slow down now, so I'll get off on Flamingo instead of Trop. Hang on." He cranked the wheel and powered off the freeway. "Hold on. Gotta make that light." The major pressed down on the accelerator while strangling the wheel. He skidded right and merged onto The Strip.

In the rear of the bus, the aliens held onto the seat backs to keep from tumbling into the aisle. When the bus passed the Bellagio fountains, they peered through the tinted windows. "Ooh... Aww..."

"They like the water show?" Carlos smiled back at them.

"We have no such displays on Areth," Sunny said. "And there are so many people here."

Major Bay chuckled. "It's still early. Wait till noon, the freeway will come to a standstill." He glanced at her. "Yes, that's a good thing—the cops will be bogged down, too."

Traffic slowed on The Strip, affording the aliens an unhurried view of tourists strolling along the boulevard holding enormous drinks, gift bags, and cameras. The glaring signs of the hotels announcing the latest celebrity shows gave the morning sun competition. The extraterrestrials pointed at various attractions, from the Eiffel Tower to the High Roller Observation Wheel. They gazed at the pyramid and sphinx of the Luxor, and particularly marveled at the golden windows of the Mandalay Bay.

Pulling over, Major Bay parked in the 'Busses Only' lane. "Okay, everybody out."

"Now this is what I'm talking about," Sergeant Sandoval said, glancing at the entrance to the Mandalay Bay Hotel. "Excellent choice, major."

"Don't be absurd." The major frowned. "It's too high profile and would raise a lot of red flags. No, sergeant." He pointed across the street at a decaying one-story wooden structure.

The wrinkled paint might have been white at one time but had baked to a brownish-beige after decades under the desert sun. Tumbleweeds rolled across the front "lawn." A neon sign featuring the figure of a girl in a bathing suit diving into a pool had long since lost its color. A rusted sign declared—

The All In Motel–Sin City's Best Bet.

CHAPTER 29

"**Is the motel even** open?" Carlos narrowed his eyes, giving the dilapidated place another once over.

Sergeant Sandoval winced. "It looks like it's been condemned—or should be."

"Don't worry," Major Bay said, "looks can be deceiving. Of course it's open. And even if it's not, we have Prudence—our secret weapon." He pulled a lever opening the bus door. "Carlos, would you please take everybody across the street and get some rooms. I'll ditch the bus, double back, and meet you at the motel."

"I'm going with you," The Sundarian said.

"No, Sunny." He shook his head. "You stay with the rest of—"

"Together, we will blend in. The humans, I have observed, wander about in packs or couples. The lone individual stands out."

He grinned. "In packs, huh? Okay Carlos, Sunny and I will meet you back at the motel in about thirty minutes."

Carlos nodded. "Very well. Uh, major, may I have a word with you…in private?"

"Sure. Everybody off the bus. Stay together and wait for Carlos."

The aliens fell in line behind the Specialists followed by the Gatekeepers, who had discarded their Black Shirts in favor of the uniform *de jour*—colorful Hawaiian shirts and baseball hats. They all gathered on the sidewalk—just another group of tourists ready for a day of fun and sun on the world-famous Las Vegas Strip. Sunny strolled to the back of the bus.

Carlos stood over the major who sat behind the wheel. "The Sundarian is very special to me. She and I have been through much together."

"I agree, doc. Sunny is quite special."

"Please, *señor*, be vigilant. Make certain no harm comes to her."

"Listen, I don't intend to—"

"And I expect her back in exactly thirty minutes."

"You don't have to worry about—"

"Not a minute later. This *is* Las Vegas, after all."

"For God's sake, what's gotten into you?"

"Tell me you have protection."

"Carlos, take it easy. You sound like a nervous father on prom night. Yes, I brought protection." He lifted his shirt to reveal the butt of a firearm. "Stop worrying. It's not like we're going to elope."

"What does it mean…to elope?" Sunny stood next to Carlos.

"Uh, nothing, *mija*. Just be careful. I will see you soon." He stepped off the bus, turned back to the major, and pointed at his watch. "Thirty minutes."

"Okay, *dad*."

Sunny cocked her head. "Carlos Huerta is your father?"

"No, he's not my father." The door slid shut.

Carlos watched the bus merge into traffic on The Strip. "*Bien*, everybody, listen up. We're going to wait for the light to change green so we can all get to the other side safely. Watch for my signal." He kept his eye on the light. The moment it changed, he raised his arm over his head and shouted, "Now. Let's go. Cross the street. Use the buddy system. Nobody left behind."

The aliens, Specialists, and Gatekeepers marched across the boulevard, doing their best to blend in with the tourists. The extraterrestrial's legs and arms glistened in the sunlight, while strands of platinum hair peeked out from under baseball caps.

"Okay, come along, over here." Carlos waved the group to safety on the other side of the street. "I'm so proud of you. Not one person gave you a second look. I guess in a town like this you fit right in."

"Hey, you make a pretty good tour guide," Sandoval said. "If that physics thing doesn't pan out, at least you have something to fall back on."

"Another joke, sergeant?"

"Sorry, professor. Just trying to lighten the mood."

Puffing out his cheeks, Carlos blew out a slow breath. "No, no, I am sorry. I feel like I have not slept in a week. I'm furious at what happened to the Aretheans. I'm exhausted, hungry…I'm just, how do you say? *¿Malhumorado?* Grouchy." He led the group over a pebbled pathway to the All In Motel office. "If one more thing goes wrong, I will explode."

"Understood," Sandoval said. "I guess the sooner we get some shut eye, the better."

The sign on the office door did not help Carlos's mood. Closed for Remodeling. "*Ay, carajo.* What happens now?"

"Calm down." Prudence stepped forward. "I'm your secret weapon, remember? Give us a sec." She took Sergeant Sandoval by the hand and they hurried into the office.

Carlos kept his eye on the others. The aliens stood still—almost at attention—stiff and unyielding. The Specialists stretched, wiped away sweat, making side comments on the disrepair of the motel and the heat of the day. The Gatekeepers glanced over a wrought iron fence at the drained swimming pool. The murky green puddle festering at the bottom made the whole thing look like a giant bowl of chunky pea soup. Tall "Bob" stood apart from the group. Carlos closed his eyes and transmitted a message.

Relax, Bob. Why are you so anxious?

I am worried for The Sundarian.

The major will take good care of her. They will return soon.

Bob glanced about, shifting his weight from foot to foot. *I go to find.*

No, Bob. Do not wander off. Wait here.

I go to find. Bob backed away, turned, and ran toward the boulevard.

Carlos opened his eyes. "*No señor,* come back here this instant."

His words were too late. Bob had vanished.

"*Ay, no me digas.*"

"Don't tell you what, doc?" Sergeant Sandoval said. He and Prudence stood side by side, holding room keys. "Thanks to our secret weapon here, five rooms didn't need remodeling after all. They suddenly became available…at a deep discount."

Prudence feigned arrogance. "It's what I do. What's wrong, doc?"

"Uh…Bob…the alien…yes…well, he seemed a bit uneasy. He

decided to go and look for Sunny. I tried to stop him, but—"

"What?" Sandoval said. "Oh, this is bad, doc—real bad. Here." He gave Carlos the room keys. "Get everybody settled in. I'm going after him."

"Let's go," Prudence said.

"We're right behind you." Marissa held Tarissa and Clarissa's hands.

"Everyone listen up. I need to go alone. We can't risk everyone getting separated. Y'all just hang back and get you some rest."

Prudence shook her head. "But I'm the—"

"Yes, you are our secret weapon," Sandoval said. "That's why I need you here, with them. I'll be back in no time. Promise." He jogged back to The Strip and turned left.

"Come on, everybody, follow me." Carlos led the group over a graveled parking area to a building across from the office. Five doors were numbered in sequence, corresponding to the keys he held. Images of chalkboards and underground chambers ran through his mind. "Who wants room one?" Marissa grabbed the key. She and her sisters entered the first room. "Wait," Carlos said. "Prudence and Patricia as well, please." The two girls joined the triplets.

"*Bien.* Room number two. Mindy, Willie, Bruce, and Gregory. Coed dorms, eh? We're all adults here, yes?"

He gave the next key to the Gatekeepers, Lieutenant Sullivan, Lieutenant Meyer, and Captain Dempsey. Glancing up, he whispered, "And Jedediah if, indeed, you need a place to rest your weary head—if, indeed, you do have a head…uh…no matter, this room is yours."

Carlos saved a key for the major, Sunny, Bob, and Sergeant Sandoval. He took the last room for himself and the aliens. "In we go. We'll be roomies, eh?"

Once inside the spacious two bed suite, he switched to telepathy. *Who wants a bed?*

The aliens inched away from the mattresses.

Very well, last chance. Carlos kicked off his shoes, pulled down the blackout shades, and laid down. He peered at the aliens huddled together near the bathroom.

Are you sure nobody wants a bed? Okay, get comfortable then, and go to sleep. He enjoyed the feeling of a long overdue yawn. The aliens pattered about, selecting places to stretch out on the carpet. Were they comfortable? Carlos could not tell. At least they were far from the ice-cold conditions they had endured at The Shelter, and the outrageous heat of the desert. He closed his eyes, allowing memories of his home in Sedona to fill his thoughts. Soon, the vortex mantra weaved its magic spell. *Cathedral. Bell. Chimney. Steamboat. Devil's Bridge. Cathedral. Bell. Chimney—*

Knock. Knock. Knock.

His eyes shot open. People surrounded his bed. Faceless shapes. Strangers. Shadowy forms. The beginnings of a panic attack built until he remembered who they were. The extraterrestrials.

Knock. Knock. Knock.

"*Momento.*" Carlos slipped out of bed. "I'll be right there." He wove his way around the aliens and peered through the spyhole. "Ah, Sergeant Sandoval."

Sunlight flooded the room when he opened the door. The sergeant stepped inside and eased the door shut.

"Did you find Bob?"

"Yup. I bet you'll never guess where. Found him posing for pictures with tourists at the Welcome to Las Vegas sign, if you can believe that. They all loved it—thought he was part of the show."

"The show? What show?"

"It's Vegas, doc. There's always a show. And boy did he play to the crowd."

"A born actor, eh?"

"More like a spoiled child. Anyway, the major and Sunny are back, too."

"Ah, *bien*. So, we are all together, safe and sound." Carlos patted Sandoval's back and opened the door. "So, why don't we all get some sleep? Maybe in the morning we can—"

"Carlos." Sandoval held out his hand. "I need a key."

"*Lo siento.*" He rummaged through his pockets and found the last remaining key. "*Numero Quatro*, it's just next door. Get some sleep, and thank you for finding Bob."

Carlos locked the door and found his way back to the lumpy mattress. The aliens shuffled about the room, their thoughts sneaking into his mind. "Calm down," he said aloud, "you are safe. Nobody knows we are here." They continued their slow walk-about. Carlos watched them for a while. He couldn't be certain, but an educated guess told him their eyes were wide open, waiting...watching.

For what?

CHAPTER 30

Tick-tock. Tick-tock.

"Right there, staff sergeant, there's an ENO. Didn't take too long to locate them, did it?" Colonel Bloodstone glanced at his Omega. "Only two and a half hours, all told. Not bad for an *old* man."

"Sir, I didn't mean—"

"Drop it—that's an order."

"Uh, sir, before you said you wanted to talk."

"Piss poor timing, staff sergeant. Later."

Earlier, they had followed intel provided by Nellis drones. Glimpses of a stolen bus—a trip down I-15—a stop outside Mandalay Bay—but when the suspects departed the bus, they blended in with the tourists on The Strip and became invisible. Bloodstone used his years of military instinct to pick up their trail again.

He, along with his staff sergeant, now occupied a bus bench on Las Vegas Boulevard. He wore a yellow Hawaiian shirt, khaki shorts, and white tennis shoes. A .45 caliber Hardballer with brushed stainless-steel finish tucked into his belt completed the attire.

Staff Sergeant Benjamin De La Cuesta wore a blue Cubs T-shirt, black shorts, and sandals. He carried no weapon. "How can you be so sure he's an extraterrestrial, sir? To be honest, everybody in Las Vegas looks like an alien."

"No time to be glib. That's an ENO, all right. Look how tall he is—look at his skin, his hair color—and he hasn't said a word for at least ten minutes. That's not natural, given the obvious circumstances."

"What do you mean by that?"

Bloodstone motioned to the "island median" separating the northbound and southbound lanes of The Strip. The world famous "Welcome to Fabulous Las Vegas" sign enthralled the tourists. Every one of them held a cell phone, camcorder, or digital camera, awaiting their turn to immortalize their visit with a few pictures.

Every one of them except one. An extremely tall man dressed in a tight red shirt, white shorts, and blue canvas shoes. He posed with tourists, waving off fees unlike the "showgirls," "pioneers," and "Elvis" impersonators. The man placed his arms around families, bent over and stood cheek to cheek with female visitors, and crouched down for the younger children. Always smiling as if it were his greatest honor to be photographed with anyone requesting his presence. He looked to be having a ball, mugging for the cameras.

"You're not very observant, are you?" Bloodstone said. "The lifeblood of this city is gratuities. That man should be talking up the paying customers, hustling for tips. Instead, I haven't seen him accept one thin dime for his efforts. Not only that, look how he's dressed."

"Look how *we're* dressed, sir."

"Watch yourself, son."

"Sir, what I mean is, if he *is* an alien, where's the rest of them? Where's Professor Huerta and Major Bay?"

"Right over there." Bloodstone clamped a hand onto De La Cuesta's arm. "See? Major Bay is across the street with that girl. She's definitely an alien. Don't you see?"

"You're right, sir." De La Cuesta stood, only to be yanked back down to the bench by the colonel.

"Sit down. You'll give us away." Bloodstone spoke into a concealed microphone. "I have a visual on Major Bay. He's crossing the street to the welcome sign. I want all teams to hold your positions."

All three teams confirmed his orders.

He whispered, "I don't see Prudence Wellman."

"Sir, if you don't mind me asking, what's so special about the Wellman girl?"

Bloodstone eyed his staff sergeant, answering in a measured

tone. "I do mind." He pressed the mic again and spoke to his hand-picked team. "Keep your eyes on the tall man in the red shirt, he's an ENO. Also, the girl accompanying Major Bay is an alien. Stay out of sight—we'll let them lead us to the others." Clear confirmations arrived in his earpiece. He suppressed a smile. He'd chosen his team well—then again—they had an excellent leader.

Heavy traffic zoomed by. Even though the first signs of evening covered the valley, tourists still bunched in the crosswalk, parading toward the historic marker. Occasionally, the colonel's view became obstructed. He leaned to the left, then right, always searching for a clearer view, eyeing the median strip like a hawk seeking prey.

Major Bay and the girl marched straight to the tall man. Arms waved, fingers wagged, and poses were struck. At one point, the major tugged at the elbow of the tall man, an action the big fellow did not like at all.

Bloodstone pressed the mic. "Can we get ears on this conversation?"

"We're putting the parabolic in place now."

"Get a move on." Bloodstone viewed patience as a weakness—a waste of time. Still, he remained on the bench in silence, waiting for the covert listening device to be positioned. He stretched his neck, trying his best to read lips, a skill he envied in others.

"Parabolic's online, sir." The same calm voice reassured Bloodstone. "We're putting the audio through to you now."

Bloodstone heard an unforgiving "pop," then an annoying screech, followed by a clear transmission of the conversation taking place forty yards away.

Major Bay—We've got to get back to the motel, Bob. Now.

The tall alien shook his head, frowned, and motioned to the line of tourists.

Major Bay—Sunny, see if you can talk some sense into him.

The alien called Sunny stood in silence for a moment.

Sunny—Bob wishes to stay here and please the humans.

Major Bay—Look, if we don't leave now, the only humans he's gonna please are the ones using him for target practice.

Sunny turned to the tall ENO once again. They stared at each other in silence. After a few seconds, both aliens nodded.

Major Bay—Great, now let's get a move on.

Bloodstone whispered-shouted into the mic. "Listen up, they're leaving the median strip. We need to stay out of sight and follow them. Confirm." Bloodstone received confirmations from each team. He turned to his staff sergeant. "The alien with Major Bay spoke. Can you believe it? She actually spoke." He patted sweat from his brow. "We'll wait here till they get off the median. Then, and only then, will we rise and walk—not run—but walk after them."

"Roger that, sir."

"Good. We need to blend in with the crowd."

"Sir," De La Cuesta said, nodding toward the other side of the boulevard. "That man across the street looks familiar. I swear I've seen him before."

The colonel squinted. "Good eye. That's Sergeant Henry Sandoval."

He watched Major Bay lead the group from the median, across the far side of the street. They greeted Sandoval and continued north along the east side of the boulevard.

"Heads up now, staff sergeant." Bloodstone stood, taking baby steps at first, then quick marching to the crosswalk. He stared across the street, keeping his eyes trained on the tall alien called Bob.

A blinking walk/don't walk light forced the colonel and staff sergeant to wait. Bloodstone's eyes darted between the never changing light and Bob.

"C'mon," he raged under his breath. "C'mon you blasted light. Tick-tock, tick-tock. Okay, let's go, staff sergeant. The light's green."

The two men raced across the street to the median strip. They scurried through the tourists waiting in line to have their pictures taken with the iconic sign. Colonel Bloodstone dashed in front of a couple dressed in wedding attire. Staff Sergeant De La Cuesta waited, then ducked beneath the camera, apologizing for the colonel's exuberance. At the eastern edge of the busy median, they were forced to wait for another walk/don't walk pedestrian light.

"Blasted tourists," Colonel Bloodstone shouted. "They were thick as locusts before, now there isn't enough of them to hide behind. We're going to have to go back to the other side of the street or Major Bay will surely see us." He turned around and hurried back to the western side of the median, De La Cuesta in tow. They strode across the street and turned right, heading north along The Strip on the west side of the boulevard.

"C'mon, De La Cuesta. Don't dawdle."

"I'm not dawdling, sir. I'm literally right beside you."

A sideways glance and brusque, "On the double," put the sergeant in his place. The colonel could not tell why the crowds of sightseers had thinned. Only moments before there were hundreds of them trolling the boulevard. Now, the sidewalks were nearly deserted.

He spoke into the mic. "Come in, teams. Status?"

"Blue team," came the report, "they're heading north on the east side of the boulevard. They're approaching a church building now."

"Red team, how about you? Come in."

"Red team—we've got 'em."

"Green team—they're not going anywhere. The big fella's pretty easy to track."

"Mobile," Bloodstone said, "what's your position?"

"Still outside the Mandalay Bay, standing by."

"Good." Every angle covered. Heavy weapons were in the mobile unit, ready to roll at a moment's notice. Still, the little voice inside his head, that nagging, Negative Nelly—his constant companion, would not hold its tongue. *Twelve men are not enough for this mission. You should have gone with more. The aliens slipped away before—they can do it again.*

"Shut up." The words shot from his lips.

"What's that, sir?" De La Cuesta stared at Bloodstone.

"Nothing. Keep your eyes open."

"I swear you told someone to shut up. Maybe the sun is—"

"Is what? Getting the better of an old man? You can keep your opinions to yourself."

"They're still ahead of us on the other side of the street. Looks like they're making for that motel up ahead, uh…the All In Motel. Sir, if I may, uh…that is—"

"Stop stammering. Out with it."

"Sir, maybe we could capture the aliens. I mean, killing them seems…excessive."

"Excessive? Huh." Bloodstone turned to his staff sergeant. "What a gutless wonder you turned out to be."

"May I recommend we call Nellis?"

"Why, staff sergeant?"

"Shouldn't they be here? I mean legally—"

"So, you're a lawyer now?"

"No, sir. All I meant—"

"Can the noise."

Bloodstone focused on the operation. If the aliens were holed up at the motel across the street, he'd have to position his teams wisely. Block the driveway. Storm the office. The next step would be a bit tricky—extract Prudence Wellman, unharmed.

After that, it would be a turkey shoot.

CHAPTER 31

"Sir," De La Cuesta said, "you don't look so good."

Sweat dripped from the colonel's face and splattered on the sidewalk, evaporating in just a few seconds. He leaned against one of the green bollards separating vehicles on The Strip from foot traffic. Bloodstone gasped for air and ambled to a tree providing a bit of shade.

"This damned heat will be the death of me." He checked his watch. "God, it's almost eight PM and it's still hotter than Hell out here. Get me some water, staff sergeant."

"I'll have to go all the way back to the welcome sign, sir."

Bloodstone glared at the man. "If I'm lucky you won't come back."

Staff Sergeant De La Cuesta turned south and jogged toward the median strip.

"Good riddance." Bloodstone stood and wiped the sweat from his eyes. He peered across the street. The aliens, led by Major Bay, had vanished. "Shit." He glanced left, then right, then left again before racing across the boulevard. Car horns honked.

Bloop, bloop, bloop. A Las Vegas Metro unit pulled up to the sidewalk once Bloodstone had crossed. The colonel turned and faced the black and white like a matador staring down a bull. The officer hit the siren one more time, sending a final *bloop* into the evening sky.

"Oh, for Christ's sake." Bloodstone traipsed back to the vehicle.

An officer stepped out and approached him. "Do you have a death wish, sir? Tourists are killed every year because they—"

"I'll have your badge for this." Bloodstone reached for his wallet.

The officer unhooked the safety strap of her handgun. "Whoa buddy, don't move."

"Buddy? My name is Colonel Ulysses S. Bloodstone, and you're in the middle of a national security operation."

She rested her hand on the holstered weapon. "Relax. Take a breath."

"Lady, I need you to get the hell out of here—now."

"Lady? I'm sure you meant *officer*." She pulled her hand away from her weapon. "I want you to stop right where you are. Don't make me say it again."

"That's a big mistake, lady." He spoke into the mic. "Get this gal out of my face. Red team, copy? On the double."

Two Black Shirts emerged from the shrubbery next to the sidewalk. They stood seven feet from the officer, aiming assault rifles at her head.

Her eyes widened. "What the hell?"

"This is a military operation, *lady*," Colonel Bloodstone said, his voice a low growl. "And you're in the wrong place, at the wrong time."

"Under whose authority?"

"Mine. And I don't need a bunch of trigger-happy locals getting in the way. Do you read me? Now climb back in your police car and get lost."

"Okay, okay, take it easy." She backpedaled to the open door of the vehicle. "You boys just lower your weapons. Nobody's got to get hurt today." She kept her eyes trained on the rifles pointed in her direction and hopped back into the SUV. She floored the accelerator, leaving skid marks on the pavement.

Bloodstone eyed her departure, then turned to the Gatekeepers. "Disappear." They blended back into the bushes. The incident proved he had chosen the right men for the mission. The thought brought a rare smile to his face. He switched channels on his handheld radio. "Come in Metro Command. Metro Command, come in." He informed them of his presence in their city, invoking Nellis, the Joint Chiefs, and Governor Blakley. That should forestall the lady officer's cries of foul play.

The sun dropped behind the Spring Mountains. Bloodstone glanced up at the sign overhead. The lighted letters flickered red neon against a white background.

All In Motel
Air Conditioned
Swimming Pool

Bloodstone followed the driveway leading to the motel office. He ducked low, creeping along the gravel path toward a decaying, two-story, wooden structure. Using the shadows of pomegranate and palm trees for cover, he moved closer to the office, then leaned against the swimming pool's white iron gate for a breather. The sprinklers must have just been turned off. He knelt on the wet grass, thankful for a cool respite. Keeping his eyes on the office, Bloodstone pressed his palms on the damp lawn and patted his brow. Although hot wind raked across his face like a blow torch, the tepid water comforted him. For a moment, he had found an oasis amid this arid no-man's land.

At once, Bloodstone recalled how much fire ants loved standing water. He glanced at his hands. Several of the tiny devils crawled across his exposed flesh. He panicked, swiping at them with wild gestures. Bloodstone knew, all too well, the kind of damage these aggressive little bastards could do. Stinging. Biting. Scratching. If they happened to crawl inside the eyes or nose—no, no, no. He brushed his hands over his face, swiping again and again. Bloodstone refused to be sidelined by the minuscule enemy.

The tinted windows of the office prevented a clear view inside, but he identified two silhouettes. Neither one of them seemed freakishly tall. "I'm entering the motel office," he whispered into the mic. "Stand by."

He ran across an open area, hiding behind the columns of an overhead awning. The silhouettes did not move. He brushed away a few more ants crawling over his arm before dashing across the driveway outside the office—no longer bothering to seek cover. If he had been seen, so be it. He placed one hand on the .45 behind his back, the other on the door handle.

The glass door opened with ease, a little "ting-ting" sounding from a brass bell. A man behind the reception desk glanced up and smiled. Another man, leaning against the counter, turned back and stared over his shoulder at the colonel. Neither man appeared hostile.

Bloodstone released his hold on the concealed firearm and straightened. "Evening, gentlemen. I'm looking for some friends of mine. They're supposed to be staying here."

"Sorry, stranger," the counter man said, "ain't got no guests here. The motel's closed for remodeling."

"Speaking of which," the other man said, "I'm heading out—want to get an early start on it tomorrow." He stepped past the colonel and opened the door to another "ting-ting." The man turned back. "Nice to meet you, mister."

Bloodstone faced the man behind the desk. "I'm certain my friends said they were staying at the All In Motel. This *is* the All In, isn't it?"

"Damn straight, only one in town," the man said, a grin crossing his lips. He handed the colonel a business card. "That's me, Ryan Overton—owner, manager, chief bottle washer. But, like I said, we've been closed for a couple weeks now. Sprucing the place up a bit." He pointed toward The Strip. "Got to keep up with the Joneses—am I right?"

Bloodstone glanced across the street at the massive golden facade of the Mandalay Bay. "I'm sure they're worried about the competition." He turned back to Overton. "You must be mistaken. My friends definitely said they'd be staying here. There's about of dozen of 'em. How many units do you have?"

"Well, we got twenty-four rooms altogether, but like I said, we're closed. Now if there's nothing else—"

Bloodstone pulled the .45 and held it to Overton's head. He spoke into the mic. "Red team, I need you in the motel office. Blue team, green team, set up roadblocks. Nobody in or out. Mobile unit, stay where you are for now." He turned his attention back to the trembling desk clerk. "You're lying to me, Mr. Overton. I just followed some of my friends onto your property. What rooms are they in?"

"Honest, mister," Overton said, speaking in a hurry, "I didn't mean to lie to you. She made me do it, that red-headed gal. She put some kind of hoodoo on me or something. They took five rooms—number one to five. Right across the courtyard, that way over there, past the pool. She told me not to tell nobody. Please don't shoot."

The door crashed open. Three men wearing black uniforms and carrying assault rifles burst into the office. The little brass bell hit the floor, sounding its final "ting."

"Okay," Bloodstone said to his men. "Zip tie and gag this idiot. We'll set up shop upstairs. We should have a good view of the whole layout from there."

The red team carried out his orders without delay. Bloodstone stood above Overton. "You did what the redhead told you without question?" The man nodded, his eyes bulging. "You did nothing to stop her?" The man shook his head. "That's my girl."

Bloodstone glanced out the window, admiring the first signs of twilight. He spoke into the mic. "Mobile unit. We'll need the Range-Z in here now. We need to see what the bastards are up to. We're also going to need the tranquilizing rifle. Use the back-road entrance—quietly."

"Roger that, sir.

"Lieutenant Spears," Bloodstone said, "I believe you're a pretty decent shot from distance, yes?"

"Marksman, sir." Spears's voice came back over the radio. "I'll be there in two minutes."

Bloodstone glanced at his Omega and grinned. "Nine PM.. Time to save the world."

Tick-tock. Tick-tock.

CHAPTER 32

Carlos Huerta had never been a light sleeper, but something—a noise, a feeling—opened his eyes. He lay in the dark, listening, barely breathing. No one had banged on the door. The phone had not rung. Silence. He glanced at the red numerals on the bedside clock. 9:10 PM.

The steady drumming of traffic on Las Vegas Boulevard had not woken him. In fact, street noise produced the opposite effect. It lulled him to sleep—that, and the Vortex mantra running through his mind like sheep.

His eyes adjusted to the darkness, moving from the clock, across the bare walls, and finally settled on the mysterious shapes of the aliens milling about the room. Eight otherworldly beings huddled together. Of the million that had come to Earth, only eight remained. His heart sank.

They trembled, swaying like leaves in a summer breeze. He did not know much about extraterrestrials, but he knew how they slept—lying down, silent, with eyes closed. Something or someone had spooked them.

"What is it?" he whispered, his heart pounding in his own ears. "The wind?"

Carlos eased out of bed and tip-toed around the aliens. They shuffled back, making way for him. He peeled open the blackout shades, just enough to peek into the courtyard. The sun had been replaced by a quarter moon. Trees and shrubbery, providing shelter from the lights of the city, danced in a summer breeze. Not a soul stirred.

Intending to calm the aliens, he spoke out loud. "Don't worry. There's nothing out there. I'll turn on the air conditioner. I sometimes do that at home. The noise helps me fall back to sleep." The aliens said nothing. "Lay down. We're perfectly safe."

Shots exploded, like a riff on a snare drum, across the courtyard. The window shattered throwing glass in all directions. Carlos fell to the ground, clamping his hands over his ears. He shut his eyes, directing a message to the aliens.

Get down. Take cover.

Screams replaced the sound of gunfire. Shrieks. Howls. Cries. Carlos opened his eyes. Every alien hugged the carpet. He took cover against the wall under the window. Terrible moans filled the room.

Ay, Dios mio. Is everyone okay?

No answer. Had they all been killed?

The door joining his to the adjacent room crashed open. Major Bay and Sergeant Sandoval crawled in. The sergeant used his phone's flashlight to throw light across the devastation. Pools of dark blue blood covered the floor.

"Ay, no." Carlos trembled. "Two Aretheans, Tim and Pas are... I'm afraid they are dead."

"Carlos," Major Bay whispered, "we gotta get out of here. Follow us."

"No, I will not leave them here like this."

Sunny ran into the room. Major Bay grabbed her hand, pulling her down to the ground. Her eyes landed on Carlos. "We must leave."

He refused to abandon the fallen aliens. Sunny touched his hand. Altruistic emotions of life and death, gain and loss filled his mind. He understood the logic of moving on. They all crawled into room number four.

"This'll only buy us a few seconds," Major Bay said. "They're probably using the Z."

"Z?" Sergeant Sandoval shouted.

"Thermal locator. It sees through walls. C'mon, we should bust through these adjoining doors and group up in room number one. From there—"

Another burst of gunfire tore through the walls and windows.

Major Bay yelped and grabbed his shoulder.

"Major," Sunny said, "I can—" Another barrage blasted into the room, lasting a few seconds then came to an abrupt halt. Glass, smoke, and dust filled the air. Sunny suffered an uncontrollable coughing fit.

"C'mon," the major said, taking hold of her. "Let's go. Sergeant, lead the way."

Sergeant Sandoval crawled to the door leading to the next room. He lay on his back and kicked at the flimsy, hollow door until it gave way. The gunfire stopped. They jumped to their feet and rushed into room number three.

Captain Dempsey had already begun kicking at the adjoining door to room number two. When it popped open, an alien fell—The Shalouin, another extraterrestrial fatality. Sunny knelt next to her body, stroking her platinum hair.

The front door to room two lay wide open. Carlos chanced a quick peek outside. *"Ay Dios mio."*

"What is it?" Sunny turned to him.

Carlos wiped at his tears with shaking fingers. "Mindy, Willie T., and Bruce are outside." They lay face down in the gravel drive, their lifeless bodies scattered about in morbid poses. "They're not moving."

Gregory the Confabulator lay on the carpet in a fetal position. "They wanted me to go with them, but I couldn't. Now they're all dead—deceased, expired, departed."

"It's not your fault, my friend." Carlos helped Gregory kneel. An eerie silence covered the motel grounds. Sunny put her arms around Carlos.

Police sirens echoed in the distance. "The cops will be here any second," Major Bay whispered. "We need to get out of here. Sergeant, bust through that last door."

Sandoval hesitated. "They'll hear us."

Major Bay turned to his Gatekeeper team. "Cover fire."

Captain Dempsey, Lieutenant Sullivan, and Lieutenant Meyer lay on their backs. They aimed their handguns in the general direction of the motel's office building.

"Ready, sir." Dempsey waited for orders.

Major Bay nodded. Scrambling up onto their knees, the Gatekeepers returned fire through the window. Carlos covered his ears, the salvo rattling his bones. Sandoval kicked the final door down. Gunfire from the office tore through the wall. The bullets sank into furniture, mirrors, floorboards. The humans and aliens kept low to the ground, scampering into Room Number One. Marissa, Clarissa, Tarissa, and Patricia hugged the carpet.

"Where's Prudence?" Sergeant Sandoval shouted.

"They took her," Patricia said. "Two Black Shirts. They broke in and—"

Boom.

An explosion tore through room number two, shaking the ground. The weapons of Captain Dempsey and Lieutenants Sullivan and Meyer in room two were silenced. Red and blue lights lit up the night. Horns honked. Sirens raged. More screams. Carlos gambled on another glance across the courtyard. Metro officers dove out of their vehicles, drew weapons, and returned fire at the motel's office.

"Right," Major Bay shouted, "this is it. When I open the door, move out and head to The Strip. Ready?"

"Where'd they take Prudence?" Sandoval yelled over the gunfire but received no answer.

A gust of wind kicked up over the motel. It swirled, gathering strength, carrying bits of dirt and rocks. The squall raged, spinning like a tornado. Shrubs popped out of the ground. Lawn chairs, rakes, and shovels whipped through the air, striking the office walls. It forced the police to keep low, under the debris. All gunfire ceased, but the wind raged on.

Major Bay yanked the door open. "Go, go, go."

Sergeant Sandoval made the sign of the cross and bolted through the opened door followed by Gregory the Confabulator. The five remaining aliens used their super speed to exit. Sunny remained behind.

"Let's go." Major Bay turned to the three sisters. "Now ladies, we're out of time."

Clarissa shook her head. "I can't move."

"We will not leave without you." Carlos took hold of the clairvoyant's hand. "*Por favor,* I refuse to die here, not in this dirty little motel—*not* in Sin City."

"Besides," Patricia said, "I've prepared a little surprise for us outside. So, what do you say, ladies, are you ready?"

The three sisters exchanged glances, nodded, and ran for the door. Patricia followed.

Pop. A single shot raced through the storm, across the courtyard, and into room one. Carlos dropped to the floor, red hot pain ripping through his gut. Tears filled his eyes. He moved his hands down to his midsection, finding a hole in his flesh. Sticky warm blood spread across his clothes.

Outside, the dust devil intensified. Winds howled through the courtyard.

"Doc," Major Bay shouted, crawling to the professor's side. He put a hand under Carlos's neck, lifting his head. "Stay with me."

"It's okay." Carlos struggled to speak through the pain. "Everybody is safe. Go now."

"No, doc. You'll be okay."

Carlos raised his voice. "Protect the Aretheans." His eyelids fluttered and closed.

A soft hand came to rest on his forehead. Electrical charges raced through his body, a soothing calm filling him with hope—with promise. He opened his eyes. Sunny knelt beside him, her restorative powers rushing over his body. He put a hand to his stomach, still wet with blood, but the wound had closed—the pain gone.

"Whoa," Major Bay said. "What the hell was that?" He shook his head and wiped the professor's blood from his hands onto the dirty, yellow carpet.

Sunny glanced at the major. "We are healers." She placed her hand over the bullet wound in his shoulder.

His face brightened. "Then help my men, and Willie T. and the rest of—"

"We can revitalize that which is living. We cannot restore that which is gone."

Glaring at her, Major Bay helped Carlos up and turned for the door. Sunny followed close behind. She placed a hand on Carlos's back.

"He is angry," she whispered.

"He'll understand." Carlos reached back and held her hand.

Crossing the threshold, Carlos saw police officers taking cover on the ground just under the swirling menagerie of dust, bushes, and trash. Rocks, tools, and stray bits of earth swirled about in the funnel, pelting the walls of the motel office. Carlos, Major Bay, and Sunny turned to the left. They found themselves held in the protection of a clear and calm tunnel, safe from the raging storm.

"Patricia's surprise." Carlos beamed, glancing into the night sky. "And thank you as well, my friend."

Major Bay turned back. "What are you talking about?"

"I merely thought I would thank Patricia for her magical assistance, and Jedediah for the whirlwind—giving us a ghost of a chance."

Sunny squeezed his hand.

CHAPTER 33

The farther they ran from the motel, the clearer their vision through the "safety tunnel" became. As soon as they reached Las Vegas Boulevard, the boundaries of the corridor vanished. Sounds of the tempest hovering above the motel and occasional bursts of gunfire could be heard. Those noises seemed so distant, as if no longer involving them. Carlos still held Sunny's hand. Major Bay still led the way. Night still covered the city.

The shots, sirens, and glow of red and blue strobes drew hundreds of curious tourists from their comfortable rooms, onto The Strip in front of the Mandalay Bay. Hotel Security, Las Vegas Metro, and the Nevada Highway Patrol formed a human barrier, keeping the assembled masses off the street. Clearing the area seemed impossible. The growing crowd wanted a show—a spectacle. They jockeyed for position, seeking front row seats to the devastation.

"Carlos," Sergeant Sandoval said, "over here." The sergeant stood in the middle of the boulevard. "The cops have everything shut down. We gotta go back and find Prudence."

Patricia and the three sisters stood together near the sergeant.

"Where are the aliens?" Major Bay said.

"There." Sunny pointed toward the crowd across the street. Five Aretheans stood together amidst the swarm of onlookers. Five remained of the vast numbers who had been held prisoners in the underground facility. Not counting Sunny, and assuming Tall Bob

215

had either been captured or killed. Only five survivors.

Carlos could not breath. "What have I done? So many dead."

"You are blameless." Sunny draped her arm over his shoulder. "The time came to begin our journey. It is done. We are free."

"I wanted to prevent a holocaust. Instead, I caused it."

"No, Carlos Huerta. Your actions will save more than you can possibly know."

"But how? And why? Why save this…this… nightmare of a world? We humans are the monsters. I am the—"

"Shh." She moved her hand to the back of his neck. He calmed at once.

"How can you ever forgive me, after losing so much?"

"Breathe." Sunny offered him a sweet, flawless emotion—one that until this very moment had escaped her understanding—a smile.

Any guilt he may have hoarded, any responsibility for the atrocities the keepers of The Shelter had committed, evaporated. He returned her smile, letting the warm desert air fill his lungs. *"Bien. Entonces? Continuamos.* We continue."

"I can't believe it," Major Bay shouted.

Carlos and Sunny turned to where the major pointed. Through the darkness, in the distance, two Black Shirts stood on either side of a red-headed girl. They held her arms. A third man in a Gatekeeper's uniform—older, pompous—directed their actions.

"Prudence," Sergeant Sandoval shouted.

"That's Colonel Bloodstone." Major Bay ran toward the man.

"Out of the street," a policeman ordered. "Move it—off the street."

Major Bay barreled through the uniformed officer. Sandoval rushed past them both, making a beeline for Prudence. Carlos and Sunny followed.

Breaking ranks, police officers encircled the three sisters, Patricia the Witch, and Gregory the Confabulator. "Back on the sidewalk. Move it."

Sandoval stopped just short of Prudence and her captives. "What did you do to her?"

They stood at the intersection of Reno Avenue and Las Vegas Boulevard. Most of the looky-loos made their way south toward the All In Motel. Only a few onlookers covered the sidewalk here, most remained behind the safety bollards. Police had stationed no crowd control at this location. The two Black Shirts not only secured Prudence by the arms, but they also supported her unconscious body. Each pulled a sidearm, turning it on Sandoval.

"Stand down," Colonel Bloodstone ordered, stepping toward the sergeant. "Back off. We have what we came for. We're leaving now." He drew his .45 Hardballer but held it down by his side.

Major Bay arrived, followed by Carlos and Sunny.

"All of you," Bloodstone said, making sure the new arrivals got a good look at his firearm, "stay where you are. I have no desire to hurt you, professor. Nor you, major." He focused on Sunny. "The ENO, on the other hand…"

More police cruisers rushed down the boulevard. The colonel lowered his weapon, concealing it behind his back. Additional officers raced by on foot. Emergency vehicles sped toward the All In Motel. Like spectators at a Las Vegas hypnotist show, the crowds followed the glow of red and blue lights. When the onlookers thinned, Bloodstone raised the .45 again.

"No, colonel." Sunny lifted a hand over her head.

Bloodstone dropped the weapon, his mouth falling open. His face changed from pink, to red, to blue. He clawed at his throat, a desperate gurgle coming from his mouth. He fell to his knees in anguish.

The two Black Shirts released their captive, turning their guns on Sunny. Sandoval jumped forward and caught Prudence. In an instant, the Black Shirts crumpled to the ground as well. Behind them, five aliens, all grinning, nodded to Sunny. She released her hold on the colonel, freeing him to roll into the gutter.

A hoarse, high pitched declaration spilled from Bloodstone's lips. "Your time's up." He pawed at the ground until he found the .45, picked it up, and waved it at Sunny. His lips formed what might have been a grin, his narrowed eyes on The Sundarian. "Tick-tock."

Both Carlos and Major Bay jumped in front of her. Bloodstone steadied the handgun, taking careful aim at Sunny. He squeezed the trigger but a man wearing a blue Cubs t-shirt jumped from the crowd and grabbed hold of the colonel's arm, making the shot miss.

"De La Cuesta. Are you insane?" Bloodstone rose to his knees

217

and aimed the Hardballer at the man.

"No, sir." De La Cuesta backed away. "Not anymore."

Bloodstone fired, his bullet tearing through the C in Cubs on the man's shirt. De La Cuesta fell backward, clutching his chest. Bloodstone turned the weapon on Carlos.

A passing white police transport bus veered and jumped the curb, its momentum crushing Colonel Bloodstone under its wheels. The driver jumped out and glanced beneath the chassis.

"Tall Bob?" Carlos blinked in shock.

Bob glanced under the vehicle again, then turned and grinned. "Sk-wee-ishh…" His first attempt at speaking came out as more of a noise than a word.

"How in the hell did you get this bus?" Major Bay slapped Tall Bob on the back.

"I watch. I watch you."

Two helicopters circled overhead, flooding the street with blinding searchlights. Despite the transport bus mishap, Metro kept their focus on the shootout at the All In Motel. Squad cars, SUVs, and ambulances clogged the street, making their way to the motel in a slow parade.

"Hey, welcome back." Sergeant Sandoval helped Prudence to her feet and held her tight. "You okay?"

"I am now." She wrapped her arms around him.

The small group of aliens led by Sunny, along with the humans led by Carlos, hopped aboard the police bus. Major Bay took the wheel.

At the front of the bus, Carlos turned to face the others. *"Bien, vamanos amigos."*

"Where to, doc?" Major Bay started the engine.

"I want to go home…to Sedona. But first, we must visit an old friend." He turned to Sunny. "You say you can revitalize that which is living, *si?*"

She nodded, her eyebrows rising.

"Bien, we need to go to The Mojave Hospice Center."

"Will do." Major Bay pulled his cell phone out and checked the address. "We're eventually going to need gas, food. How are we going to pay for—"

"We can help with that." Clarissa, Marissa, and Tarissa pulled their hands out of their pockets. Golden dust, pebbles, and rocks shone in the streetlights. "Will this be enough?"

"Oh yeah," Major Bay said with a laugh. "That'll do just fine."

The triplets shoved the gold back in their pockets and winced when the vehicle inched away from the scene, crunching over the remains of Colonel Ulysses S. Bloodstone.

"Bump-bump." Tall Bob grinned. "Bump-bump."

CHAPTER 34

Carlos Huerta truly loved everything about living in Sedona, Arizona. Well, everything except the Javelinas—they could get a little aggressive at times.

Nobody from the government, military, or Gatekeeper ever dug too deep into the professor's disappearance. According to an official release, he, along with other employees at the Nevada Test Site, were killed in an unfortunate accident during the Red Flag air combat exercise at Nellis Air Force Base.

In his will, he left the entirety of his estate to his sister, Sylvia Huerta. The woman, also the beneficiary of his million-dollar life insurance policy, took a bus from Phoenix, Arizona and settled in the small *casita* on the property. She leased the main five-bedroom, four-bath house to a group of scholars led by a Dr. Samuel Hasting. Their stated purpose—an extended study of the preternatural powers of the Vortex.

The story satisfied the neighbors, although tales of the late professor's affiliation with a secret government project studying extraterrestrials surfaced every now and again. Rumors sprang up on the internet. A syndicated radio show promised to expose the truth—someday.

Henry Sandoval cleared his throat. "So, what are you thinking about, doc? You got that look on your face again."

"Oh, just how much Lilly would have loved to see her kitchen now." Carlos smiled at the young sergeant. "The people, conversation, and laughter—she would have loved it all." He savored the morning ritual of breakfast prepared in "her" kitchen— eggs, muffins, toast, potatoes, pancakes, orange juice, and coffee or tea. The aliens were not keen on eating meat, so it never made the menu. From the large oak table, everyone enjoyed fabulous views of the Coconiño National Forest, the sandstone hills, and snow-covered peaks in the distance.

Nothing thrilled Carlos more than conferring with his good friend Dr. Samuel Hasting. He believed their daily confabulations about space and time, physics and philosophy, science and religion, kept his mind sharp. But, of course, he knew the truth. His fountain of youth stemmed from his proximity to the extraterrestrials. He had never felt better in his life. In fact, all the humans benefited from their relationship with the Aretheans.

Patricia the Witch always insisted on washing the dishes. Tall Bob dried. Like magic, cleanup took only a minute or two. After the meal, Carlos and Sandoval strolled about the grounds, discussing the latest weather, news, and environmental issues. Prudence occasionally joined them, holding hands with the young sergeant.

Every day, Major Bay took his usual early morning jog around the perimeter of the property, checking for any breaks in the fence line encircling the park-like setting. He kept an eye open for strangers and anything out of the ordinary. Once, a group of Javelinas breached the gate. It took all day, and most of the residents, to herd them off the professor's land and back into the forest. Although the pig-like animals snorted and scowled, with a wave of Sunny's hand they became submissive. Eventually, the Javelinas departed peacefully and without incident.

On most days, Sunny and the other aliens spent their time attempting to summon a monolith from their home planet of Areth. What came so easily to Sunny in the past, proved impossible for her now—well, almost impossible. The aliens gathered in the backyard, formed a tight circle, and held hands. With eyes closed, they bowed their heads and chanted.

"Pillin kom interwinde en Earte."

They kept it up for hours, both mouth-speaking and projecting telepathically. Sometimes a tall object would materialize, glowing from within and gleaming under the bright desert sun. It would manifest for a moment or two, then vanish. The aliens were not deterred. After a deep, collective breath, they would begin anew.

Days turned into months and the years passed.

Sunny and Major Bay had two children—twins. Clarissa, Marissa, and Tarissa acted as midwives. Both boys were healthy and carried the distinctive large eyes and glistening skin of the Aretheans. Their waves of short black hair came from the major. He could not have been prouder. Sunny did not yet know if they inherited her powers—only time would tell. She did hope, however, one day they might all visit Areth.

They named the children Jose and Dillon, after First Lieutenant Jose Pagan, and Captain Dillon Quarrels. Sunny's idea of honoring the humans who saved Carlos Huerta's life.

"I'm afraid summoning a Pillar is beyond my powers," she said, confessing to the major as they watched the shadows of sunset crawl across the walls of their bedroom. "I don't know what else I can do."

"Have you tried involving Prudence?" the major said.

"We have. Her abilities are extraordinary, to be sure, but more is needed."

"Then use more."

"What do you suggest?"

"Why not tap into the powers of Clarissa, Marissa, and Tarissa. I'm sure Patricia would be more than willing to pitch in, as well. Hell, why not include Carlos, Hank, Dr. Hasting—me and the children, too?" He propped up on his elbows. "I'll bet with all of us chanting, something's bound to happen. Of course, I don't mean to tell you your business. You are, after all, The Sundarian."

Wrinkling her nose at him, she got out of bed. "I am Sunny, not The Sundarian." She stopped, her eyes going wide. "But I do see the logic. Aretheans, humans, and Specialists all working together to restore the balance. Yes." She scampered from the bedroom, darting down the main hallway to the kitchen and called out names. In a few minutes, the others gathered around her. She explained the plan.

"We've all seen you in the backyard," Patricia said. "At times you were so close, I could actually see a Pillar materialize. I wanted to help but chose not to be rude."

"Nonsense," Sunny said. "Everyone is welcome. We all need to do what we can to restore the Earth." Major Bay entered the kitchen holding his sons, one in each arm. Sunny beamed. "To restore our home."

"I'll help, as well, if that's alright." A woman's voice called out.

Carlos turned to see his sister enter the kitchen. "Of course, Sylvia. Of course." He crossed the room and hugged her. "In fact, I insist."

"We all insist," Sunny said, taking her by the hand. "You're more than welcome."

"And of course..." Sylvia raised a finger upward. "...don't forget about him."

Carlos made the sign of the cross. *"Ay, Dios mio.* Yes, of course our Lord is always invited to help—"

"No," Sylvia said, "I mean that ghost who's always flying around. I've seen him at all hours of the night and day, swooping down and flitting about. I must admit, I'm not too sure who—or what—most of you are, but any friend of Carlos..."

"Ah, yes, Jedediah," Carlos said. "He is always welcome."

"Right," Major Bay said, "that settles it. What do you say we get started?"

The aliens nodded and filed out the kitchen door, down the two steps, and into the backyard. Clarissa, Marissa, and Tarissa laughed and spoke in excited tones on their way down the stairs. Major Bay carried the two boys, following Sunny, Prudence, and the sergeant into the clearing just beyond the *casita*. Patricia and Tall Bob held hands, joining the others under the fading light of the desert sky. They formed a circle in the backyard. Jedediah soared overhead, stirring up the waxy leaves of the California Fan Palms.

"Everybody, please close your eyes," Sunny said. "Sylvia, concentrate on the image of a towering Pillar. For the rest of you, we've all seen it, when we were underground at The Shelter. Let your minds summon the picture of that large transparent shape. Remember the details. The way it glows from within, the smooth texture, the thunder and lightning."

Wind picked up and clouds formed above the property, blocking out the sun. A low rumbling shook across the upper Sonoran Desert.

"Pillin kom interwinde en Earte..."

The aliens joined the chant Sunny began, followed by The Specialists. Carlos and Sylvia added their voices.

"Pillin kom interwinde en Earte. Pillin kom interwinde en Earte."

Sheet lightning lit up the darkened sky. Jedediah twirled in the turbulent wind. Thunder resonated, again and again, through the heavens.

"Pillin kom interwinde en Earte."

Out of nowhere, a monolith popped into existence. It hovered in the center of the circle, glowing a bright blue. Again, sheet lightning skittered through the air. Thunder boomed like a kettle drum. Sunny opened her eyes and beamed. "It's working. Pillin kom interwinde en Earte."

The Pillar, once solid, began to fade until it vanished. Silence.

"How perplexing." Gregory the Confabulator shook his head. "What happened?"

Clarissa turned to Sunny. "Did we say the chant wrong?"

"No," Sunny said. "you voiced a perfect chant. I don't understand."

"I have an idea," Samuel Hastings said. He conferred with Carlos whose eyes lit up with each word.

Carlos approached Sunny and whispered in her ear. "Cathedral. Bell. Chimney. Steamboat. Devil's Bridge."

She nodded. "Just so."

The circle formed again, everybody holding hands. Jedediah dove into the center of the group, then spirited up into the sky. His antics were met with joyful expressions by each of the participants, especially the children.

"Okay, everyone, close your eyes," Sunny said. "This time, Carlos is going to lead us in a new chant. Carlos?"

He nodded. His voice started out low, a bit nervous, then picked up volume. "Cathedral. Bell. Chimney. Steamboat. Devil's Bridge. Cathedral. Bell. Chimney. Steamboat. Devil's Bridge."

One by one, the Aretheans, Specialists, and humans took up the mantra, the words floating high into the ether. "Cathedral. Bell. Chimney. Steamboat. Devil's Bridge."

A fluttering shape appeared in the middle of the circle, wind, clouds, lightning, and thunder raging overhead. Jedediah danced about like a plastic bag in a storm.

The object in the center of the circle took on a firm outline, gleaming, solid, and real, planting itself in the middle of the circle. A Pillar. The expression of sheer delight Jose and Dillon wore, their

225

mother shared.

"It's here," she shouted. "The Pillar is here."

"The power of the Vortex," Carlos said.

A flash of lightning lit up the sky. Three aliens marched out of the Pillar. Sunny and Tall Bob moved forward, welcoming them. The Specialists applauded while the children ran about the backyard, laughing and shouting. Carlos brushed a tear from his eye.

The three new arrivals smiled at Sunny, gave her a quick bow of the head and exchanged silent, telepathic pleasantries. The other aliens greeted them.

"I'll get some clothes for our visitors," Sylvia said, darting back into the house.

"We're going to have to go on another shopping spree," Sergeant Sandoval said. "Look."

The Pillar glowed again. Four more aliens appeared. They marched in single file toward Sunny, stopped, and bowed.

"I'll go shopping with you this time," Prudence said to the sergeant.

"It's a date."

"Welcome to Earth." Sunny hugged the new arrivals. "We have much work to—"

An intense flash lit up the backyard, accompanied by the sound of thunder. Carlos squinted at the manmade terror in the sky. A missile. Jedediah expanded, forming an umbrella over the estate. His form sizzled from the rocket's impact.

"Everybody," Major Bay shouted, scooping up the twins, "Code Red. Quick, this is not a drill."

Specialists, aliens, and humans ran back into the house. The new arrivals were shown the way by Tall Bob and Sunny.

Another streak of light shot across the sky. Jedediah absorbed the blast, letting out a terrible howl. He vanished. Carlos slammed the backdoor, following everyone into the basement. Major Bay had already pulled aside the plywood covering up the entrance to the escape tunnel. A string of light bulbs illuminated the way. Prudence spoke into her cell phone. "Please hurry. Yes, this is for real."

Sergeant Sandoval waited for everyone to enter before securing the sheet of plywood across the tunnel, then followed the professor into the passageway. The shaft led away from the estate, running straight to the base of Cathedral Rock. For the past two years, Major

Bay and Sergeant Sandoval supervised while the aliens performed the excavation. The extraterrestrials proved themselves expert miners.

Not until well past midnight did they reach the end of the tunnel. Major Bay used a shovel to knock back loose rocks and brush. Exposing the opening allowed clean air to rush into the tunnel. "Let's go, everybody. Quickly now."

One by one, they emerged from the ground, making their way down a small ravine to a paved area—Cathedral Rock Trailhead. The only vehicle in the lot, a black Mercedes Benz Sprinter van, waited with motor running. The group jogged to the van, and the doors opened.

"Took you long enough," Benjamin De La Cuesta said. "I thought you'd never make it."

"You're a good man." Sunny gave him a warm smile.

"It's the least I could do for the girl who saved my life."

Everybody climbed into the luxury vehicle and settled in. Quarters were quite cramped. The escape plan had not accounted for the additional Aretheans.

"I heard the explosions from my house," De La Cuesta said. "When the lightning started up, I figured I'd be hearing from you. Hang on everybody."

The van pulled out of the parking area and onto Back O Beyond Road. Carlos stared through the window. Sylvia sat next to him. He closed his eyes, held her hand, and said a silent prayer for Jedediah the Ghost.

Sylvia stirred. "What are the odds of repairing the Earth now?"

"Our odds are better than good," Carlos whispered. "We are here, we are alive, and we now know how to create a monolith. This is not by chance, *Sylvita*. Sometime ago, a good friend of mine reminded me what Einstein once said. 'God does not play dice with the universe.'"

Rick Newberry lives in Las Vegas, Nevada. He regards Sin City as a unique backdrop for his works of fiction. Mr. Newberry has been published in *The Writer's Block Anthology* series, placed second in the 2014 Las Vegas Flash Fiction competition, and his Sin City Trilogy was completed in 2017. Published by The Wild Rose Press of New York, the series includes *Sin City Wolfhound* (2015), *Sin City Daemon* (2016), and *Sin City Mystic* (2017). *The Theory of Insanity* (2019), published by NewLink Publishing of Las Vegas is a new look at time travel, the afterlife, and saving the world — a world which may not want to be saved.

His latest novel, *The Vast Configuration,* is a fresh take on the idea of alien visitations. In November 2011, the White House released an official response to two petitions asking the U.S. Government to acknowledge formally that aliens have visited Earth. According to the response, there is "no credible information to suggest that any evidence is being hidden from the public's eye." I beg to differ. *The Vast Configuration* is published by NewLink Publishing.

Mr. Newberry is married to Betty, a Registered Nurse, and they have one son, Samuel, a talented musician. They live in a section of Las Vegas known as The Lakes with their rescue Schnauzers, Lil Bit, Bandit, and Rufus.

CPSIA information can be obtained
at www.ICGtesting.com
Printed in the USA
BVHW042242251121
622522BV00014B/425

9 781948 266284